ADVANCE PRAISE FOR *49 MILES ALONE*

"A twisted and suspenseful story about survival in its many forms. You'll race to the end."

—Jessica Goodman, *New York Times* bestselling author of *The Counselors* and *The Legacies*

"Natalie D. Richards's latest crackles with tension and desert heat. This pulse-pumping survival thriller is not to be missed!"

—Kit Frick, author of *I Killed Zoe Spanos* and *The Reunion*

PRAISE FOR *FOUR FOUND DEAD*

"[*Four Found Dead*] teems with rich character interactions and propulsive action as slasher-flick ambiance takes over the nostalgic setting."

—*Publishers Weekly*

PRAISE FOR *SEVEN DIRTY SECRETS*

"Richards's knack for blending exciting nail-biting plots with realistic and engaging characters results in yet another riveting page-turner."

ist

T0284368

"A serious thriller for readers itching for a good mystery, and also a cautionary tale about abusive relationships and how they can escalate into violence."

—*School Library Journal*

PRAISE FOR *FIVE TOTAL STRANGERS*

"A twisty thrill ride that will leave you breathless. I stayed up after midnight just to see how it all ended."

—April Henry, *New York Times* bestselling author of *Girl, Stolen*

"Richards is a master of tension… Suspense fans will get all the ups and downs of a well-paced narrative, but they may never want to drive on a snowy road again."

—*The Bulletin of the Center for Children's Books*

PRAISE FOR *WHAT YOU HIDE*

"A taut, compelling mystery and a compassionate realistic fiction novel all in one."

—*Kirkus Reviews*

"A chilling, small-town mystery…this page-turning story of teens helping each other through dilemmas will attract and inspire readers."

—*Booklist*

ALSO BY NATALIE D. RICHARDS

49
MILES
ALONE

49

MILES

ALONE

NATALIE D. RICHARDS

sourcebooks
fire

Copyright © 2024 by Natalie D. Richards
Cover and internal design © 2024 by Sourcebooks
Cover design by Nicole Hower
Cover images © Nico De Pasquale Photography/Getty Images, Gary Mayes/Getty Images
Internal design by Laura Boren/Sourcebooks

Published by Sourcebooks Fire, an imprint of Sourcebooks
P.O. Box 4410, Naperville, Illinois 60567–4410
(630) 961-3900
sourcebooks.com

Cataloging-in-Publication Data is on file with the Library of Congress.

Printed and bound in Canada.
MBP 10 9 8 7 6 5 4 3 2 1

To Jody

For more reasons than there are pages.

ASTER

know I shouldn't leave her. She is across the room, blond hair swinging. Hips shimmying. I imagine her on the trail, her brow furrowed as she peruses a map. Her hands calloused and steady on the sandstone walls of a canyon. The Katie I know is missing. This Katie is different. Giggly. Bouncy. Drunk.

This party reminds me of a kicked anthill, bodies swarming and frantic. Girls in laughably high heels. Boys in baseball hats and unbuttoned flannels. Half-empty plastic cups on sticky kitchen counters. Inane conversations swallow up every inch of air that isn't already permeated with the endless *thump thump thump* of club music. The tiny bathroom is the only reasonably quiet and empty space here. I'd know, because I've spent half my time in there, gripping the sink and staring at my reflection.

I debate a return trip. Third time, and I haven't needed to pee once. But that's not really what I want to do. I want to walk out of this loud, nasty college apartment and never look back. A Nerf football whizzes through the living room, inches from my face. A peal of laughter rises over the music. My stomach squirms. I hate every single thing about this night.

Katie is still in the corner. Dancing with her hands up over her head with a tall boy I do not know. Not that I know any boy here. Or any person, for that matter. I only know Katie. She's the reason I'm here. Said it would be fun if I wanted to come along. She did not tell me to stay, but I know it's the right thing to do.

Too bad my feet don't give a damn about what's right.

They help me push up off the stained couch. Standing is even worse for a moment, with all these people. All these bodies. And the music. The bass line that has crawled under my skin and hammered at my ears since we walked in here an hour ago.

Another laugh, shrill, bright, and familiar.

Katie.

She is no longer dancing. She is leaned against the wall, her smile a remnant of the laughter I just heard. The red plastic cup in her hand tilts precariously. There is a small group around her, three boys and another girl, and Katie is smiling and smiling. She looks okay. I think she is okay.

"Where's your drink, girlie?"

I turn and assess the speaker. Male. Twenty-ish with a mop of messy brown hair and an *aw shucks* grin beaming above his Vineyard Vines polo. He's definitely talking to me. My hands curl into fists, but I keep the irritation off my face. Manners first.

"I could get you a drink," he offers. "If you're shy."

"No. I'm fine." I look away, remembering a quick, "Thanks though."

A snicker follows my words. I look again, spotting another one beside the first. Taller and blonder. A little mean-looking in the eyes. My muscles all constrict at once and I feel my polite smile flatten. Not in the mood doesn't even begin to describe me in this moment.

"She's been too good for us all night." The blond's eyes lock on to me like I'm a target. "She's one of those types. Aren't you?"

I narrow my eyes at him.

"Ignore him," the first guy says. "But if you change your mind about that drink…"

"I won't." I hold his gaze so it's clear I'm not being coy or what-not. I do not want a drink. And if I did, I would not trust him to procure it. There is exactly one person in this apartment I trust, and given the number of red plastic cups she's gone through tonight, that trust is wearing a little thin.

Someone petite pushes between us, and I take my chance. I ease my way past the brunette, choosing him because I don't like the blond. Don't like either of them, really. Or anything else about this party, and all I want is to get out.

Right now.

I move for the kitchen and past it to the door with the scratch in the paint and the rickety lock chain dangling by the frame. I force myself to stop and look back, to find Katie. She's still in that corner, her cheeks pink and smile so wide.

I'm surprised when she notices me, but she does. She catches my eye, and I see her expression change. Just a little, but it's enough. That's her uncomfortable smile. Having me here is making her uncomfortable. And that's all the permission I need.

I open the door, hoping for quiet and the smell of something cool and crisp. Columbus isn't like Moab though. It's huge, for one. And I am on a campus of fifty thousand or something like it.

So I smell garbage and gasoline. And I hear traffic and the thump of that same awful music booming through the thin wall of the apartment. I walk down the metal staircase, across the parking lot, and east until I find Indianola Avenue.

I head north, wishing I were on a quieter street. A longer walk. A half a dozen states away. At least I'm alone. Barely a mile and a half to my aunt's, but I don't know it well enough to find my own path. I stick to the route I know. There is a point when the neighborhood shifts. Matching chairs and potted mums appear on the porches. Flowerbeds and curtains in the windows. As I turn toward Aunt Julie's house, I see the signs for Glen Echo Park.

Tempting. The tall trees and cold air sound delicious, but it's all but one o'clock in the morning, and I'm not in Utah. I have no idea what a park in Columbus might hold at this time of night.

Aunt Julie's house is small, blue, and pristinely kept with a wide white porch and matching rockers. I slip through the side door, using the code she provided. A combo of Adam and Katie's birthdays. The lights are out except the one in the kitchen. Adam is only home between semesters now, so it's just Aunt Julie and Katie. Well, and me for this weekend.

I climb the stairs, which creak all the way up. Some part of me expects my aunt to open her bedroom door. To poke a bleary head out and ask me where I've been. Where Katie still is. It's the same way I've expected my phone to buzz since I left the party, Katie asking me why I left or letting me know she's five minutes behind me.

Instead there is silence. I slip out of my jeans and crawl onto the air mattress set up beside Katie's bed. Our backpacks are already side by side near her closet. Hope bubbles up in my chest, a reminder that this weird weekend is almost over. Tomorrow we'll have breakfast, and Aunt Julie will drive us southeast, dropping us at a point on the Buckeye Trail.

Our first hike outside of Utah will be different, sure. But it will also be the same. I close my eyes, imagining the sound of our feet on the trail. Wondering what the nights will feel like here. Will we make good miles on the first day? Or maybe we'll need time to adjust?

At some point a door swings open and wakes me up. It's not Katie. I sit up, groggy with sleep and surprised by the smudgy almost-morning glow in the room. Aunt Julie is in the doorway. Across from me, Katie's bed is still piled with the clothes she discarded while getting ready earlier.

"Aunt Julie?"

"I'm sorry, Aster. I need you to get up." Her breath shudders in and then out. "It's Katie."

The shape of her name is wrong. Everything is wrong. There are dark hollows beneath Aunt Julie's eyes. Tear tracks on her cheeks. My mouth opens with a question, but I hold it in. There is something in the air in this strange gray room. Something in the stillness that answers the question I won't ask.

I don't need to ask.

I already know something terrible happened.

KATIE

I check my phone in the trailhead parking lot because I do a lot of pointless shit these days. This exercise is particularly worthless because after hiking the canyons of Utah every summer since I was little, I know damn well what I'll find. Zero bars. Not even that cute little *SOS* symbol that assures me in a pinch I could alert some sort of authority. Want to know a hiking-in-Utah tidbit? Reliable cell phone service is a myth the minute you wander behind a giant slab of orange rock.

"Are you sure you're ready for this?" Mom asks from beside me in the Jeep.

"I was born ready," I deadpan. I push my sunglasses on as I say it, dialing my campy act up to something truly film-worthy.

Mom smiles too tightly in response, and I smile like I don't notice the tightness. We've been playing this game since we boarded the flight to Salt Lake City. It's a game where Mom pretends she's thrilled about this backpacking trip, and I pretend I don't know she's faking it.

Uncle Mike and Aster hop out of the front of the Jeep and check the notice posted near the single-stall outhouse. Vile. Inside the Jeep, Mom and I swelter as we play the game of who is going to get out and start the goodbye process first. We wind up getting out at the same time, so it's a tie.

"Katie." Mom's hands on my arms are as feather-soft as her voice. I want to flinch and pull away, but I stay still and patient and quiet. "You know you don't have to do this."

"I want to do this," I say, dropping the campy act. Now I go for hey-you're-kind-of-embarrassing-me quiet. "It was my idea, remember?"

"It was your idea in Ohio when you were surrounded by your things and your friends. You may have felt safer there."

Well, joke's on her, because I haven't felt safe there in eleven months. I'm probably not going to feel safe here either, but hey, the scenery's nicer.

"It will be good to have a break from those things," I say.

A beat passes, and then Mom brightens. "I could still go with you."

I snort. Mom's idea of roughing it is being forced to pee in a gas station bathroom.

"I don't think a four-day hike through the Utah desert is really your thing," I say. "Besides, this is a Aster-and-me thing. Always has been."

"And always will be," Aster says.

Mom and I turn to see Aster behind the Jeep. My cousin and I have barely spoken since Mom and I drove down to Moab last night, and this is the first time I'm getting a good look at her. She maybe looks thinner than I remember? Who knows. She's always been scrawny, and I've never wondered about it before. I've also never had a hard time talking to Aster before, but like every other thing in my shitstain of a life, talking to my cousin is different now. Different in the way that we barely ever do it.

"Well," Uncle Mike says. "Remember what I said about rain, and keep an eye out for the triple R."

"I will," Aster says.

"The triple R?" Mom asks.

Aster nods. "Rain, rattlesnakes—"

"And rapscallions," I say with a grin. Because I've always loved that word, especially since my no-use-for-fancy uncle introduced me to it.

Uncle Mike winks at me and then kisses the top of Aster's head. They are practically the same person, all bone-straight hair and abundant freckles and knobby elbows. Meanwhile Mom and I look like nature threw us together as a practical joke. She's tiny and dark with elfin features. I'm tall and blond and curvy everywhere a curve is possible.

"Well, that's about it. Make good miles. Check in at night," Uncle Mike says.

Aster taps the pocket in her backpack that holds the aging GPS tracker. There are newer, shinier models, but Aster is a devout believer in the church of off-grid. She doesn't even bring her phone. I do on some trails, but this one is notorious for having a seven-day stretch of trail with zero areas of service. Weird marketing slogan, but hey, who am I to judge?

"And most of all, stay safe," Mom says.

Aster tilts her head. "This is a statistically safe trail. I've outlined fairly ambitious mileage, but it would be easy to adjust to a more modest pace if necessary."

It's like reliving every other hike we've ever experienced. Uncle Mike handles supplies and Mom worries herself sick and Aster creates an ambitious but pragmatic hiking plan. She's good at that—good at plans in general.

"I know. I'm just having second thoughts about this idea," Mom says softly, the fear clear on her face.

Oh, hell no. I put on my backpack. "Well, I'm eighteen now. A real live high school graduate and everything," I say with a goofy grin. "I think it's sort of my time to lean hard into all my terrible ideas, right?"

Mom just stares at me. She stares until it feels like she's peeling back my breezy expression to see the shivering, terrified version of me she picked up at a hospital eleven months ago. I don't know what I hate more—the fact that she still thinks I'm that girl or the fact that she might be right.

My therapist is always telling me that *both things can be true.* She means I can be a hot mess express and a happy, capable woman at the same time, but that's always felt like nonsense to me. I change tactics with my Mom though, softening my tone. "We are going to be great. Plus we have the satellite GPS thing, so we can check in each night. And reach out if there's a problem."

I know just how to deliver these lines, because my job in life is to make everyone feel better about everything. I'm excellent at my job. So excellent that I've spent plenty of time successfully comforting the many people who are sad that I was raped.

Uncle Mike pats Mom's arm and moves to close the Jeep's tailgate. "I'll leave water and snacks at the drop point. See you at the pickup lot by lunchtime on Thursday."

"It's a little more than twelve miles a day," Aster says. "Closer to dinnertime is my guess."

Uncle Mike winks at me. "I think we'll be lucky if Julie doesn't have me there waiting at dawn."

My laugh sounds a little flat to my ears, and my body feels strange and wooden when each parent hugs us.

"I love you," Mom says, and then she looks at Aster too. "Both of you."

"You too," I say.

"Four and a half days," Uncle Mike says, opening the door to the Jeep.

"Forty-nine miles," Aster nods.

"Your dad would love to see you out here, Katie," he tells me.

Then he and my mom are in the Jeep and the engine is starting and holy shit, I don't want to do this. I want to run after them and ride the twenty miles back to Moab while my mom pats my knee and tells me it's okay and that I don't need to do anything I don't want to do. I want to curl up in a corner of Back of Beyond Books. I want a coffee and a scone from Love Muffin, and then maybe I'll watch the tourists buy crap they don't need from shops up and down the main drag.

Instead I stand like I'm made of stone while the Jeep crunches out of the lot and onto the road and behind a ridge that swallows up the rumble of the engine in an instant. The silence is so heavy and complete that for a moment I think something has happened to my ears. Maybe one more part of me doesn't work right anymore?

I turn in a circle, panic bubbling up in my middle. What if we forgot something, or what if we go slower than twelve miles a day? Or, God, what if we get lost, and we're just stuck out here? There is no one here! No cars, no trash in the can beside the map. We are already completely and utterly alone.

I turn in a slow circle, feeling the certainty of our solitude. And instead of my fear frothing higher, it begins to dissolve into the silence. Eerie as it is, I feel calm.

Aster crunches slowly toward the trail, the sound amplified in the quiet. I release a heavy breath and listen to her steps and the buzz of a fly moving past and the hiss of my shirt fabric when I move my arms. That's all there is out here, just us and the fathomless stretch of the desert.

I close my eyes, and for the first time since it all happened, there is no echo of his laughter. No sounds of a lock turning or picture frames thumping the wall or the rustle of fabric and zippers. When I look again, the trail rolls out, narrow and rocky and orange. Pinyon pines and junipers twist their gnarled arms toward the sun on either side of the path. The narrow strip we'll follow meanders east, where I can see a tall outcropping of rocks and small clusters of trees in the distance. There are two canyons side by side. That's where we're headed—the start of the real trail we're after.

Even from here, I can see black streaks of varnish along the walls and giant chunks of rock heaped here and there along the base where they've fallen. They're a good reminder that for all its stillness and quiet, southern Utah holds plenty of danger. But I'm not afraid of the desert. I'm not afraid of dehydration or flash floods or even being alone. The last eleven months have taught me that people are only thing worth fearing.

ASTER

MILE 1

The connector trail to our primary route winds past a few so-called points of interest. A mediocre overlook. A panel of graffiti-covered rock art. And a climbing area. That's the one place where we're likely to run into traffic. After that, we'll cut off the main trail to the forty-six-mile section that winds up and down a series of long canyons with small stretches of high desert between. According to the trail logs, we have a decent chance of having the remaining forty-six miles to ourselves.

Perfection.

A gnat buzzes past my ear, and I swat it hard. Things should improve on the bug front once we're away from all these cottonwood trees. So far, that's the only improvement we need. The weather isn't too warm, and Katie is doing well with her pack. Doing well with everything, actually. Normally I wouldn't have expected anything else. She's always been capable. But that was before.

What happened at that party changed her, and I don't know this new Katie. Not really. Is she a fighter? A wild card? A victim? She is a survivor. That much is clear, even if I'm not sure what it means.

The wall of the east canyon is growing closer, blocking out the view of the one we will actually enter. The east canyon isn't passable anymore. After a serious flash flood hit the Moab area two years back, the original trail through the east canyon was washed out beyond use. It's not optimal to follow an unmapped route, but at Back of Beyond Books, I managed to find a couple of detailed hiking notes from trail guides. Dad thinks the trail will be marked and finalized through the west canyon next year, but it is not official yet. Which is sometimes the best kind of trail.

We stop at the top of the slope, and I check the spiral-bound, multipage map—another score at Back of Beyond. All the peaks and ridges line up. Should be good to go. A triumphant shout echoes off the canyon wall. I look up.

Katie's tension sharpens every angle in her face.

"Climbers, most likely," I say in explanation.

Twenty yards later, we spot them. A slim green rope bisects an eighty-foot slab of sandstone. A man is crouched on a ledge sixty feet up, jostling something in his hands. He laughs again, and it's the kind of laugh that only comes out of a certain kind of man. A generalization, but when he swings wildly from his belay line with a Tarzan call, I feel justified in making it.

His partner is at the bottom, looking impatient. He flips his dark hair out of his eyes and spots us. Tenses and looks us over, probably searching for gear. The climbing route here is anchored, but it is too narrow to accommodate more than one or two climbers at a time. If we were here to climb, we'd be waiting on them.

I'm glad we're not waiting. I can't stand watching adrenaline junkies like this climb. They are the ones that my dad ends up scraping off the side of a canyon when they fall. Being my father's daughter has taught me there are plenty of mistakes you don't come back from out here. And with climbers like this, it is never a matter of *if* a mistake will happen. Only when.

"Hey, hey," the dark-haired one says with another hair flip. "How goes it?"

"Good," I say, not offering anything more than a tight smile. Katie says absolutely nothing. To pass them, we'll have to be in close proximity though.

So I'm not surprised when he continues the small talk, looking away from his belay line just long enough to glance at our packs. "You headed out on a long one?"

Katie stumbles behind me, going still. Tense. Silent. Which is fantastic, because she's usually the one who does the talking. Being a social butterfly does not come naturally for me. I force myself to emulate what I remember Katie doing. Katie from before at least.

I stop and turn, trying a pleasant expression that feels uncomfortable. "Yes, we're headed out for four days or so."

"Cool, cool, us too." He looks up at his partner, who is now playing with a rosin bag and making guitar noises, and laughs. "Jesus, sorry about that. I'm Carter."

"Nice to meet you," I say. Not that we've actually met. I don't see a real reason for Carter to have either of our names. But still. Manners matter. "You're doing a multiday climb?"

"No, no. We're camping here tonight."

"Hi!" The partner booms from overhead, drawing the word out until it means something more. "You two looking for a climbing lesson?"

My smile withers when I look up at him. "Definitely not."

Carter chuckles. "Sorry. That's Luke. He's—"

"You sure you cuties don't want lessons?"

A sigh from Carter. "Well, he's a dick. Obviously."

"We need to go." Katie. She's behind me. Hands clenched into fists. Her cheeks have gone very white. Not because she's sick or in pain. No. She's frightened.

"We should head out," I say.

"Maybe we'll see you out there," Carter says. "We don't head out until tomorrow afternoon though."

"Dude, are they going south?" Luke asks from the wall.

"We will be well ahead by tomorrow," I say.

"Wait for us!" Luke yells. "You can totally go with us!" He laughs and swings from his belay again. A pendulum moving back and forth. Back and forth. "We are real good company."

"Dude, knock it off!" Carter calls back. Then he shakes his head. "Sorry about that. Good luck out there."

"You too!"

Katie pushes past us with a wave, heading south.

"Don't go, blondie!"

"Shut the hell up!" Carter shouts. "Switch that damn relay!"

One stiff wave is all I offer them. Then I follow Katie. She's moving fast so I have to work to keep pace.

"Are you okay?" I ask.

"Yeah, I'm fine. Just want to get a move on."

She's lying. But we keep moving, and I keep my mouth shut. Ten yards up, and I hear Carter shout.

"Did you switch the cam?"

"Nah, I don't have it. I'd need a huge one."

"We have them down here."

"Too much of a pain in the ass."

"Dude, that cam isn't big enough. You need to use—"

A sharp zip tells me it's coming. One of them yelps. Another swears. All of it happens at the same time. I see Luke falling and falling. Arms, legs, and that thread of a rope that is not linked to a proper mechanism.

It is one second. Maybe less. Luke's body hurtling down. My heart climbing into my throat. Katie frozen to the stone beneath her. I should cover her eyes, because she should not see—

Luke's body jerks at the end of his rope. Carter is at an angle, heels dug into the ground to hold the belay steady.

"Oh my God," Katie whispers.

Carter groans. Katie takes a shuddering breath. And Luke? The damn idiot laughs.

"Let's go," I say, but Katie is still looking. Her hand is at her throat. She is clearly relieved. Not me.

The only thing I feel is rage.

"Let's go," I say again.

I march forward without checking to see if she follows. I do not look back. Not once. I keep my eyes on the next ridge.

A quarter of a mile later, I spot a short wooden sign in the center of the trail. At one point I'm guessing this offered mileage information about the east canyon. Now an orange sign is bolted across it. *Danger. Trail Closed.* It looks like a temporary detour sign. But trail repairs can take years out here. Decades if it they aren't in one of the big parks.

Most hikers will take the hint and turn back at a sign like this. But we are in the footsteps of another kind of hiker. A thin trickle of people who wondered if there was a chance of getting through the other canyon. Those are my kind of hikers. I spot the narrow ribbon of path winding through the scrubby desert.

"That's our trail," I say.

"That? It's like six inches wide. Are we sure it isn't a critter trail?"

"Most trails started that way. Buffalo paths and whatnot."

"Well, then. Lead the way, buffalo girl."

We march on another hundred yards or so before stopping to check the detour notes. Two boulders sit on the south side of the canyon opening, just like the notes promised. That's the spot we should enter. So far so good.

A soft sigh behind me. Katie. She's pulling her water bottle out of the side pocket, and a twinge of worry flits through me as she drinks. She looks strong. Calm. Happy. Then again, I thought she looked happy at that party, too, so what the hell do I know?

"All good?" I ask.

"Mm-hm." She looks back over her shoulder. "That guy. The one who fell. Do you think he's going to get down okay?"

"No way to know." I turn back to the trail, hoping she'll drop it.

"Well, I obviously didn't want to take lessons or whatever the hell he was talking about. But still…" She scrunches her nose. "I don't know. Should we have checked to make sure they were okay?"

"No."

"No? Wow, talk about a hard-line stance." Her laugh is a token offer at best.

A raven cries in the distance. It feels like a warning to tread lightly. Maybe I should. This Katie might prefer a candy-coated truth. She would almost certainly like to know I'm not a heartless monster. She has already had her quota of heartless monsters. But I have never lied to Katie before. Now doesn't feel like the time to start.

"Some people don't want to be helped," I say. "They want to believe they are indestructible."

"No one is indestructible."

"No," I say. "But he made his choices."

"True," she says, her gaze taking a faraway look. "I guess they could have asked for help. They knew we were still probably close."

"Exactly," I say. "They didn't ask, and I am not out here looking for people to save."

Katie laughs, but I am not sure I meant it as a joke. And when I think about her clenched fists and white cheeks, I am not even sure what I said was true.

KATIE

—

MILE 2

'm maybe two miles in, and I'm delighted to report that I have not, in fact, died of a cardiac event. It's kind of a miracle really. My recent trauma hasn't proven to be a great workout motivator for me. Not that I can really blame the rape for this one. Actually, thanks to a victim support group, I have a membership to a nice cushy gym with all the bells and bows. But gyms have men and motion and, worst of all, mirrors. I don't really do mirrors these days. Or either of those other things, for that matter. I do occasionally pant out a mile on the ancient treadmill in our basement, so there's that.

"We're going to have to climb down and back out," Aster says, pointing ahead.

"Like, we're going to need to borrow that dude's rope, or we're just going to have to clamber over some rocks?"

Aster takes a long drink and shakes her head. "Just scrambling, but the notes use the word *challenging*."

We share a smirk. Challenging on a hiking guide can mean all kinds of things, but around here it usually means this-is-going-to-be-a-giant-pain-in-the-ass. I look back at the narrow trail we've been following and spot a wider section a few yards ahead with a few low rocks. The rocks look good for sitting, and I don't think I'm the first one to notice, because I also spot a small plastic storage bin. It's weighed down with smaller rocks to keep it in place, and *LOG* is written across the side in giant markered letters.

"Ah, the death book," I say.

"Mostly the logs are used to determine trail use. And to communicate conditions and information. Especially important here since part of this is not technically an official trail."

"Sure, fine, but it's far more exciting to think it's there to aid recovery groups in finding the remains of some dumbass who wandered off a cliff. Has your dad ever used them?"

Aster's pack rustles, something small—maybe a zipper—jangling softly with each step. "Dad's team is usually after survivors. Not that he hasn't had his share of body-recovery missions. Also, you don't have to be dumb or reckless to die out here."

"Fair point. Remember when you helped me write my fifty-ways-to-die-in-the-desert paper for AP Enviro? Wasn't one of those stories I used true?"

Aster nods. "A tourist couple who died on their honeymoon after heading out for a hike with a single bottle of water. That was a while ago though."

"I still wish I would have added that one about the dude who broke both legs when he decided to climb a Class 3 while holding a beer."

"Dad did drag that guy out. Good lesson in why flip-flops are never a wise choice when climbing." I laugh and Aster tilts her head.

"He was drinking. Could have been that."

"If it was a single beer, I doubt it. Flip-flops get my vote."

She laughs. "Since I don't drink, I'll have to take your word for it."

Heat zips up my neck. "What's that supposed to mean?"

Aster's shoulders go tight, so I know she can feel the way the air has shifted. Her eyes turn soft and wide, like she's completely innocent. Like when she said she'd have to take my word for it, she somehow didn't mean I'd know all about how much beer a person could handle. Because I'm such a world-class drinker or whatever? It's bullshit. I've gone drinking exactly three times in my life. The first two times I barely drank enough to feel it. And the third time? I wound up in the hospital with a rape kit souvenir.

"I don't understand what you're asking," Aster says.

"Sure you don't. Did you say that because you think *I* would know all about drinking?"

Her hands go up. "Katie, I didn't—I didn't mean…" She takes a steadying breath. "I thought we were joking."

I'm already winding up my next smart remark, but then I remember that Aster doesn't lie. She tells the truth when I wish she wouldn't. About haircuts and homemade dinners and grades that missed the mark back in high school. She's a devoted truth teller.

"Weren't we joking?" Her voice is small.

For the span of a breath, I feel something swell and stretch between us. It's the terrible, invisible thing, the thing we don't ever, ever talk about. Not when she walked into my hospital room and not any time since. Even now, we aren't talking about it, but it's right there. Right under her worried eyes and inside the aching hollow in my chest.

"I'm sorry," I say and then, because I'm ridiculous and strange and very, very broken, I laugh. "I can't expect everyone to tiptoe around me. I actually hate it when people do."

Aster rolls her hands into fists and releases them. She looks miserably uncomfortable, so I guess my work here is complete. I sigh. "Maybe we should check that log and do the whole sign-in thing."

Aster is at the tub before I finish the sentence. The book she retrieves resembles a cheap, boring spiral notebook, but I know the look of it. The waxy cover and the sound of the paper under her hands tells me it's a weatherproof notebook.

"Nothing earth-shattering," she says, handing it over.

I scan the notebook too. There's nothing official or formal about this, but hikers have made their own rules. A blank line between each entry, and most entries come in a name-then-date-then-notes-on-the-trail format.

September 15—Heading south. Day 3. Shit ton of mud. Extra socks required.

Meg and Collum Adkins—Sep 26—Heading north. Getting picked up at the trailhead two miles north of here. Long east-west switchback is poorly marked. One troublesome character near the south terminus. The marked springs were low at best. You'll need to bring at least a third of your water.

Pete/Jack/Tanner—Sept 29—Heading north. Floods. Mosquitos. Map mileage off.

RF—Oct 2—Heading south, day one! Stoked!

"Troublesome character?" I ask.

Aster waves it off. "That was a while ago. They would be long gone by now. And frankly, we don't have much worth troubling over, unless someone wants an ancient GPS."

"Or your dad's trail mix," I say. Then I point at the last entry. "That's two days ago. Do you think we'll run into them?"

Aster shakes her head. "Doubt it. Unless they're moving super slow. Or pulling an out and back."

Out and backs aren't uncommon, letting hikers enjoy the thrill of backpacking somewhere remote without the commitment of twenty or thirty miles until the next trailhead. I think of Carter and Luke, and hope to God that's what they're planning. Because I hate the idea of them on this trail, creeping up behind us mile by mile.

"Katie, I'm sorry if what I said insinuated anything."

"It's no big deal," I say lightly, but unlike Aster, I lie all the time, and I'm damn good at it. At least when it comes to this, I am.

"All right," she says softly. It stings when she says it and it stings when she turns to leave a quick note in the log and it stings even more when she doesn't look back. Which is ridiculous. I told her it was no big deal. But deep down inside, I guess I'm a passive-aggressive jerk who wants her to read my mind and somehow know that I don't want her to ignore this weirdness. And I don't want her to acknowledge it either. I want her to magically give me the ability to let her throwaway comments roll right off me like they used to. I want to be the person I was before, and deep down, I'm such a mess that I want her to fix it. To fix me.

A raven cries, calling for a snack. Or calling me out on my bullshit, maybe. Who knows. I spot it perched on the side of an orange slab of rock, its beak slightly open. Nothing feels more like Utah to me than the sight of that bird with its cocked head and glossy black feathers. It cries again, a dry, gurgling plea that sounds like my most beautiful memories and my darkest hours, and it makes me feel more alive than I have in eleven months.

"Looking for a handout?" I ask softly. The raven hops closer, tilting its head this way and then that, because it's one hundred percent hoping I'm going to toss a Frito or a rotting chunk of hot dog or something. But if I can forget the scavenger side to this bird, having it close to me feels like magic.

It stays with us for the next four miles. And those miles are slow and crappy with lots of boulders and loose stones and patches of prickly pears that force us to dodge and weave our way along the canyon floor. By the time we stop for a late lunch, I'm working on a potential blister on my left heel. My shoulder is sore and the socks I picked are making my feet sweat. And fine, I leave the raven a tiny piece of seed-studded crust from the peanut butter sandwich my mom packed, but Aster hasn't said a single word since we left the trail log, so this dang raven has been my sole source of interaction.

Aster rustles the map across from me. She's a little pink from the heat now that it's in the mid-eighties, and when she looks up, her faint freckles blend into the flush across her cheeks.

"I think that note in the log is right," she says.

"Which note?"

"The one about the mileage being off. The journal guide I bought said five miles, but the map..." She shakes her head and thrusts the map at me, pointing at a spot that looks pretty much the same as every other spot on the map. "I need a second opinion. Does this look like that outcropping across from us? I think it stairsteps like the map. And back a half a mile or so ago, we had that big curve like this."

She taps at another place, and I dutifully stare down at the slim tip of her finger.

"That looks right to me," I lie. Or maybe I don't lie. Who knows. I was so ravenous and shaky for that last mile, I don't think I would have noticed if Big Bird passed us on the trail. And all these maps are just slight variations of the same lines and blobs to me, anyway.

Aster frowns. "Definitely a problem. This route is substantially longer."

I shrug. "Okay, so we hike a little longer than we thought. No bigs, right?"

"I think we still have three miles until the end of this canyon. And the guide goes into a lot of detail about a challenging scramble on the climb out."

I wince. "There's that word *challenging* again."

"Climbing isn't what scares me about this," she says, and there's a hush in her voice that sucks the humor right out of me. "Katie, we've still got a couple hours to go. We might be dealing with that climb in the dark."

ZERO MILES

She wakes up to die. She sees nothing. Hears nothing. Her body won't move, though every nerve and tendon tries to fix that. She feels them, the jolts and jabs. An unscratchable itch that snaps at her.

Move.

Twist.

Writhe.

Get away from the pain.

The pain is an animal or many animals. They climb up her back and bite at her limbs, and it should end soon. It *has* to end soon. She begs for it. Screams and screams until her ears ring and her breathing grows ragged. Then she realizes she is not screaming at all.

She is silent.

The fact scares her. And there are more. One, two, three, she lines them up. She cannot speak. She cannot see. She cannot move. The thoughts sink softly into an abyss, and she wants to follow, wants that deep, dark stillness.

If she is lucky, she will die soon.

ASTER

---

9 MILES

Darkness arrives in canyons quickly. The sun hasn't fully set, but everything is cast in murky shadow. My headlamp illuminates narrow slivers of the world around us. Jagged boulders like broken teeth. A sheer wall of rock on the right. The trail, narrow and rutted, before us. Which begs the question: am I following a true path or a wash channel where hard rain cut grooves into the canyon floor?

I stop to double-check the guide and find the balanced rock that's noted. Try to remember the curves we've passed. Katie shifts on her feet behind me, and I wonder how she's holding up. We haven't spoken much.

"So are we getting close to the end of this canyon, or are we planning on giving up and climbing one of the walls out?"

"No," I assure her. "I think we're very close. I'm concerned about the climb in this light."

"Can we camp here and climb out in the morning?"

"Not safely. It's October."

I turn in time to see her brow furrow. Her face is flushed, and the hair that's pulled loose from her ponytail is dark with sweat.

She tilts her head, her chin the pointed end of her heart-shaped face. "Are you thinking it could rain?"

"Always possible."

My headlamp illuminates about two hundred feet ahead in spot mode, which I'm using, but the beam is narrow. It's like piecing together the canyon through a peephole, but it all matches up. We have to be all but a quarter mile from the end now. Except I should see the end if we are. Shouldn't I?

"Do you need to rest?" Katie asks, presumably because I'm not moving.

"I'm just trying to get my bearings and whatnot. It's dark, so I don't know when this canyon ends."

Her laugh is soft. "Aren't you the one who always tells me we can't get lost in a canyon?"

"I'm also the one who says to be cautious when it's dark."

A beat of silence. The wind whispers at the other end of the canyon. The smell of sage—pungent and green—brings back memories of countless other hikes. A thousand other mistakes or setbacks I've overcome in the past. Without snapping at anyone.

"I'm sorry," I say. "That was uncalled for."

"Yeah, but I get it," she says. To my surprise, she doesn't sound annoyed. "Shit can go downhill fast out here."

"Yes," I say. I suppose *downhill* is a reasonable term to use. Minor inconveniences can quickly turn into life-or-death catastrophes in canyon country. A small leak in your water bladder. A sudden rainstorm. A twisted ankle.

That last one is reason enough to take our time. I can't have anything bad happen on this trip. After what happened to her—after that night—I just need everything here to be right for her. For both of us.

I close my eyes briefly. They're burning and my throat feels raw. Allergies, maybe? There are plenty of things in bloom right now, and one of them must really be getting to me.

"I didn't mean to push you," Katie says. "It's just getting cold and way windier, and frankly it's kind of creepy down in this canyon with the walls bringing all the doom and gloom."

"I understand," I say, though I only understand pieces of what she's saying. It is cold and windy, but there is nothing creepy about these canyon walls. In fact, these ridges are currently keeping the worst of that wind at bay.

I press my palm to the rock, still warm from the sun that's been hidden from us for the last hour. Gratitude surges through me. My hands and feet are resting on the bones of this planet. I will never not be amazed out here.

I start forward again, sand hissing and hissing as I walk. The wind is cold on my face, but my jacket is keeping my body warm. A raven cries, suddenly and unexpectedly, and Katie jumps, swearing. Little late for a raven, but one has been trailing us, so I'm surprised at her reaction.

I turn, careful to keep my headlamp out of her eyes. "Are you okay?"

"Yeah, just…" There is such a long pause that I think maybe Katie's not going to finish. But then she does, her voice small and quiet. "I'm freaked out. The dark…it sucks."

"I won't let—" I cut myself off abruptly. Because that's not true anymore is it? I already let plenty happen to Katie. I look away. I tell myself it's because I am scanning the trail for danger, because it feels easier than focusing on how hard it is to face her.

"I know you won't let anything happen," she says softly, finishing the thought I wouldn't. I walk faster because I can't stand that softness. Not from her. But Katie stops walking altogether. "Aster?"

I cringe before I look at her. It's not forgiveness in her eyes though. Just honesty. "I still trust you," she says.

I swallow, and my throat feels thick and scratchy. It could just be the same thing that's making my eyes burn. Or it could be Katie's words. Probably that.

"I mean, I know you know what you're doing out here." The words tumble out of her in a rush to fill the silence I'm leaving. "Obviously, you know. You're, like, an expert."

A vague humming noise comes out of me. No response seems appropriate. She should not trust me. I am not an expert. It is impossible to know what you're doing out here. There are so many wrong things about her words. Where would I start? I suppose silence is preferable.

"Okay, my turn to ask if you're all right," Katie says.

I nod awkwardly, having no clue of where to go from here. Is it a joke or a jab? These sorts of things used to be clear. As long as I can remember, Katie has been a person who gets me. But what was always much stranger is that I got her too. Since we were kids, I knew what she needed. I could sense her mood. I always picked up on her silent cues and whatnot.

Until I walked out of a party and left her alone with a monster.

We start moving forward again. While we walk, I bite down on my water valve and take a long drink. The water is far from cold at this point, but it still soothes my raw throat. Every time I blink, my eyelids burn. My fatigue is intense, which makes me worry about the *challenging scramble* the guide promises. A simple hop up a couple of boulders would feel challenging right now. What is going on with me?

"Shit," Katie says, voice sharp with alarm. I whirl automatically, feeling my stomach drop.

"Something moved," she says. "By that rock."

I freeze. We are maybe thirty minutes after sunset. Prime time for rattlesnakes, scorpions, and black widows to be awake. Moving. Hunting. Striking.

There is no rattling, which is marginally reassuring since the rattlesnake is the only one that could deliver a fatal bite. But any sort of bite would create more delay and misery on a day that's starting to feel like a whole lot of both.

"Do you know what it was?" I ask.

"I know it was on the ground. I think it moved near that rock."

"Reptile? Mammal? Maybe a lizard?"

"Maybe? I don't know. I didn't get the chance to ask it for some form of identification."

"Probably just a lizard," I say, and then I look down, keeping my headlamp beam on the large rock between us. An edge of the rock hangs over the path. The trail is maybe eighteen inches wide here with two foot ledges opposite the rock Katie is watching. Logically, it's highly likely this is not a dangerous animal.

But it could be a rattlesnake.

It's the right environment. Right time of day. The least convenient possible moment for a snakebite, which often seems to coincide with when they happen.

I tilt my head and switch my beam to flood for a wider view. A shadow moves. Could be a snake. A lizard. A kangaroo rat. Unless I reach down to yank up the edge of that rock, I'm not going to know for sure.

I shake my head. "I can't get a good look at it."

"You know, it's fine. I'll go over." Katie sounds bright about it, and as soon as the words are out, she finds handholds and hikes her feet up onto the wall. Katie has always been a solid climber, and this is a basic move. She works her way a few feet left until she's past the stone with its mystery creature. I step back to give her space to land next to me.

She dusts her hands off, and I grin. "You are still a pro."

"Hardly, but—" She cuts herself off and points. I turn my beam and catch a better glimpse of the yellow, waxy body peeking out from beneath the rock. Just a sliver of exoskeleton and I know.

"Whoa," she whispers.

Giant desert scorpion. Not particularly aggressive or dangerous, though they sure look it. It scuttles backward on eight jointed legs, its tail curled up over its back like an invitation. Its yellow body would all but melt into the color of the rocks during daylight.

"Not something to worry about," I say softly, but a strange feeling curls in my stomach watching those yellow legs undulate.

Some people consider scorpions to be a sign of change. Danger. Even death. One legend tells of the scorpion that was carried across a river only to sting the creature who bore him safely to the shore. Because in legend, stinging is the scorpion's way.

I am not afraid of scorpions. And I do not believe in legends. But when we move on, I can't stop thinking of that story. The centuries-old warning. The last time I missed a warning, Katie was assaulted.

What happens if this scorpion is a warning too? A warning of change. Danger. Death.

KATIE

---

10 MILES IN

I t is colder than a polar bear's ass by the time Aster stops. Adding to that, my feet have passed sore and are moving into just-cutting-them-off-might-feel-better territory. But while Aster starts double and triple checking her map, I dig my hoodie out of my backpack and find another problem waiting for me in a decidedly empty interior pocket.

I do not have my headlamp. I also do not have my emergency deck of cards or my tiny stash of Velcro straps or my ring of safety pins. I can picture all four of these items lined up neatly in the ready-to-pack zone on my dresser. Except I didn't pack because we were running late for our flight and had to bolt out the door, and I'm pretty sure Aster is not going to love this.

I sigh and tip my head up to look up. The stars are out, a bright glittering blanket with a glowing gray smear stretching diagonally across the sky. It's the Milky Way. In Ohio, there truly isn't a single place where you can see it like this. One more reason my home state isn't the home of my heart anymore, I guess.

"I think we are out of the canyon," Aster says. Her voice sounds gravelly. Apparently, she's not an endless font of energy either. "We still have the rocks to scramble up ahead, but that's about it."

"I don't see the climb," I say. I don't add that I can't see much of anything.

"It's straight ahead."

Aster adjusts her headlamp beam, and I see a haphazard-looking heap of boulders and above it, less clearly, a dark horizontal line. That has to be the ledge. And if I remember right—and I might not because Aster loves to rhapsodize trail notes the way some women love to talk about romance novels—there is plenty of flat, clear ground there good for camping.

Aster is still perusing the scramble area with her headlamp. Maybe she won't even notice that I don't have mine. Or maybe she'll have an extra. Or maybe I'll sprout wings and fly up to the top. Who knows. Something chitters behind us, and something else clicks to our right. All the night creatures are coming to life.

I try to scope out the kind of scramble we're dealing with. The rocks are like cubes of ice spilling from the lip of a cup into the canyon floor. The light beam swings away from the wall and over to me.

"Where's your headlamp?"

"Um, about that…"

Aster blinks, her expression blank.

My answering laugh is short and strained. "It's a possibility that I may have left that at home. And by *possibility*, I mean *probability*. And by *probability*, I mean I one hundred percent left it on my dresser along with several other less important items."

Aster takes a breath to answer and then sneezes loudly.

"Bless you."

"Thanks." She frowns and then sniffs. "Are your allergies bothering you?"

"No they never do out here." Now that I'm looking, I notice Aster is pale. Her eyes are heavy lidded, and she's been sniffling for a while now. "Do you even have allergies?"

"Not that I recall." She shakes it off. "Come on; let's figure out how we are going to do this."

Aster doesn't have an extra headlamp, but she has a pen flashlight that we clip into my ponytail. It's not perfect, but it's better than no light at all, and I need my hands free to make this climb, so we're going to make it work.

Under normal conditions, I truly live for stuff like this on a hike and am forever trying to talk Aster into a real climbing trip. But it's dark and windy, and thanks to nine hours on the trail, my arms and legs are overcooked noodles.

Aster moves her head slowly, taking in the ascent. "Starting from the right makes sense."

She's right. There are three short, wide boulders with fairly flat tops. "Yeah, and the one in the middle is twice as tall, but see that horizontal lip almost halfway up?"

"Yes."

"That will make it easy. That's not the piece I'm worried about." My gaze drags to the real problem—a single smooth and narrow rock bridging the space between the middle boulder and the top of the cliff. It's maybe eight feet tall, which isn't much. But since it's sitting on top of a pile, it will leave us thirty feet up for a few dangerous moments while we try to heave ourselves to the top of that rock and the ledge of the ground beyond the canyon.

We start out strong, hopscotching up the first three boulders. On the next rocks, Aster goes first. She's slow and methodical, and I follow the same route. Between the low lighting and my trail-weary muscles and the arctic wind whipping across us, there are dozens of ways I could slip and crack a bone—or my whole face for that matter. Or we could get bitten or stung by some living thing hiding in the pitch-black crevices I'm poking my fingers into. Cool as that scorpion was, it was also a reminder that there are plenty of happy-to-sting-us things crawling around this desert with us.

"This section up here is tough," Aster says, sniffling again as she finds a solid toehold on the obelisk rock.

I hoist myself the rest of the way up the boulder before it and wait for her to grab the lip of the cliff overhead. Her boots scrape at the sandstone as she inches a foot higher. Once she grips the cliff, I approach using the same path. It's maybe nine feet tall without a lot of helpful divots for climbers, but there are a few bumps and grooves, and frankly, I've done more difficult bouldering at climbing parks.

I situate myself halfway up the rock and hear Aster grunt as she heaves her body up over the ledge of the cliff. Her boot slips. Above me the ground snaps. Sand sprays down, pebbling my head and shoulders. I close my eyes and press my body to the gritty boulder, my heart pounding.

Aster hisses above, and it sounds like she's in pain.

"Are you okay?" My voice wobbles.

"Cactus," she says, which doesn't feel like much of an answer.

My head swims and opening my eyes doesn't help. There is a gap now, between the rock I'm on and the sandstone ledge above. Whatever crumbled above changed this situation. The gap is slightly wider now. It is going to be a bigger reach to get to that ledge. Maybe just a few inches, but enough to make me think. Can I reach it? Will it crumble when I grab hold? Will I fall? Who knows? But staying here isn't a good option either.

My hands shake on the rock, and the pressure of my heartbeat pulses behind my ears. *Get a grip, Katie.* A fall would truly bust me up, but no one is dying on this pile of rocks. But I hate this feeling. I hate the way it makes me think of plastic cups and loud zippers and frames thumping against a dingy bedroom wall.

No. I grit my teeth because I will not, will not, *will not* think of that night. Not here in this place that might as well be a whole other universe.

I take a steadying breath and let it out slow. I find my met-aphorical big-girl socks, pull them up high, and get on with it. Pushing off and up with my right foot, catching the ledge with a too-hard smack of my palm. My fingers grip, and then it is all autopilot. My foot moves, my muscles contract, and I heave myself out of the canyon and onto the ledge.

It's all a bit anticlimactic, me flopped onto my back like I've run a marathon while the Milky Way looks down with its arms full of galaxies.

Aster hisses, and I sit up, my hair-tie flashlight flopping at a strange angle. I yank it free, tugging a few stray hairs with it, and finally, I see her. She has one pant leg rolled up, and her sock—white this morning—is dark with blood.

"Shit, ouch!" I say. "Are you okay? What did that cliff do to you?"

"Cactus," she corrects. "There was a prickly pear against the wall. I couldn't see it."

I see part of the prickly pear in question, a few of its green thorny paddles snapped off, quills jutting in dozens of directions.

Aster groans softly, and I unlatch my pack, setting it down to search for our tiny camp lantern. It pops open with a satisfying click, and a small bowl of light surrounds us. Lousy for hiking but not half bad for sitting around camp or assessing a cactus attack.

"You've got to look sharp out here, right?" I say, looking for the first aid kit.

Her laugh is more of a cough.

"I mean, I know you're a little stuck—"

"These are terrible puns, Katie."

"That's the whole point. Get it? *Point?*"

I find the tweezers in the pack and move closer to offer them up. My stomach constricts at the sight of her ankle, all gleaming and crimson and awful. She grabs the tweezers with bloody fingers and catches me looking.

"I think it looks worse than it really is."

"Well, good. Because it looks a bit like the cactus shot you in the leg with a Glock."

"An extreme exaggeration," she says. Aster rips open an antibacterial wipe, and the odor dredges up a murky memory in the back of my mind. When she pulls on a neoprene glove, it snaps into perfect focus.

I am on the edge of a hospital bed, and there is a tall nurse beside me with warm eyes and a steady voice and neoprene gloves. She tells me her name, she tells me where I am, and she tells me about the kit. She brings me a warm blanket, which she tucks around my body like I'm a little girl, and it is so kind. But when I hear the rustle of that blanket, the sound of fabric shifting against fabric—the nausea rises in me so fast that I'm vomiting before I even know what's happening. And she's right there with a pink plastic basin, her hand on my back, featherlight but somehow strong enough to hold me together while my world blows apart.

"Ouch."

Aster's complaint pulls me back, but she is still focused on her work. I blink away my memories, letting the clicks and chirps of night creatures drown out the noise in my own mind.

Utah is a million miles away from the therapy sessions and the mental check-ins and the doctor's appointments for my neck pain, which has been constant since that night. Since he pushed me down with his hand on the back of my head and took everything beautiful away from me.

Or tried.

I feel something steely and hot take root in my stomach. He did not take this place and these moments from me. *No one* will take this from me.

"Well," she says, breathing a little hard as she shucks her glove and collects her bloody gauze into a Ziploc bag. "That was unpleasant."

"How can I help?" I smooth my ponytail with shaking hands. "Do you want a bandage or tape, or maybe a piece of wood to bite?"

She laughs. "Maybe one of the two-inch bandages and some antibacterial cream?"

I find the bandage and cream, and then, a scream tears through the night.

I launch to my feet, but the sound is everywhere and nowhere— shrill and rasping. It wedges itself into my darkest, coldest places.

I start forward but stop because I don't know where to go. I don't know how to help or where to run, but standing still feels dangerous.

The scream cuts to silence. It's so fast. I hold my breath, sure I've misplaced the sound. Lost my hearing. Something. But whatever I heard is gone. The wind blows and the crickets sing and the desert closes around that scream like it never happened at all.

ZERO MILES

ick, pick, pick.

She can't place it. She floats and spins in a sea of pain, and she can't place this new thing. A sound? A feeling? Is it her heart stuttering? She thinks maybe this is the end.

Pick, pick, pick.

Three hard jerks drag her up from the fog. Stabs of pain that feel different than the others. Her eyes open to a dark smear overhead. Crushed blueberries. Old bruises. Maybe she is not awake at all.

Pick, pick.

Her nerves fire once. Twice. She comes back to her body on the second buzz. She was gone, and now she is here. Just like that.

She is stretched out long, something hard beneath her. Cold air moves above. The pain is everywhere. Inside her bones and skin. And then her blood.

She blinks again. Grit in her eyes. Tiny spots of white against the darkness. No, not spots. Stars. She is outside. Somewhere cold and hard. So quiet.

Pick, pick, pick.

Stab. Stab. Stab. She lifts her head. Just enough to send a wave of agony rolling though her temples, crashing down her neck and shoulders. Her vision slowly pulls itself together. She sees herself. A blue shirt. Dark pants. A large black bird perched on her right thigh.

Pick-stab-*pick*-stab-*pick*-stab.

She cries out, her body jerking. Her head, suddenly too heavy, falls back to the ground, but she feels the bird's weight lift from her thigh. Hears its wings beat. It perches nearby, cocking its head.

A raven. Its beak gleams in the darkness, wet and dark with blood. She watches as it opens its mouth. She doesn't know which one of them screams.

ASTER

---

10 MILES

Katie bolts upright, head swiveling and eyes only half-awake. "What is that?"

Her voice is raspy with sleep and fear, but mine is raspy with something else. "Coyotes."

"It's not what we heard last night?"

"No. Just coyotes." I swallow, wincing.

I don't know what we heard last night. That sound was farther away—but it was not coyotes. It was a scream. Lingering. Frightening. Human. There are plenty of reasons for humans to scream though. I reminded myself of every one I could think of while we set up the tent last night. I kept thinking of them until I fell asleep.

"Are you sure?" Katie asks.

The coyote howls again as if answering her. It is a little farther north now. A few seconds later, another answers. And then another. It's an all but endless loop of wailing in the distance.

"They are moving off." My voice sounds worse than hers, which has little do with sleep. "Heading north. The way we came."

"How do you know?"

"They arrived about twenty minutes ago. Sniffed around, but I hit the side of the tent a few times and spooked them."

Not before they spooked me. I woke to one of them snuffling and snuffling, its snout separated from my head by six inches and a thin layer of vinyl. Alarming. But not the most concerning part of my morning.

"And you don't think that was what we heard last night?" she asks.

"No."

Katie looks at me with wide eyes. She wants me to elaborate. To explain and reassure her. I tuck the guide I've been reviewing back into my backpack instead.

"What was that scream then?" she asks. "Was it some kind of animal?"

Suppose I was too hopeful expecting her to drop it.

"Honestly, I don't know." It's true. Mostly.

"Do you think someone was in trouble?" she asks.

"People scream for all kinds of reasons."

"It scared me," she says. "It sounded like someone was fighting for their life."

"Or someone saw a scorpion. Or stubbed their toe. Or any number of things."

She looks unconvinced, but I have more pressing issues than a single scream from nine hours ago. My fingers discreetly test the tender, swollen glands beneath my jaw. I also have a stuffy nose, a sore throat, and a headache throbbing in step with my pulse.

No chance I can blame this level of misery on allergies. Not that I have any idea what this is. It could be a run-of-the-mill summer cold or the start of a miserable case of flu or Covid or whatnot. I clear my throat, sending waves of pain through the area.

"You don't sound right," Katie says. "Are you sick?"

The coyote howls again. It's much farther away now. Katie tilts her head to see me more clearly. Telling her feels risky. She's already nervous about that stupid scream.

"Maybe," I answer. No point in elaborating. It could be a cold. No reason to rile her up over a stupid cold.

I push my sleeping bag down around my waist. My head thrums with the motion. I find my first aid kit and work two ibuprofen out of a plastic packet while Katie watches in the darkness.

"How sick are you?"

"Not very."

My water bottle has an inch of lukewarm water. I take the pills and rub my temples.

"Aster?" she prods.

"I have a cold. Not a big deal."

"Look, I'm not trying to be paranoid, but how long have you been sick? You fell getting up the cliff yesterday and ripped up your ankle…"

The pain in my head tightens. "And?"

Katie pulls her ponytail out and refastens it with quick, angry movements. "Did you know you were sick when we started out? Because it's not like you to fall, and now you're suddenly sick as hell, and it feels like a bad idea to tackle a forty-nine-mile hike while sick."

"Do you think I would intentionally start a forty-nine-mile hike if I knew I was ill?"

"I don't know."

"You seem to be implying it."

"Okay, fine. Maybe it's just me, but I'm not crazy for asking. Everybody in my life is being extra careful around me. Hiding everything they don't think the poor little victim can handle."

"I have never called you a victim."

"No, you actually never call me anything." She spits the words out. "You've barely spoken to me at all since this shit went down."

"I am speaking to you now. I spoke with you to plan this trip. Remember?"

"Yeah, I do. But you also failed to mention that you might be coming down with bubonic plague or whatever."

"I didn't know!" I blow my nose and drop my volume. "And you're being dramatic. I'm not dying of tuberculosis here."

"Fine, I'm dramatic. But I'm always dramatic. That hasn't changed, but you are acting different. And I have to know that you can still tell me if something is up out here."

"I can and I will." But will I? Am I even telling her how sick I am right now?

"Okay, fine. Do you think you can still do this? Because you look like maybe you can't."

My laugh is hard and angry. "It's a damn cold, Katie. I figured I would probably live to fight another day. But maybe I'm wrong. Maybe we should send for the rescue helicopter and call it."

She is very quiet. Outside, the light is shifting, the pink of dawn giving way to an impossibly bright morning. It gives me more light to watch her not move. And to think about the irony of my dramatic outburst and her stoic response. My face goes hot with shame.

"That was unnecessary," I say. "This headache is making me a jerk. I'm sorry."

Katie squirms in her sleeping bag, wriggling her shoulders and arms free.

I wait for her to react. I wait for her to call me out for shouting. It would be valid and justified, but she just blows out a heavy breath.

"I'm sorry that you have a cold," she says. "And I'm sorry I made it some weird you're-hiding-shit-from-Katie thing. I recognize my actions were unfair."

It's such an unusual choice of words that I can't help but to repeat them. "Your actions were unfair?"

Katie laughs. "Yeah, that's therapy for you. Mom pays a hundred bucks a session for that fancy vocabulary. Now are you still worried about mileage or what?"

Abrupt as the topic change is, I am grateful. I blow my nose. "Not worried. But I suppose we should try to move at a good clip to get to the next canyon."

"How far away is that from here?"

"Two and a half miles? Give or take."

"That's nothing." She grins. "Shoot, we could probably sprint that two miles."

"Optimistic," I say, and we clamber out of the tent. The morning air is brisk enough to send goose bumps up on my arms.

Katie shrugs, zipping up her jacket. "I believe in us. Even if you are Typhoid Mary at the moment."

"Just a touch of consumption."

"Well, you know what they say—"

Katie cuts herself off, her eyes gone wide. She's looking at the trail to the south, to the way we should be headed. And then I hear it. Footsteps. Moving fast. I spot a man in the distance, moving north.

We haven't seen another human being since the climbers. And this man isn't cruising along with trek poles and a heavy pack. He is running. Small pack. Good shoes. Hat pulled low.

"Trail runner," I nod at his muscled legs and measured stride. "Good one, I'd bet."

Two years ago, Katie would have called out the moment he was near enough to hear. She would have offered a greeting. A drink. An inane comment about the trail or the weather. Now she stands beside our tent with her fists clenched and her face gone pale. She looks like she might bolt. Will she?

The guy is fifteen yards away and closing fast. A flicker of unease runs through me. No reason for it. Except Katie. She is so clearly terrified. I think of the scorpion's waxy, golden back. A warning that some creatures are built to harm. Nothing in this man strikes me as dangerous, but what do I know? A year ago, I walked away from something that would break my cousin. I don't know danger when I see it.

But Katie might.

I keep her in my line of vision as the runner approaches, his eyes forward. Katie edges behind me like he's holding a gun. But he's just running. He doesn't even look in our direction.

"Morning," I say automatically as he passes.

He nods succinctly but does not slow. And does not move his eyes from the trail.

As soon as he's out of earshot, I whirl to her, my hands dropping gently to her shoulders. She jerks away before I can speak. Shakes her head like she's trying to shrug this whole strange moment away.

"Katie, what happened? Do you know him?"

She shrugs and gives a laugh that isn't funny at all. And then she drags her hands over her face. She's shaking. "No, I'm sorry. He was just… It seemed like he was coming right at us. Didn't it seem like that?"

I cringe before I answer. "Not to me."

"Not at all?" she asks. I can still read her well enough to see she's desperate for my agreement. Desperate to feel less alone in that feeling.

North of her, I can see the trail runner climbing down into the canyon. From his Patagonia T-shirt to his worn Merrells, he is all but a poster child for outdoor enthusiasts everywhere. He does not look like a threat.

I want to know what Katie saw. And why she's afraid. I want to know how bad this all is, but I won't ask. I'll do the same damn thing I've done since I sat in the plastic chair beside her hospital bed. I'll give her space.

"Light is weird in the canyons in the morning," I finally say. Because I want to give her something.

Katie looks over her shoulder. Her posture makes me wonder if she wants to leave. If she's going to change her mind. That thought sends a bolt of fear through me. If we quit now, we'll lose another year. And I already know this might be the last year.

It's hard to accept. Katie and I have been running around the Utah backcountry since her father died and my mother split. We were seven. Dad was only related to Aunt Julie through marriage, but they were in the same boat. Both forced to deal with raising kids on their own. Both hundreds of miles away from any real family.

Dad invited Aunt Julie and Katie to stay while Adam attended some high-octane engineering camp at BYU. We were nine. And it became a thing. Adam went to some academic camp or another, and Katie and Aunt Julie came here.

It's hard to imagine a world where Katie and I aren't running around in the desert, staining our sneakers orange and scraping our knees on slickrock. But last year, I could see a change in her. Even before the party. The careful waves in her hair. The pretty dresses lined up in her closet. The delicate gold chains around her neck.

When this trip is over, Katie will go back to Ohio. To college, where she's starting spring semester. To whatever else comes next in her world. Because Katie's world isn't here with me anymore.

But she is here now.

"You ready to see if you can keep up with Patient Zero here?" I ask.

"Oh yeah. I'm beyond ready."

Her grin makes her look like the real Katie, the one from before. If I squint just right, I can almost pretend it is real. I can almost believe this trip will be enough to bring her back.

KATIE

---

14 MILES

By the time the sun is fully risen, Aster has us packed and on our way. She's been coughing and blowing her nose approximately every fifteen seconds, but she's also kept us trotting at a good clip. If stubborn resolve was an Olympic event, Aster would absolutely take home a medal.

I don't really get colds, so I'm not worried about the coughing. Mom says even as a baby I had a freakish immunity against all things respiratory. Even Covid barely kept me down for a weekend, but still, I truly don't get her commitment to hauling ass all over Utah at top speed, snotty nose be damned.

But Aster isn't one to quit easily. And by *easily* I mean *ever*.

We reach the mouth of the canyon, but she doesn't quit then either. She marches like it's a mission from God until she's standing at the foot of the scramble. My water is running low and the sun is beating down and a pair of ravens is watching us from the gnarled branch of a pinyon pine.

"Six boulders down into the canyon," she says. "That look right to you?"

I count them out like I'm on *Sesame Street*. Tall one, short one, short one, tall, tall, holy hell that last one does not even look possible. "Yeah, it looks right. But I'd love to meet the yahoo that called this a scramble."

Aster snorts. "It does look challenging."

It is worse than the last one and takes twice as long. Aster looks a little wobbly and winded when we finally reach the canyon floor. She blows her nose with a tissue that's so worn and soggy, I can tell she doesn't have many to spare.

I check our surroundings, spotting a narrow trench cut through the center of the canyon floor. I don't see or hear running water, but it looks mucky in the channel. Plus there are bugs. Bugs usually mean water, which is good news because we're getting low.

The bad news is, I don't see a trail. Other than the strip of sand at the bottom of the canyon, I can't see anything that even resembles a trail.

"We're not supposed to be on sand here," Aster says in her new I-smoke-two-packs-a-day voice.

"Are we supposed to be on the right or left side of the canyon?"

"North side," she says absently.

"You might as well give me longitude and latitude."

"Sorry. Left."

Canyons are like snowflakes, and this one has nothing in common with the one we traversed yesterday. That one was all smooth, gently curving walls. Today, we are facing slabs of rock and enormous boulders. The whole place might as well be a sign that reads, *Not for Humans*.

"Look for a cairn," she says.

We scour the area for one of the telltale graduating stacks of rocks that mark trails, but instead we find a set of footprints. They are small and evenly spaced. My mind drags up a vivid memory of the scream we heard last night. A reminder that we are not entirely alone out here. Aster said there could have been a lot of reasons for that scream. But she only mentioned the ones that wouldn't scare me.

I think of the trail runner who was racing right toward us with vacant eyes. The climbers with their boys-will-be-boys comments. The hiker from the book, RF, moving in the same direction we are. I don't want to run into them. I don't want to run into any of these people. Goose bumps rise on my arms. I rub them away and focus on the trail of small prints.

"Are these a kid's footprints?" I ask.

"Maybe."

"Why would a kid be all the way out here alone?"

Aster takes a closer look at the tracks, and I shift on my feet, feeling uneasy. Could that scream have been a kid? How far away could we hear something like that? Would it echo off the walls out here?

"Could be a small woman," she finally answers. "And they might not be alone. Most hikers would choose to walk on the slickrock. Too much sand in the shoes on that path."

"Yeah, okay. That makes sense." It is sensible and logical and I need to chill. This is not an omen. It is a set of footprints. That's it. I have to stop being this way. I came out here for the specific purpose of not being a scared little shell of a person anymore.

"Got it," Aster says.

I'm not sure what she's talking about until I see her outstretched finger. She's pointing at a cairn stacked on top of a boulder. My eyes follow it a few yards to the right where I see another. Just like Aster mentioned, we opt for the slickrock ledge that runs parallel to the loose sand and those strange, tiny footprints. It is narrow and shadowy, but it's cool and relatively smooth for walking.

"See those? They're claret cups," she says, pointing at a wad of dead-looking cactus spikes that looks nothing like the claret cups I remember with their striking scarlet blooms. "The path will run behind those and sort of double back on itself on the other side of that fin up there."

She moves her finger to point at an eighty-foot-tall blade of orange rock, the kind that crops up all over southeast Utah and, as far as I know, almost nowhere else on the planet.

We follow the trail from one cairn to another, heading steadily south through the canyon. We're tucked close enough to the wall to keep us in shadow, but the sun is creeping higher in the blue sky, and when I step to the edge of the trail, the heat is delicious. The formations in the canyon are wild, swooping whorls of solid rock, like this whole section was squirted out of a tube or poured from a pitcher.

Before I know it, I'm stripping my jacket off, and we are walking into a new canyon, this one wide and shallow at the entrance. No scrambling at all, just some weaving around enormous hunks of rock until the walls stretch high on either side of the path.

"There are petroglyphs in this canyon and a spring too," she says. "We should pass a small window in the next mile, and then the petroglyphs half a mile beyond that. We can check them out when we're getting water."

"Do we need to get water? We're picking up the stash tonight."

"Right. Unless the road is impassable and Dad can't get there."

Alarm prickles through me. "Is that a possibility?"

"It's probably a fifty-fifty. That road is a mess. But he'd just leave it at the next drop. That one isn't prone to flooding. It's just a pain because it's so far off the main drag."

"Well, let's hope for today. I could use a bit of that trail mix of his. He better remember the peanut M&Ms. I live for the M&Ms."

Aster laughs, which sends her into a coughing fit and then a sneezing fit and finally a honk-like-a-goose nose-blowing episode. Gross and pitiful all at once. A mile or two later, Aster's bag emits a long beep with a succession of shorter beeps. The pattern repeats, one long beep followed by three short. Not a message then—those are two short beeps. This must be a weather alert. Instinctively I search the skies, but they are blue and clear. A single wisp of white drifts overhead. It's hard to even imagine rain in skies like this, but skies change.

"Weather alert," she says.

"For this violent case of blue cloudless skies we're having?"

"Just means something could be on the way. I set it to alert for anything within forty miles."

"Well, what's the warning?"

"Storm headed this way," she says, looking at the GPS screen. "Small, but it's bringing heavy rain. High winds. Some hail."

"Sounds dreamy," I deadpan. I focus on making my expression as bored as possible. Maybe if I look bored, she won't notice the way every muscle in my neck and shoulders has gone tense.

Storms in the desert are a whole different animal. I do not relish the possibility of being drenched out here. Or getting stuck or swept away in a flash flood.

"I could have sworn there was nothing on the radar in the whole southern half of the state," I say.

"There wasn't." She shrugs and coughs "It could shift. It's still sixty miles away, moving about thirty miles an hour. It could miss us."

"So it could hit in two hours?"

"Or not at all. Hard to tell." She shrugs it off.

"But we are literally in the bottom of a canyon. As in a place where floods love to happen."

"It is not an optimal situation," she admits. "but I'm not overly concerned."

My pulse is moving from a trot to a canter, but Aster is cool as a cucumber. She shifts her pack to dig out a second map, and then she studies everything, looking back and forth between the two maps and the weather alert on the GPS.

"Okay as much as I'd love to live in not-a-care-in-the-world land, I'm currently reliving that trip in eighth grade when that lightning storm hit a cottonwood like ten feet from our tent."

"It shouldn't be like that." She frowns. "I don't think."

"Very reassuring."

"We should consider speeding up though."

"Look, I can keep up with your gimpy ass, but I think thirty miles an hour is a bit beyond our abilities."

"Outrunning it is not reasonable, but we are standing in a wash."

"Not great."

"And we have been descending for the last mile."

I look up at the walls, which tell me she's right. Then I notice the distinct patterns and crevices under our feet. No more loose sand here; this is all packed hard and etched with grooves. Evidence of where water has run before. Aster is right. Every canyon has the capacity for flooding, but this one has obviously flooded recently.

"Okay, so I know it might not rain. But if it does, how dumb is it for us to be in this canyon?" I ask. "In layman's terms."

Aster doesn't answer right away. She looks at the canyon and checks her watch and runs her finger along the trail map. Then she blows her nose and looks up.

"So the options are limited. If we turn back, we might not make it out of the canyon before the rain hits anyway. We would also be six miles behind and could be stuck if this canyon floods badly enough."

"Even if it doesn't flood, mucky trails are probably a guarantee." I scrunch my nose, remembering the short hike we'd taken in August of my ninth grade year. Monsoon season in Utah, and I was scraping thick sticky mud out of my boots for a week.

"I'll take whatever's behind Door Number Two."

"Door Number Two is that we press on," Aster says. "Keep a quick pace to make sure we hit this section of the trail."

She taps the map.

"Why that section?"

"The trail rises well above the canyon floor and follows a ledge on the canyon wall for nearly a mile. I'm guessing because the plants and cottonwoods are too densely packed for a good trail at the bottom." Aster shrugs then. "There's also the chance that the rain passes us by."

"And if it doesn't?"

"As long as we can make a mile, a mile and a half tops, we'll be climbing. That's the long and short of it. If we need to do anything at all—and we might not—we just need to get to higher ground. The elevation there is twenty to forty feet above the bottom of the canyon. It's not a slot canyon, and this isn't a big storm."

"So if it floods—"

"It is just as likely not to," she says, interrupting me.

All this reassurance is decidedly not reassuring. I don't relish the idea of fortyish miles trekking through hellish mud or contending with crossing flooded washes, but I don't need to be mollified either. And it feels like she's waving off my concerns.

I push back the flyaway bits of hair that have escaped my ponytail and try to keep my tone playful and light. "Okay, I know you don't want to be an alarmist, but level with me. What's the absolute worst-case scenario? If this is one of those situations where we're going to end up interviewed on a survival documentary—"

"What are you even talking about?"

I force out a laugh, trying to show her that this is all *ha-ha-no-bigs*. "I'm just saying if we need to phone a friend to check on this weather or whatever, you can tell me."

Aster's face tightens. "We don't need to call someone. There isn't anything to call about. This rain could veer five miles south or north, so can you just stop worrying?"

"I'm not worried! I just want to talk through our options. I want to make sure we talk about our plan in case this weather is the real deal. Because what happens then?"

"I don't know, Katie. I guess we get wet. It's not worth stressing over, I promise."

"Stop treating me like I'm a child."

Aster stops and looks at me, and I should soften my tone, but I can't. Heat is crawling into my cheeks, and I am tired of this. Tired of being coddled and babied and written off like a person that has to be *handled*.

I cross my arms. "Look, if we can't find an overhang or

something to shelter us, then rain could be bad news. You're the one who taught me that, Aster."

Her face is blotchy, and I can't tell if it's her cold or her embarrassment doing it. But she nods at me, and when she speaks, her voice is level and calm.

"Yes." She presses her lips together in thought.

"Okay," I say. "What if we dug our ponchos out?"

She nods. "That seems logical. We can keep them handy and arrange our packs to make sure nothing vital gets wet."

Aster tilts her head, and I can tell she's seeing something behind me. Something that confuses her. When I turn, all I see is the canyon wall towering in front of me, with giant gaping vertical crevices to the left and right.

"Do you see something in that crevice on the right?" she asks.

"Shadows and rock," I say automatically, but then I see a shape in the darkness, something small. Crow-sized but plump, with a rounded head. I shift to the right, and I can see it more clearly, body compact and tucked tightly against the wall. Its large, round eyes are unmistakable.

"Holy shit, is that an owl?"

"Yes."

Aster's voice is like gravel, and when I turn back to her she is sheet pale with a thousand-yard stare. Before I can ask her what's going on, she turns away. Then she's in the business of rain preparation, retrieving her poncho and shifting around gear. I don't know what happened to the everything's-totally-fine Aster of five minutes ago, but that owl unnerved her.

We shift the GPS and our IDs and money into a waterproof pouch. We also take the time to work plastic grocery sacks around our sleeping bags for an extra layer of protection. Wet clothes can be changed, and other stuff can be dried, but a wet sleeping bag is absolute hell. We were rained out once a few years ago on a short trip. It was the last night, which was a good thing, because neither of us slept a wink.

Once we are as waterproofed as possible, we march single file along the trail, which, true to Aster's word, climbs within a half a mile of our last stop and stays at least twenty feet above the bottom of the canyon after the first climb. Below us the vegetation grows thick, and the canyon bottom narrows. I spot a slurry of mud and some unidentified plants and trees pushed over, most likely from the last flood that rushed through. A prickle of unease runs up the back of my neck.

Are we high enough to be safe? Are we at risk of lightning here or some other thing? Who knows. I search the sky for clouds and the canyon floor for proof of alarming levels of flooding. Neither appear.

Most of the flood remnants stop several feet below the height of the trail. I do spot one exception on the opposite side of the canyon, where a small pocket canyon in the wall across from us collected water until it gushed up over the edge. The water's long gone now, but there are frothy stains on the rock and mineral streaks and hunks of vegetation tangled in green-brown waterfalls spilling over the top edge of the pocket.

I force myself to stop thinking about all the ways I could wind up in a cautionary documentary created to underscore the perils of canyon hiking in Utah. And despite what Aster thought I was getting at, I also don't want to call home, because no version of that action would result in us being allowed to continue hiking.

Mom would have me on the first plane back to Ohio, and I want to be here.

Hell, I need to be here.

Aster pushes us at a hard pace. Her coughing is growing worse, and she makes us stop once so she can dig out two more ibuprofen. I offer to check my first aid kit for cough medicine. I'm sure I have something—Mom sends me with a pharmacy—but she waves me off, because apparently hiking at top speed while hacking up a lung proves you're a real woman.

She finally allows us both a real break when she sees the hammer-shaped rock formation that tells us we're getting close to the petroglyphs and the spring. The trail dips as expected, but I can also see where it quickly rises back up maybe thirty yards ahead. I think she mostly stops because there is a wide alcove on the canyon floor that provides a safe and somewhat private area to relieve our bladders, and God knows those aren't coming frequently today.

Ten yards or so south of our makeshift restroom, we spot a gurgle of water flowing through a crack in the wall. It's barely more than a seep, but even the sight of it sends me reaching for my water bottle. I drink heavily, leaning back against the canyon wall.

I'm breathing hard. Sweat has soaked through the back of my shirt and it's got to be closer to noon because the sun is merciless now, without so much as an inch of overhang to be found in any direction.

Aster cannot stop coughing. I unshoulder my bag.

"What are you doing?" she asks, blowing her nose.

"I'm getting the cold medicine you refused earlier," I say. "You're being ridiculous."

"We really need to be quick down here," she says. "I am fine."

"You're a walking NyQuil commercial." I find the pills in a plastic packet. "Just take them. Besides I need a hot second to recuperate a bit."

She accepts the medicine without any more fuss, then moves quietly to the spring where she starts filling a collapsible jug.

I frown. "Aren't you going to filter that? I mean, as much as I like the idea of a little cholera for the road..."

"Dad said to let water sit a few hours before filtering if we can. Gives the silt time to settle to the bottom."

"Gotcha," I say. "I'm still hoping we get to the stash before we have to drink filtered shit dredged off some sand-coated rock."

She laughs. "Probably cleaner than the tap water we will pick up."

I step off the wall and move toward a section of shade. Maybe ten yards from the spring, I spot familiar white shapes up high on the canyon wall. I move until I can see them better.

"Did you see?" I ask. "The petroglyphs."

Aster gives them a brief glance before returning to her water, but I can't stop staring. The longer I look, the more shapes I see. A long squiggly snake and a circular swirl and a deerlike creature with elaborate antlers. Awe sweeps over me in waves. Petroglyphs are easy to find around here, which always blows my mind. Someone— lots of someones—left their mark on these rocks an unfathomably long time ago. Now their bones are probably mingled in the dust beneath my feet, but these symbols are still here. Proof that this desert wasn't always so empty.

Aster caps the water and hooks it inside a compartment in her bag to distribute the weight. I force myself to drag my own back- pack off the dirt. I'm hungry and I'm hot and my shoulders are—

The sunlight fades abruptly, cutting off my thoughts.

"Damn it," Aster breathes.

I look up, and my curiosity chills into dread as I spot the thick, cottony cloud drifting across the face of the sun. It's far from overcast, but the endless stretch of blue I saw earlier is long gone. Now there are clusters of puffy clouds marching in rows overhead. The break from the heat would be a relief if it didn't tell me that rain is very likely on its way.

ZERO MILES

She blinks and the darkness turns to blue. Blinks again and it is gray. Time is a seesaw. Moving fast. Moving slow. Maybe not moving at all. She closes her eyes, but she is still awake. Still alive.

She catalogs her parts and pieces. Her head pounds. Her left arm hangs like a dead weight from her shoulder. Motionless. Numb. Her right leg is a black hole of roaring pain. Invisible hammers and knives hacking into the sinew and muscle. And then bone.

Thunder rumbles and her eyes dart. Past the gray of the sky and the shadow of a tall, dark wall stretching up. A curved orange rock beside her.

She remembers in fragments. The weight of the pack on her back. The warmth of the sun on her face. She hears the echo of her own laughter. A trail. A companion. A fight.

More thunder. She swallows, her throat sensing the promise of rain. Of water. Thirst proves stronger than her pain.

She tests the fingers of her right hand. One. Two. Three. Four.

The joints are rusted, but they move. They turn the palm up. Bend the wrist.

Pins and needles fire as she inches her fingers across the grit of the sand. Finds the edge of her hip and the pebbled fabric of a belt around her waist.

A pouch. Her fingers remember the way. The zipper and the flap. The collapsible silicone cup inside. One raindrop, cool and fat, hits her cheek. Her thirst is a whip, driving her faster. The cup tumbles from the pack just like her body bounced off the canyon wall. And when it lands, she remembers something else. Two hands planted in the center of her back.

And a single, hard push.

ASTER

17 MILES

The first peal of thunder sounds while we are heading downhill. We stop as if we aren't certain, but there's no guessing game here. The low distant grumble is unmistakable. Katie locks eyes with me.

"Well, that doesn't sound like it's going to miss us," she says.

"No."

I look up. The canyon wall next to the trail is sheer and featureless. Just like Katie predicted. We might as well be hiking down the middle of Potash Road. If Potash Road had another canyon wall instead of the Colorado River running alongside it. The sky—or the portion that's visible—is a blanket of gray framed by the canyon's walls now. Not a sliver of blue in sight.

"Ponchos would be a good idea now," I say.

The map rustles in my back pocket as we tug them over our heads and packs, but I leave it where it is. The map hasn't changed, and unlike the first canyon, this section is not new. It's well documented. The mileage will be close, if not perfect. This canyon is nine miles long. We've walked five of them. Maybe five and a half. We have all but zero chance of getting out of here before the rain arrives. I suppose I have known that since the first cloud appeared. The second weather alert fired a few seconds later, and to Katie's credit, she didn't say a word.

The alert told us nothing the sky didn't already promise. Storms in the area. Moving generally south. Same speed as before. What neither the alert nor the map told me was that we'd have no cover.

I pause to cough and blow my nose. And then I keep moving. We are going to get to higher ground. That's our best bet now. Katie matches my faster pace as we head downhill. It feels counterintuitive, but I can see the trail climbing in the next thirty yards or so. It is harder hiking, but every yard we gain in altitude eases the knot in my stomach.

Up is good. With a little luck, there won't be any flooding at all. Or minimal flooding confined to the canyon floor. Or the rain will be brief and light. Whatever it is, it will be fine. It has to be.

I pause to blow my nose. My ears feel clogged too, every sound tunneled and distant.

"Hey, are you seeing this trail?" Katie asks, nodding ahead. "It seems really steep."

"It is."

Annoyance pinches her features. "Okay, and that's not an issue?"

"Why would it be an issue?"

"Because I felt raindrops. Rain will make all of this slick, won't it?"

"The rain should still be a few minutes out," I say, "Just keep moving, and we should be fine. It won't climb like this forever."

But then I feel a drop too. Another. And then three more.

Above us the sky is darkening. Turning ominous. I keep moving and hear Katie following. My quads are burning from the endless uphill slog, and to my shock, it does not level off. It's like we're climbing an endless flight of stairs.

Another rumble of thunder, and then the skies open up. The rain turns on like a faucet, so fast and hard there is no time to react. It roars, pelting our ponchos and packs with brutal force. Raindrops sting the slivers of my wrists that are exposed.

And then the wind hits. The impact of it pushes into my backpack, shifting my balance forward. I pitch my feet wider to ground myself. Katie makes a sound beside me. Her arms fling out wide, and I see her step to the side awkwardly. She's off-balance.

She's too close to the edge. Even through the sluicing rain, I can see that. My heart thumps faster, and I snag her by the back of her pack. I haul her to me and then shuffle us both to the canyon wall. Lightning strikes. The crack reverberates off the sandstone walls. Another flash instantly follows.

One Mississippi, two—

The strike is so loud I feel it in my teeth. I close my eyes and keep my hand gripped on Katie's arm. Water sprays inside my poncho, stinging my face as I turn to her. It's hard to see in this mess. Hard to hear or think, even.

Katie stumbles awkwardly. Shifts on her feet.

"Stay on the wall," I warn.

"I'm trying."

"The wall will help," I say. I pull the hood of my poncho forward as I turn. It dips down into my field of vision, but I turn my face to the rock, and there is definitely less rain this way.

"Turn toward me," I say, tugging her so that our outer shoulders touch. Our bodies form a triangle with the canyon wall. Then we press the top of our heads together, and thunder claps again. So close I feel the vibration in my bones. But our faces are no longer getting pelted. Better yet, the wind isn't shoving us toward the edge of a thirty-foot drop. It's not great, but it's better. Manageable.

Then the hail starts. Katie swears when it starts, a downpour of cold gravel that pelts our backs and shoulders as the wind howls and howls through the canyon. Hail is not generally a good sign. It indicates a strong storm. Lots of rain. Maybe flooding.

"Well, this is a magical moment," Katie says.

She is less than a foot away, hair soggy and plastered to her flushed cheeks. Her smile is lopsided and absolutely genuine.

I laugh even as my throat burns and my nose runs. Water rolls down my neck. It pools at the top of my hiking boots. All the precautions that felt silly an hour ago may not be enough to keep us dry.

Suddenly Katie yelps, her body jerking toward the wall. Her eyes widen.

"What's wrong?" I ask. "Is it the hail?"

"It's the trail. My right foot. The water is cutting a trench."

She's right; the water is running fast down the trail's incline, channeling through the hard-packed low spot at the base of the canyon wall. The water will cut ridges all the way down the slope. Perfect for twisting an ankle or catching a boot.

My poncho billows up into my face, and I push it down. Water runs everywhere. Down the back of my shirt. Between my shoulder blades. Sliding around the curve of my waist until I shiver. My bones ache, and my skin is buzzing and tender from the hail.

Another boom of thunder, this time so loud we both jump. The sound pounds at the sky, bouncing back and forth off the sandstone walls. There is nothing to do. Nowhere to hide.

"We just have to hold on," I say.

"I know."

We stand in silence as the storm rages. Katie's eyes are closed, but there is a tightness in her jaw that looks like confidence. I am staring at the trench growing deeper by the second, and I do not feel the same certainty. My mind whispers about the scorpion from yesterday. The owl from this morning. There have been omens out here. Warnings I have ignored. What did I drag us into on this trail?

I shake off the question and the memories. Remind myself that legends aren't logical. That owls and scorpions are simple desert creatures with no more magic than my little finger. Storms are not malevolent beings coming after us. All of this is simple science. That's what I need to focus on.

There are real things that pose danger right now, and I need to remember them. The edges of the trail will be soaked and weak. Rocks could shift and slide. Floods could rage. We have plenty to fear without supernatural stories.

"Aster, is this still stable?" Katie asks, gesturing at her feet where the rain is cutting fast-moving rivulets through the sand.

"There is rock beneath, but we should be careful."

Part of me thinks the best option would be to keep moving. Find a portion of trail with a less severe grade. Our feet closest to the wall are sinking deeper into the trench, which isn't awesome. But moving feels dangerous with this wind and on this sort of incline.

The hail eases back into rain, and maybe it's lighter than before? How long has this been going on? At least ten minutes.

Maybe close to fifteen? I close my eyes tight, trying to hone my other senses. Trying to ignore the chill that is growing worse by the minute.

And then, as suddenly as it started, it is done. The rain stops, and we lift our heads to look at each other. We are pale and dripping in the shadow of the sandstone. I turn slowly around, pulling my left boot out of the trench near the wall.

The canyon is transformed. Rivulets of water rush. Mist clings to the rock. Slender brown ribbons of water spill down the sandstone walls. Everywhere, there is dripping.

I take a tentative step away from the wall and dig a soggy tissue out of my pocket to blow my nose. My steps squelch in the thick wet mud. My boots are trashed. Katie's don't look much better. I venture just close enough to the edge to see better. On the canyon floor, a new brown river tears through the earth, dragging sticks and rocks along with it.

"Wow." Katie's voice is flat and hollow.

"Yes."

"That was…"

"Yes."

She looks around, her wet hair clinging to her heart-shaped face in clumps. "Do you think the flooding will get worse?"

"Hard to be sure. The rain moved in from the north, which is a lower elevation. I think the worst of it will be closer to where we started, but flooding is unpredictable."

"You never know in Utah, right?"

I nod. "True."

"I'm almost afraid to ask how wet you are."

"Short answer? Very."

"Ditto."

"But I think my pack was probably spared the worst of it. We need to find a place to change. Check our things. Dry what we can."

Katie laughs. "I'm not sure anything attached to me in any way is dry at this point."

"We have to try."

"Could be interesting since we are literally surrounded by rivers and waterfalls."

I cough and push the hood back on my poncho. I feel congested, achy, and chilled to the bone. Thunder grumbles in the distance, but above us, the gray sky is already clearing, smudges of blue mixing with the gray to our north.

"It will clear," I say. "The sun will help."

Twenty minutes, and the universe proves me right. The sun is already at work drying my hair, but progress on the trail has slowed to a crawl. We're trudging uphill through mud. We're exhausted and hungry. And worst of all, our clothes are wet. Chafing becomes our next challenge.

It starts the way chafing always starts. An annoyance. A minor irritation with each step. Between the thighs. Under the backpack strap on my waist. At the edge of my bandaged ankle. But irritation is only the start. It turns quickly to discomfort. And then pain.

I scan the path, eager for an opportunity to strip down and get things dry, but it's nothing but mud and canyon wall as far as the eye can see. We do our best with an anti-chafing salve, but it is awkward to apply fully dressed, and everything's too wet for it to work properly.

The next mile is slow and awkward. We are plagued by gnats and mosquitos. My inner thighs scream with every step. I am sure we will both have raw, red welts where our wet clothes have rubbed. We have to stop. But where? Everything here is wet or sticky with mud. The sheer featureless walls stretch as far as the eye can see.

The problems of this trip lay themselves out to be counted. Bad mileage. My illness. The rainstorm and all the new problems it has dragged in its wake, and I can't help but think of that scorpion again. Of the owl watching in its hollow.

Another half a mile. Maybe more. We stop again for more salve. Dry spots are appearing on some of the rocks, and the mud is getting tackier. My sock is rubbing at the cut on my ankle, sending little fiery bursts of pain through my leg with every step, but it's okay. We're almost there.

The moment the trail widens, I scan for an area to rest and resituate ourselves. Two sickly-looking juniper trees stoop near a slim boulder, maybe four feet high. A wide flat rock that resembles a bench sits in front of it. Looks like nature's equivalent of a couch and a coatrack. Best of all, they're on a small ledge above the trail.

"Looks good," I say, pointing.

"It's not exactly a Hilton, but I'll take it." Katie drops onto the low rock and carefully pulls off her poncho.

I yank off my poncho and unsnap the chest strap on my backpack. After a coughing fit subsides, I wave at our surroundings. "We need to check everything. And we need to make sure we use moleskin anywhere the chafing is serious."

"No checking necessary. Everything is a disaster. I'm a walking rug burn." Katie pushes her hair off her face again and again. She's scowling. "I'm also somehow still drenched. Like you could wring me out like a sponge, except now that we've hiked wet, I'm like drenched and steamy."

Her knees are pulled up to her chest. She's whining. And she's not doing a single thing to improve this situation. I bite back the urge to snap at her. Where the hell is the Katie I hiked with two years ago, the one who leaps into decisive action after a crisis? Is she even still in there? Or is this all that's left? The Katie who has been assaulted. The one who's under the care of a chiropractor. A crisis counselor. A sleep clinic for God's sake.

"Let's check," I say gently. "It might not be so bad. We were wearing ponchos, and we both have good bags."

"You can't be serious, Aster. We might as well have taken a swim."

My irritation is flaring. I take a steady breath, trying to calm myself. "I am serious, and we don't know until we check."

"I know I'm miserable."

"We're both miserable," I say, and a coughing fit cuts off anything else I might add. This is not what I do. I plan the route and supply lists, but Katie is the cheerleader. The solutions girl. The comic relief. I don't know how to do those things. And Katie has forgotten.

My pack settles perfectly onto the low stone, and I feel a rush of gratitude at the sun's warmth. Starting out I worried about the unseasonable heat. Now, we're lucky to have it. Without the sunny skies and high temps, our gear might not dry. Wet gear means cold nights. I'm not sure I'd do well with a bout of hypothermia in my state.

I sort through my pack, finding a few damp things in an external pocket. The main interior compartment is impressively dry by comparison. Mostly, I need to change my clothes and let my shoes dry a little.

I yank off my boots and wince at the pain in my ankle. Then

I strip off my shirt. Drape it over the shorter juniper. I peel off my soggy socks.

My sports bra and underwear feel drier than I'd expected. Nothing left to do now but wait.

"My pack is pretty..." I trail off when I spot Katie's face.

She is frozen. Her face is pale, and her hands are clenched. It's her eyes that scare me most. Wide and dark and fixed on absolutely nothing. She looks catatonic.

"Katie?"

She flinches and I step back, giving her space. Maybe giving myself space. Something about the way she forces a smile is deeply unsettling. Almost frightening.

"Yeah, sorry. I haven't checked everything," she says.

"Do you need help?"

"I don't think..." She looks like she's struggling for words. Irritation flares through me. She's still dressed in sopping clothes. Not one item in her pack has been pulled out, so she can't possibly know what's wet. She's like a cranky child right now. One who is refusing to offer any help.

"Let me see," I say, forcing a calm tone.

She makes a face. "Don't you have your own pack to deal with?"

"Everything that matters is fine. Just need to let my boots and clothes dry a bit."

"Lucky you," she says, sounding tired.

My jaw clenches. "You may be lucky as well. It doesn't look like you've checked your things. And you need to get out of your wet clothes so they can dry."

"You're right," Katie says with a sigh. She pulls open her bag in slow motion. Then tugs loose a pouch that may have extra clothes but leaves it on the rock beside her. Her sleeping bag stays tucked inside. Her wet shoes still laced tight over sodden socks. Instead of doing a single useful thing, she goes through her lunch sack. Takes a sip of water. Lines up soggy granola bars. Whatever this is, it's not helpful. And it's pissing me off.

I move in and take her pack.

"I've got it," she says, but she doesn't take it back.

My neck and face feel hot as I yank out her sleeping bag. Dry, thankfully, so I set it aside and feel for other issues.

"You don't need to do that," she snaps.

"Someone needs to do it."

"I'm perfectly capable, Aster. I told you to stop babying me."

"This isn't babying you. This is me waiting on you."

"Waiting on me for what?"

I throw up my hands and feel my head throb. Can't tell if it's my cold giving me the headache, or Katie's attitude.

"You can't continue to hike in wet clothes, Katie! That's why we stopped. To dry out. Check bags. Change clothes."

"Well, I'm sorry if I'm not doing that fast enough to suit you. I'm exhausted and hungry, and my food's ruined."

"So? There are always things outside of the plan."

She scoffs. "This isn't a tiny little inconvenience! I barely slept last night and you have a nasty cold and we're both soaked to the bone. And as a bonus? Every trail is going to be a mess."

"So what do you want to do? Call for a rescue because our granola bars got wet?"

Katie's eyes narrow to slits. "I didn't say I wanted you to call anyone. But if I did suggest calling it, would that truly be so ridiculous?"

"It would certainly be par for course for this trip," I mutter.

"What the hell does that mean?"

"It means you have been looking for reasons to call this off since we got here."

She flushes instantly. "Bullshit!"

I tick them off on my fingers. "First it was my cold, and then it was the storm—"

"Yeah, I was totally crazy for thinking that storm might be a problem!"

"It *is* a problem, Katie! That's what backpacking is, dealing with one problem after another in some of the most beautiful settings this planet has to offer!"

She grows quiet then. My chest aches with the memory of other hikes. Other problems. We had to backtrack three miles for a map once. Another time we ran into a hornet nest and got stung four or five times each. There have been cold nights and sunburns. A hundred problems and plenty of bickering, but plenty of laughs too. Our best memories forged in our worst debacles. Those trips were nothing like this.

We were a unit. True partners. Now, it's like she's a thousand miles away. Somewhere I can't reach.

Which means all of this didn't work. This whole damn trip was about bringing her back, and it failed. I drop her bag in defeat. "It's fine. You want to pull the plug; we'll pull the plug."

I pull out my old Garmin and set it on the rock. Then blow my nose and work myself into my backup outfit. Faded leggings and a long-sleeved wicking T-shirt. Not as perfect as what I was wearing, but it's dry and cool and took up almost no space in my pack. A fresh pair of socks has me feeling like a new person.

When I look up, I'm surprised to see Katie standing. Her arms are prickled with goose bumps and her lips are nearly blue with cold. "I'm staying," she says. "I just need to change."

The words hurt like pressed bruises. She means her clothes. She has to mean her clothes. She's already changed everything else.

ZERO MILES

The cup rolls out of reach. *No! Please!* She struggles and stretches, but it's useless. She holds back a sob. And then squeezes her hand into a fist. Thunder in the distance. It's coming. She needs to be ready.

She finds a rock first. Shaped like a peanut. Comfortable in the hand. She pushes it beside her hip. Maybe it will help her think. *Think.*

What she needs now is the bandana. Five-in-one cooling rag. Last minute purchase. Man behind the counter said *must-have.* When the rain soaks it through, she agrees. All that water trapped. She squeezes it into her mouth. Sucks it down her dry throat. Over and over, this ritual. A baptism and last rites rolled into one.

The rain stops. The sky clears. No more thirst. If she dies, it will be some other way.

Above her, orange stone rises. A canyon wall going up. Twenty feet? Thirty? There is a rim trail. She remembers the view. The push. And her scream.

But she does not remember the fall.

KATIE

---

20 MILES IN

My hands are shaking and my heart is pounding and it feels hard to breathe. It's not the cold, though I'm pretty sure that's what Aster thinks. It's not leftover fear from the storm either. I actually like storms, and storms in the desert are some of the coolest around.

No, my shaking hands and chattering teeth are about the fact that I have to peel these wet clothes off after listening to Aster peel off hers. It is bad enough to hear someone else undress. The rustle of fabric, snap of a button, or slide of a zipper—all of it brings me back, and all of it makes me sick.

But I can handle that. I've had no choice. In classrooms, people take off coats or hoodies. Public bathrooms? I truly can't begin to describe that hell. But this? I will have to stand here, out in the middle of the wide-open Utah desert, and get naked. Or mostly naked.

Aster did it without even thinking. She just yanked off her clothes, and wandered back and forth between my pack and hers in her skivvies or whatever. I used to be like that out here. I used to pick ridiculous underwear to make us both laugh, my boy shorts cluttered with dancing donuts or cartoon dogs. On particularly hot years, I'd threaten to hike naked, and part of me was genuinely tempted.

But not now. Especially since we are not alone out here. I think of Luke's voice on that wall. The way every word curled into a warning in my gut. We don't know how fast they're moving or if they might catch up.

I can barely stand to get undressed in my own bathroom these days. I have to lock the door and turn the water on full blast so I don't hear the sound of my zipper and the rustle of fabric being pushed down my legs. The noise is nauseating, but nothing is worse than feeling air against my skin. I don't want to feel any of those sensations—hell, I don't even want to be *in* my own skin, so anything that makes me more aware of it is out. And trying to do it knowing someone could come traipsing down the trail at any moment? Nightmare.

Aster looks at me, her brow furrowed. She doesn't speak. We're playing a game where we pretend we are very polite strangers. Currently we are tied for the win.

I raise my hand to the hem of my shirt and feel my stomach roll with nausea. And Aster's face grows even more pinched and concerned and curious. No, not curious. Confused. Like everyone else, she's looking at me like a person she doesn't know anymore. But confused or not, she's still Aster. So she carefully angles her body away to give me privacy.

I rip my clothes off in an awkward, miserable rush. I leave them inside out and crumpled in the dirt while I yank on my backup pants and a long-sleeved warm-up shirt from my single laughable year on the cross-country team.

And then it is done. My feet are bare, pink chipped polish peering up at me, but the rest of me is covered and safe. Aster doesn't turn, and I don't tell her I'm done. I fix my pants and shirt and stretch them out on the rock to dry, and finally, when I'm checking a brutal pair of blisters that are popping up on my Achilles tendons, Aster slowly and carefully turns around.

My face feels like it has been lit on fire. I hate that we are like this, shuffling around each other like vague acquaintances stuck on the trail together. I scope out my first aid kit, but it's soaked beyond saving, having been stuffed at the very top of my pack.

Aster, who has watched me get heel blisters on every hiking trip we've ever taken, offers me two magical blister bandages. I don't know who invented these glorious things, but I place one on each tendon and pull up my clean, dry wool socks.

Once we're packed up again, I find my secret stash of dark chocolate caramel turtles packed beside a tiny freezer pack that lost its cool hours ago. I always bring turtles to reward us for the really awful days. When I offer her two on a strip of paper towel, she takes them. In return, she offers me two strips of beef jerky and her last bit of Uncle Mike's trail mix. Basically our whole friendship has been reduced to Boo Radley offerings on a dirty boulder in the desert.

I eat every last morsel of everything, and it's like a drop in the ocean. I'm suddenly ravenously hungry and very aware that unless we want to skip dinner tonight, this is going to have to do. Backpacking food never feels like enough to keep me full. Especially today, when the only other thing I have to consume is this endless awkward silence between us.

Aster taps out a quick message on the GPS, probably knowing that her dad, or more likely my mom, is aware of the weather situation. Rain finished. All good now just drying out. She shows it to me before sending and I offer her gum and frankly, I don't know why the hell we're not speaking at this point.

Maybe we're just too tired or maybe we've run out of things to say or maybe what happened at that party broke more than I even realized. We are half a mile down the trail when the silent treatment breaks, and it isn't thanks to either of us being the bigger person. The GPS beeps with an incoming message.

Aster stops and retrieves it from her bag. I reapply sunscreen while she opens the text and reads. Then, maybe forgetting about our not-speaking-to-each-other situation, she looks up at me.

"Dad couldn't make the drop."

My face goes cold in a single downward wave. "What?"

She turns the GPS for me to see. "Flash floods. The road's washed out."

"Even for the Jeep?" I ask. But the message on the screen tells me what I need to know.

Unable to drop stash. Roads flooded. Attempting Angels Pass now. Watch your elevation. Substantial flooding.

"What road is he talking about?" I ask.

Another message beeps in.

PS. Petty theft reports on an adjacent trail out of CR. Drug paraphernalia too. Be alert and keep your distance from unsavories.

I take a deep breath and, thankfully, feel a strange steadiness anchoring me. "What exactly is an unsavory, anyway? And *CR*? Is that ranger code or whatever?"

Aster paws through her maps and guidebook. "*CR* is Capital Reef. *Unsavory* is Dad's term for anyone up to no good on a trail." She finds whatever map she was looking for and blows out a hard breath. "So we should talk about this. It will take more time to get to that drop."

The word *unsavory* repeats itself in my mind for a moment. Up to no good. Drugs. Thefts. There was that mention in the trail log too. How afraid should I be of these people? I feel squeezed by bad possibilities. The climbers behind us and maybe criminals ahead. We chose this trail for the views and the challenge, yes, but also for the solitude.

I take a deep breath, but my calmness is intact. "Okay, let's think. How far are we from the first stash?"

"Still four miles. We were supposed to get there at dinnertime."

"And we could camp after that?"

"Theoretically yes. But that's a lower elevation. It could be flooded. That could create more delays."

"It's okay," I say. And to my surprise, I absolutely believe this. "We won't starve in two days. We can salvage the granola bars, and you still have some stuff, right?"

"Not much."

"Well, we have filters for water, and God knows after that rain, finding it is not going to be a problem for a few days."

"True…" Aster turns up the end of the word like a question. She looks like she has no idea how to read me in this moment.

Who could blame her? My anxiety decides to loosen its

stranglehold *now?* I came out here to prove something to my mom and to Aster and most of all to myself. But mostly I've been a tense, sensitive little shit the whole time. So what is this? Aster is clearly uneasy now. Why am I so calm?

I start pacing, solutions taking shape in my mind. "Food is trickier, but I have some turtles left, and the water-logged granola. We're not going to die of hunger. We might need to order and eat a large pizza each on our way back into town, but we're okay."

"Right," she says. "But Katie, it has to be bad. If Dad can't get through—if he's telling me to watch our elevation…"

"I know," I say. "I know it's bad."

And I know the thing she isn't saying—the reason she's finally giving in to the worry. Uncle Mike is on multiple rescue teams. He knows how to traverse roads to get to people in every kind of condition. So if he can't get to us right now, then no one can.

We are completely isolated.

Aster, who has obviously already processed this fact, is quietly panicking by the boulder. Or she's as close to panic as Aster gets, her hands clutched in front of her while she thinks. She quickly taps a reply to her father on the GPS, then checks her map and thinks some more.

Strangely, even as I watch her spin herself into a stress-mess-on-slick-rock, I feel calm. My shoulders are loose and relaxed, and as bizarre and impossible as it seems, I swear my senses are sharper. Everything is clearer: the soft gurgle of the stream at the bottom of the canyon and the sharp clean smell of sage and the shiver of a lizard easing its way back out of its rain shelter into the sun.

"We should hit the second stash end of day tomorrow,"

she says. "But we have to cross another wash. Which could be flooded."

"Eh, maybe not. If it's flooded, we'll wait. Things dry fast in the desert, right? Water never lasts."

"And it always comes in the wrong quantities," she says, and then she repeats a mantra I've heard Uncle Mike say a thousand times. "Nowhere near enough or way too much."

She sounds so much like her dad in that moment that I laugh. It releases a delicious feeling through my whole body. Aster looks at me like I've completely lost all sense and logic, and who knows? Maybe I have. Everything has sort of gone to shit, but I'm truly happy.

"You've been nervous all day, but now you seem...unusually relaxed." Her voice is cool and assessing. Classic Aster. "What about this moment makes it better for you?"

"We're on our own," I say. I feel a beat of surprise when the words are out. Is that the truth? Is that really why I feel better about all of this? "You and me against the world. Isn't this what we do best?"

I meet her eyes for a beat, and this is different too. For the last twenty hours or whatever, I've been beside Aster. Hiking and eating and getting the worst sleep I can remember in years. Physically we haven't been more than a few feet apart since we hit this trail, but there have been galaxies between us.

I have felt them. And I also feel them shrinking in this moment.

"You like that no one can get to us," she says softly.

"Yeah."

"Why?"

"Because nothing bad has ever happened to me..."

Aster waits for me to continue. The words stall out somewhere between my heart and my throat, but she finds them. And she offers my own truth back to me with a steady voice.

"Nothing bad has ever happened to you when you were alone."

ASTER

---

23 MILES IN

The canyon drags us through hell. Mud. Mosquitos. More chafing. But it deposits us into paradise. The climb out is all but a stroll up a flight of stairs. After the climb we emerge into an endless landscape of desert. Two mesas tower in the distance, flat topped and nestled in heaps of crumbled red rock.

"Holy shit," Katie breathes.

I stop short, stunned at the sight. There is too much to take in. The cloudless blue sky. The grove of pinyon pines before us, their withered roots finding life in the smallest crevices and shallowest bits of dirt. There is plenty of beauty here. But the flowers steal the show.

"What is all that?" Katie asks, waving vaguely. "The purple?"

"Blue pod lupines." I've seen them before, of course. They are tall as far as wildflowers go, with multiple spires for each plant. Each spire is topped with rows of small purple flowers.

There are hundreds of them. Few words do justice to the way red rock glows in the late afternoon sun. But when you combine that with a field of vibrant purple flowers? All the adjectives I know feel inadequate.

The glory holds us captive until a coughing fit drags me away. I drink after it settles and catch air bubbles in my water tube. Water is low enough that I'm not positive we'll make it the full day. But we're already behind on mileage. I'm not stopping to filter water unless it's absolutely necessary. We need to keep going.

"You know, would it kill people to leave a cairn or two?" Katie asks. "Because it doesn't feel much like a trail."

"The guide mentions this area being poorly marked."

"Okay, we just cruise on and hope to God we aren't lost?"

"We should be fine as long as we head southwest." I do not add that the guide was quite specific about keeping to a particular ridgeline on our right. That ridgeline isn't visible, thanks to the storm that drenched us earlier and is still leaving the ridge in question shrouded in haze.

Katie darts around a cluster of yuccas, her steps loud on the rock. "Let's just hope we find a better camping site. My old bones are sore."

"You're eighteen."

"Getting older every day. And you're nineteen. You can't afford to sleep on rock. Hell, you should probably start looking into your senior discount options."

"Very funny. Slickrock should end here soon."

Should have ended already, really. Katie steps up on a large flat rock, and a cicada begins to buzz. Except it is not cicada season.

Her blond hair swings. "Okay, so we—"

"Freeze!" I whisper-scream the command, but Katie complies instantly.

In the sudden silence, the buzzing sound is immediately clear. Not a cicada. Not a grasshopper. A rattlesnake.

Some piece of the old Katie is still in there. Because she realizes it's a snake and remembers all the right things to do. She is motionless. Silent. Watchful. Only the paleness of her cheeks and the speed of her breath reveal her fear.

"I'm looking," I say, searching the ground around her. I don't know where it is. What it is. How pissed it is.

"Have you found it?"

"Not yet," I say, being careful not to move.

Could be a Great Basin rattlesnake. We're just far enough south that they might be more common here. But it sounds familiar, and if it is, then it's something I've seen closer to Moab. Which means we are probably looking for something quite small. And nasty.

Katie's trembling. I can see it now in her fingers, which are splayed at her sides.

"It's okay," I say. "You're okay."

"I know I'm okay," she says, and then she notices my gaze on her hands. She huffs. "I'm just hungry, and I get shaky."

All the more reason why we need to find this rattlesnake, so she doesn't tremble in the wrong direction, spook a rattler, and end up bitten. The buzzing continues. Katie turns her head in the same direction I'm looking.

"It's to my left," she says. I agree. "I can hear it, but I can't tell how far away."

I nod and scan every cactus and rock. The buzzing rattle continues. Nothing. I blow out a frustrated breath. "Where the hell is this snake?"

The buzzing abruptly stops. My chest tightens. I scan the sand. The rocks. The—

There.

"Got him," I say softly. "Right there under the flat rock. The one under the sage bush to your left."

"What sage bush? How far?" Katie's voice is tight, but not panicked. Her eyes scan the area, but she's looking too close.

"Three feet to your left."

"So I'm safe where I'm standing?"

The snake coils tighter, scales pulling the long tail into a spiral. "Five feet would be better."

She arches a brow. "Yeah, half a mile would be better. But we're not working with that kind of buffer."

"True."

The snake continues to slither in on itself, its pale flesh marked with rectangular blotches. It is small enough that someone might think it's young, but I know better. Despite their petite size, the venom of a midget faded rattler packs a serious punch.

I look right of the snake where Katie is standing. To the broken boulder she's eyeing. The snake gives a short rattle and then stops. Now's the time.

"Go for that boulder," I tell her.

She nods and moves smoothly to the right. The rattling resumes, the snake coiled up in warning. Its head lifts, its rattle a steady buzz in the quiet. Katie sees it now and her focus intensifies.

"Is that a baby?"

"No. It's a midget faded rattlesnake," I say.

"Wait, shit. Shit. Isn't that the super toxic one?" she asks.

"Yes."

"It's so little and pale though," she muses softly, tilting her head. "It's like the Aster of rattlesnakes."

A laugh bursts out of me, loud and unexpected. It makes her laugh too. And it's good, this moment. This isn't the girl who fears runners and can't handle some rain. This is the real Katie. The part of her that I miss the most. And I want to hold on to it.

We hike maybe half a mile when the storm moves off the ridge, and I can see it clearly. Can see, too, that we are off. I search the rock formations to our left and the scrubby field to the right. There are supposed to be some broken-down fence posts and other remnants from an old farm. But I don't see anything close to that.

And then I see paw prints in the path. Clear as day. Which tells me the scant bits of trail I've picked up might not be the one I'm after. This is a critter trail of some sort. Fox maybe. Or coyote.

We can't be that far off though. We haven't gone more than a mile or two. So we just need to find the old farm. I keep the ridge in front of us and shift slightly, aiming for a raised area of slickrock where we might see better. If Katie notices, she doesn't mention it.

The sun is dipping lower. My water is down to dredges. All my chafed areas are burning. When we reached the higher ground, I look again. Search the field to my left a little, but there is nothing. No fence posts and no cairns promising a trail in any direction.

The topography looks mostly right, but it's hard to be sure. Trails in the desert are always trickier after a hard rain. We walk a bit farther, staying due south. I think of pulling out my old heavy-duty compass, but resist. Then a series of three rock fins appear dead ahead. They are not familiar. And they are not in the guide. It's absolutely a feature that would be in the trail notes if it were right on the trail.

I check the guide again. My stomach drops.

"We're not on the trail," I say, feeling a little breathless.

"What?"

"We lost the trail. This is not in the guide."

"How far off are we?" Katie asks. She still sounds completely calm. But that won't last.

We are running out of water. It's getting dark. And at this particular moment, we are lost.

ZERO MILES

The rain felt like the end, but then the sun returns. Changing her clothes from soaked to damp. Warming her skin. Giving her light. A lizard emerges from rocks, watching her. Spines circle his yellow head like children drawing the sun.

Her cheeks feel tight and hot. She walks her fingers back to her bag. Finds a mashed granola bar. A tube of lip balm. A map she'll never use. She drags that five-in-one rag over her face. Drapes it like a funeral shroud. Outside, hungry flies buzz.

Time passes, or it doesn't. She remembers, but not enough. She feels things. Grief. Terror. Loneliness.

No.

She grabs that word and strangles it. Loneliness is nothing but trouble. Loneliness is the reason she's here.

KATIE

---

25 Miles In

A ster stops me so solemnly, I'm convinced she's going to tell me, that *sometimes-moms-and-dads-can't-be-together-but-it's-not-your-fault*. Which would be ridiculous, since my dad died and her mom took off, so we already know all of that. Instead, she tells me again that we've lost the trail.

"Okay," I say, and then I shrug. "So we're a little bit lost."

"Not exactly lost. We just need to…recalibrate. We need to consider our options."

"Um, finding the trail? Isn't that the only option?"

"No. We have a few others. Camp here. Keep going in the dark. Or call home."

"Well, frankly, Aster, those options all suck ass."

"That they do."

"Camping on slickrock is out. Calling home feels a little theatrical since we're only sort of lost and only got that way in the last ten minutes."

"Hour, maybe," Aster corrects. "Not ten minutes."

"Fine. Hour. But if we call home, my mom is going to flip her shit. I'm not ready for that yet."

Aster nods. "So we're down to our third option, which is to keep going in the dark."

I snort. "It was ever so much fun last night. Maybe we could find a really difficult collection of boulders to scramble. I can cut my ankle this time. But seriously, it's fine. It's not quite dark. We can just backtrack a bit or whatever."

I'm one hundred percent on board with a screw-it-let's-see-what-happens approach, but Aster doesn't wing it with anything. She probably game-plans before picking up a sandwich for lunch. Her focus has been bouncing between her trail notes, her map, and her ankle. Now that I really look at her, I can tell she's not just planning. She's still nervous.

When she spots me looking, she taps her map book. "We only have about forty-five minutes of daylight left. I think we need to figure out where we are first."

"When's the last time you were sure we were on the path?"

"A little before you ran into that rattlesnake."

I rub the center of my forehead which is aching. "So that's like a mile and a half?"

"Maybe. I think so."

"Can we find any of this on the map?" I gesture vaguely around us at various rock formations and sandstone fins. There are ridges in the distance too, though they probably look pretty much the same as they did a mile ago.

She coughs and jabs an angry finger at the map. "That's the whole problem. We're in the middle of those two enormous switchbacks."

I nod, remembering the sections she pointed out where we'll head nearly due east around a particularly steep, inhospitable ridge and then will spend the next several hours of hiking going in the opposite direction around the same ridge. Feels like there should have been an easier way, but just-head-south is impossible in canyon country. But it will be worth it. The third day of our trip will include several miles on a narrow cliff that curves east and climbs just enough for us to see the whole trail we've followed. Nothing beats a distant view of wonders you've already seen up close.

I realize Aster hasn't continued. She's still staring at the trail guide, glowering.

"I'm guessing this is not a scenario where we can wing it," I offer.

"Absolutely not," she says. "But every damn feature in this section is so vague, I feel like we *are* winging it. Look at this!" She stabs at the map and then gestures around. "It could be any of this! Or maybe some totally different park in Idaho. This author should be beaten."

I laugh. "Isn't it all the same author?"

"No, it's cobbled together. Different hikers complete different sections. This section was apparently authored by someone who has never given directions in his life."

Another laugh. "Okay, grouchy, let me look. Bear in mind, it's all hieroglyphics to me, but I'll try."

But instead of checking the map, which is absolutely written in a foreign language, I look at Aster's puffy eyes and red nose and general looks-like-hammered-horseshit appearance. "How are you feeling?"

"Stuffy as hell. It's messing with my ears. I can't hear right."

I smirk. "Maybe that's why you're yelling."

"Ha ha."

"We need to get somewhere where you can sleep."

I check the map and see what she's talking about. I've never been good at topography maps. A bunch of blobs and various symbols. Is it another language? Do people take a class for this? Who knows. But Aster usually does know, and she's clearly perplexed.

"Show me something that we know *is* right," I say.

She points at one oblong blob with concentric blobs inside it. "That's the mesa there. And this is the ridge of the next canyon."

The features are too large to make it clear where we got off track.

"So what are we looking for?"

"A farm. Or a grove of pinyon pines." She pauses, checking her notes again. When she looks back up, she rolls her eyes "Or, and I'm quoting here, 'turtle and chicken rocks.'"

I turn around in a slow circle, scanning the horizon in every direction. My shoulders tense. I don't know the map the way she does, but nothing she's describing looks anything like what I'm seeing. Are we actually lost?

I push the thought back out of my mind. "This happens every trip, right? We've always figured it out."

"I know. I do. But I don't know how far off we are, and I don't know how much extra time we need to get to the new drop spot. And we are running out of food."

My stomach cramps in solidarity. She's right. We gobbled up the rest of the turtles after the rattlesnake, and I know we have enough food for a pretty meager dinner and breakfast. After that, we're completely out. Long-distance hiking like this is hard when you aren't hungry. I don't even want to think about it with the added suck factor of skipping meals.

"Yeah, I could do with some replenished snacks," I say, trying to think. She coughs and winces, her eyes flicking to her ankle. I sigh. "First things first. We need to take a look at that leg. And we need to figure out how to use that mesa and anything else we can see to find our way back to the trail."

"It's going to get dark fast. We should probably just deal with my ankle later." Aster coughs again. It's getting worse now. I remember Adam—who was always sick growing up—would be worse at night with a cold. Mom would prop him up in bed and run that vaporizer thing that always smelled like Vicks. And Adam would still cough so much it'd keep me up all night.

"We're better off camping here than we are letting gangrene set in," I say. "I don't want to have to cut off your foot."

"Thank you for thinking of me," she says.

"I am thinking of you! I don't even think we could find you a stick to bite around here, let alone a shot of whiskey."

Aster consents with a laugh, and we settle onto a low ledge on the side of one of the sandstone fins. I find the first aid kit and the headlamp in her backpack, and she sets to work pulling up her pant leg and unraveling the waterproof tape that's kept our ankles dry.

It's a slow process that looks painful. The tape may have kept us dry after the rain, but when she peels down her sock, it's clear her other bandage didn't stay in place. It's twisted and half-loose, most of her sock and all of the bandage stained with red streaks. The skin around the wound is pink and puffy, but we are getting low on first aid supplies. Do we have enough to bandage this in a way that will keep it from getting infected?

"That tape trick might not have been the best idea," I muse, "but you'll probably keep the leg."

I tug the tent out of Aster's pack and look around for the least miserable section in this sea of sandstone. The sky has turned blue-jeans dark, and the bright dot of Venus glitters like a diamond low on the horizon. Tiny taps sound nearby, a slow, rhythmic chitter that distracts me from the problem of no good place to camp. Right now, I'm interested in what I'm hearing. Something small is moving across the coarse sand and rocks near my feet. Maybe a little lizard? I pull out my flashlight to search and the beam lands right on a scorpion cruising up the toe of my boot.

I shake my foot hard and send it flying.

"Holy shit!" I shudder, all of the hair on the back of my neck standing up.

Aster straightens in alarm. "What is it?"

"A scorpion was on my shoe."

"Another one?"

I hold up a hand to keep her from speaking. Because I think I heard the scorpion again, scrape-tapping its way across the ground. "Did you hear that?"

"The scorpion on your shoe? No. Why, is it still there?"

"I kicked it off when I totally lost all composure, obviously. But I think it's coming back for me." I'm searching the desert floor feeling both silly and frantic. There's a small dead cactus and a ridge in the slickrock, and everything looks like a scorpion. I'm half convinced I can feel it crawling up the nape of my neck. It is everything I can do to not start one of those bizarre shake-all-of-your-clothes-just-in-case dances to pluck off any undetected creepy-crawlies.

"I'm sure it's gone," Aster says. But she doesn't sound sure. And in the quiet that follows, there is no doubt something both creepy and crawly is moving across the ground nearby.

Aster frowns and reaches for her pack without standing up, retrieving the flashlight I'd clipped into my hair last night. But this time, she twists something near the head of the flashlight, and the beam shifts from white to purple.

Black light. Perfect for those weird glow-in-the-dark paint parties they threw in junior high and for finding scorpions in the desert. Scorpions, for reasons I'm sure Aster knows and I have zero interest in, glow fluorescent under black light.

She scans the ground near me and finds the scorpion in question maybe two yards away from us.

"What the hell," she breathes. She isn't afraid of scorpions. Aster isn't afraid of much of anything, but I think something about this is unnerving her.

As far as I can see, it's doing pretty standard scorpion things. Its tail is curled up over its back, and it's moving steadily toward the base of a fishhook cactus. But the rhythm of the creature's undulating legs does not match the tiny *tap-tap-tapping* nightmare that I'm still hearing.

"Aster, that's not the one I'm hearing. There's something else. Something closer to you."

Aster makes a dubious sound, but slowly moves the purple beam across the ground. Light sweeps my feet and the flat boulder beside me, and then the boulder she's sitting on.

"Doesn't look like—" Aster's words cut off with a rustling as she quickly stands.

"Is there another one?" I ask.

She steps back closer to me, holding her pack. "Yes."

She holds the beam steady on the boulder where she'd been sitting moments ago. A scorpion glows bright in her purple beam, still and steady and not even a foot from where she'd been sitting. We watch it swing its pinchers left and then right. And then something else moves at the base of the boulder.

I gasp as her flashlight beam catches a third, smaller scorpion on the ground, trundling over a scrubby plant.

"What is this, some sort of scorpion convention?" I ask, feeling crawly all over. I shake my pack and pluck my shirt away from my chest over and over. My hair and arms and eyeballs are itching. My body is a thousand percent convinced there are scorpions everywhere.

Aster is uncharacteristically squirmy too, shaking her pack and double-checking the area. "Must be a good area for prey. That has to be it."

"What do you mean *that has to be it*?"

"I mean there has to be a logical explanation. This is real life, not some old myth."

I look at her. "What myth? There's a scorpion myth?"

She shrugs, looking sheepish. "There is supposedly an old Navajo belief that scorpions are a warning. I don't know if it's real or just urban legend."

"Okay, then maybe don't mention it? Especially while we're chilling in the center of Scorpion Grand Central."

"Right. Of course. So"—she looks around, like she's trying to compose herself—"I suppose we can just shuffle a few yards down from here and set up camp."

I continue to look at her for a long, long moment. "Aster. If you think I am going to pitch a tent anywhere near a place where we have seen not one, not two, but *three* scorpions, you are truly mistaken."

"What do you propose we do? It's too dark to find the trail."

"I don't have a particular destination in mind, but no chance will I rest my head tonight within half a mile of this scorpion symposium."

"I really don't think—"

I hold up my hands, because I think I hear something in the distance, and this time it isn't a scorpion. Or anything else with an exoskeleton.

I tilt my head, for a moment hearing nothing but my own breathing. The vaguest whisper of a breeze. Then it comes again. It could be a raven. I know that. Or another bird. Birds can sound deceptively human from a distance.

But then I hear it again. A shout. High-pitched and not that far away. Aster turns toward the sound of the noise.

"I hear voices," she says.

"Me too."

I see the vaguest impression of light maybe a quarter of a mile south of us. We take a few tentative steps to see it better. When our angle improves, the source of the light is very clear. It's a flashlight beam.

We are not so alone after all.

ASTER

---

25 MILES IN

*P*etty theft and *drug paraphernalia*. Those are the first phrases that come to mind when I hear the voices. Under normal circumstances I wouldn't even need Dad's warning. My interest in approaching strangers during a hike is always low. But never say never. The quickest and most efficient way to find a trail you've lost is spotting another hiker on that trail.

So we pick our way across a quarter mile of desert in the dark. It is slow going. We're not quite backtracking, so we can't quite retrace our steps. The other hikers—two of them as far as I can tell—are northwest of us. We came from a northeasterly direction.

"This is a cactus minefield," Katie says, weaving around a barrel cactus.

"I know," I say, blowing my nose. My ears pop and crackle when I do it. The darker it gets, the worse I seem to be feeling.

The embarrassment of this situation isn't helping. I should have known by the slickrock that we'd missed the trail. The rock was supposed to open into a scrubby field, and it obviously did. I just somehow missed it. Stupid mistake, and I know better.

"Are you sure this is a good idea?" Katie asks. She's behind me, and all that easy, relaxed demeanor is gone.

"I think they're on the trail. It would be good to know where that is."

"But the unsavories." Her voice wobbles a bit. "Your dad said something about theft, right? And drugs?"

"He did. We will keep our eyes sharp, but if they're coming from the south, they might have important trail updates."

"Okay." She sounds unconvinced.

"To level with you, Katie, they are on the trail. Which is more than I can say for us. Once we're back on the trail, we can all but pretend we never saw them."

"But they will see us tonight, right?"

Hard to imagine a way for us to get close enough to them to be sure we are back on track without alerting them to our presence. But she's so clearly tense about this situation, I'm reluctant to admit it to her.

Katie used to love running into other hikers. But now, she enters paralysis when we cross paths with a twentysomething in running shoes. I don't know why I keep forgetting she is not the person she used to be.

"We just need to make sure we're on the trail," I say.

"Okay," she says again.

"But let's start talking a little louder."

"What?" Katie frowns. "Why?"

"Hiker etiquette. It tells them we're near and gives them time to prepare."

"That makes sense," she says softly, but her shoulders are hitched up. Lips thinned. Fists clenched.

I touch her arm and speak very softly. "If you don't want to do this, we can…"

I trail off because I'm actually not sure what we can do. We could maybe find a clear area and camp here. But we're close enough now that they're likely to see us setting up. And then that will seem weird. Because we're off-trail in a sea of cactus plants. A place no one would choose to camp.

"No," she says softly. "This is stupid. I'm being stupid."

"You're just nervous."

"Well, I need to stop seeing monsters around every corner," she says. And then she raises her voice with a goofball smile. "Because I am turning into a total weirdo."

Across from us, I see the beam of a flashlight bobble and then rise. The two hikers are little more than shadows in the dark, but their flashlight moves in our direction. Nervous whispers come from the twosome. I lift a hand in greeting to assure them we are friendly, but it's Katie who speaks.

"Hello there!"

Her voice has gone singsongy and bright. This is Katie in front of adults. Katie at a store. Katie introducing friends. It is a version I knew well, but now it feels false, and that falseness pisses me off. It's not fair. I know that. But it's also been eleven months. When do I get the normal Katie back again?

The thoughts are shameful. As penance, I force myself to recall images of her in the hospital bed. Neck bruised. Hands shaking. Eyes empty. Remembering that will always make me ache with sadness. And guilt.

We are ten yards from the camp when I can make everything out. There is a single hammock strung between two boulders, but there's also a tent bag nearby. Two people sit on rocks beside these items, one petite with a mass of springy, curly blond hair, and another almost comically tall and broad-shouldered a few feet away. The curly-haired hiker waves enthusiastically, her slim legs silhouetted by their camp lantern.

"Hi there, come visit!" she says, her voice bright and cheery.

Katie stops midstep. Tension rolls off her in waves. She looks left of the camp, into the vast expanse of dark desert. Is some part of her considering bolting?

"Thank you," I say.

"I sure hope it's okay that I offered," she says, voice all but plucked from a preschool teacher. "I hate that awkward waiting thing, you know? Where people just look at each other and don't know what to say or where to start."

The blond's laugh rolls out like a melody. Like we are the happiest thing to happen. But the man behind her doesn't look up. Beside me, Katie smiles and smiles, but I'm not sure who she thinks she's fooling. These two, maybe. Herself? Almost definitely.

"I totally get that," she says as we step into the clearing where they've made camp. "Thanks for ripping off the Band-Aid. I'm Katie and this is Aster."

"I'm Riley," the blond says, piling her mass of curls on top of her head. She's thinner than me and shorter than Katie. So small, she could double as a sixth grader in the right clothes. But she's not a child. She's probably a touch older than us. Early twenties, for certain.

Riley turns, hands on her narrow hips. "Wow, Finn, you've got to put down that strong-and-silent-type card and introduce yourself."

Finn stands up and Katie stops moving. It's brief. A stutter in her approach, but one that I notice. Then she's moving forward again, slowly sliding her pack off one shoulder. Her knuckles are white where they grip the strap, and her eyes? Her eyes are locked on Finn.

Riley points at Finn. "This fellow is Finn. He's got that quiet alpha-male energy, you know?"

Finn's eyes dart between Riley and us. It's odd. His expression tells me maybe we interrupted something. But Riley acts like we are all but the brightest spot in her day. After an awkward pause, Finn offers a tight smile. He has short dark hair and a prominent brow that gives the impression of glowering. His features add up to handsome but forgettable.

"Has it been a long day of hiking for you?" Riley asks.

"Ten hours," I say, feeling every one of those hours in my feet, joints, and—maybe most of all—my sinuses.

"Wow," Riley says. "That's super intense. You must be wiped out."

"A little," Katie offers, her voice small.

"Well, you should join us for dinner!" Riley says, and she actually gives a little hop. Then she snaps her fingers and retrieves a bag. "We have so much food. Like way, way too much."

Finn looks at her blankly and then looks down at his feet.

"Not uncommon," I say. "People tend to worry too much about food and not enough about water."

"We were actually just talking about whether to leave it on the trail tomorrow morning." Another one of those singsong laughs. "We totally don't need all of this."

"Well, thank you," Katie says, sounding a little more like herself. "We're actually really low on food."

"We didn't underpack," I say, because I don't want these two to see us as unprepared novices. "We have a supply stash being dropped, but the first location was rained out."

"Did you guys get caught in that storm?" Katie asks.

Finn suddenly looks up, locking eyes with Riley. Something wordless passes between them. A secret. One that brings a flush to Riley's cheeks. Her grin reveals a dimple in her left cheek. "Um, we totally lucked out. We were near an overhang, so we just stayed there. Rode out the rain."

Katie snorts. "We weren't so lucky. I swear you could have wrung us out like sponges."

She sounds entirely relaxed. She isn't. Her whole body is turned toward Riley and me, but she is watching Finn.

"We are probably going to have some mildewed equipment to tend to when we get home."

Finn snaps to attention. "When is that?"

I shake my head. "Sorry?"

"When are you getting to town? How much longer are you out here?"

Riley laughs. "Wow, Nosey Nate, maybe we could have dinner before you start drilling them for details."

It might be experience and not curiosity motivating his questions. If he is experienced—and given the look of his hiking boots, I'm betting he is—he knows the dangers of wet gear. "I think we will get there before any real water rot sets in. That's where we got lucky. We had ponchos and rain covers so our bags stayed relatively dry. How did your equipment do? There was a lot of rain."

Finn hesitates and then frowns. After a beat, he opens his mouth. But Riley responds first.

"We got totally lucky too. Overhang and all!" And then she bites her lip and turns to Katie. "Okay, I have a confession."

Katie pays attention, and Finn looks up. Riley blows out a sigh like she's embarrassed and tucks an escaped curl behind one ear. "We lost a lot of time because of that rain. I mean, because of me."

"How?" Katie asks. Her expression softens as she takes in Riley's obvious discomfort.

"Wow, this is embarrassing." Her princess laugh trills out. And then she shrugs her narrow shoulders. "I'm super afraid of storms. As soon as the sky clouded over, we backtracked and found shelter. And then I was totally flipped out by the flooding."

"Me too," Katie says, her smile reassuring. "We were headed through those big switchback canyons, and I kept looking at the sides to see how high it had flooded in the past."

Riley nods enthusiastically, inching closer to Katie. "Thank you so much for sharing that. It's super embarrassing to admit you waited all day instead of hiking because of a little rain. Anyway, it wasn't all bad. We started playing two truths and a lie."

Riley nods at Finn with a smirk. "Finn learned that I couldn't ride a bike until I was ten, and I learned that he was a bit of a wild child, with the mug shot to prove it!"

Katie tenses, looking at me. I just shrug. Whatever police record he has, I doubt he'd bring it up in a game if it was serious. But Finn does not offer details or laughter. He looks down as if the ground between his shoes holds a sudden fascination.

"I snuck an injured bird into my room when I was eight," I say, trying to play along.

"Wow! Super scandalous!" Riley's grin is infectious.

"I'm pretty boring," Katie says. "But I did sell a couple of history papers my senior year of high school."

"Did you just graduate?" Riley asks.

"This spring for me," Katie says. "Last year for Aster."

"My brother just graduated," Riley says. "He's a big-time climber. He'd love it out here."

Katie tilts her head and then turns to me. "I wonder how those guys are doing. Carter and…"

"Luke," I say. Noticing Riley's confused expression, I explain. "Carter and Luke were climbing near our start point. They were supposed to start out hiking today, probably around the time the rain was moving in."

Riley's brows knit together. "Wow. Do you think they maybe turned back?"

Katie laughs. "Uh, no. I don't know them obviously, but from the five minutes we spent near them, I'm guessing Luke would have tried rafting his way down one of the flooded canyons. Hell, they could catch up with us any minute."

"Unlikely," I say. "They're still a good bit behind us."

"Do you think that trail runner made it out?" Katie asks.

"Probably. Those guys can clock twenty-five or more miles a day."

"You've seen a lot of other hikers?" Finn asks. He looks excited at the prospect, which is weird since he doesn't seem thrilled to see us.

Riley slaps her knees and stands up. "You know what. Let's fix dinner while we talk. I was telling Finn earlier I could eat a whole large pizza. Or several cheeseburgers. Tonight the menu is peanut butter sandwiches. Does that sound good?"

"It sounds like a five-star restaurant," Katie says. Her eyes dart furtively to Finn, but when she smiles at Riley again, I can tell she's more relaxed.

Riley pulls out a bag of pretzels, some banana chips, and then a Ziploc bag full of candy bars. "*Oh*, look what we've got here! Care to spoil dinner?"

"I would sign away my firstborn child to eat that Twix bar," Katie says.

Another laugh like a song. "It's yours then! So tell me everything. And I super appreciate you being so nice about my wimpy moment."

"No problem at all. Maybe I can help get things ready," Katie says, but even then she positions herself farther away from Finn.

It makes no sense. First Carter and Luke. Then that trail runner. Now she's afraid of Finn who's barely said a word since we arrived. Does she think every guy is out to get her now? What about Adam? Or my dad? How does she go to the grocery store? Or buy a cup of coffee?

The truth is I don't know. Reading my cousin was as easy as breathing for years. And now? I don't know. Everything I understood about Katie from before is gone. And everything I learn about her now feels wrong.

Still, Katie is the better choice for chatting with Riley. No way could I match the relentless stream of conversation and laughter coming off that girl. In contrast, Finn is so quiet I barely know he's there. It's a welcome change, so I approach him, eyeing the long flat-topped boulder he's sitting on.

"Is it okay if I set up a water filter?" I ask. "It's easier somewhere flat."

He tilts his head like he wants to say something, but in the end only nods. Then he looks away. I resist the urge to grin. Shy and awkward are relatable for me.

"It will take about twenty minutes."

Another shrug. Okay, he might be a little more than your typical shy and awkward type, but whatever. If they were both prattling with Riley's enthusiasm, I'd be ready to tear my own hair out.

At the peanut butter station, Riley is telling Katie about her dog back home and asking about her favorite constellations. I pull out the water, double-checking the filter and connections. Finn barely acknowledges me. It's heavenly.

Unless...

I glance over, noticing his frown and hunched shoulders. Are we making him uncomfortable? Some people crave solitude on the trail. I suppose if Finn wanted to be alone with Riley, we ruined that.

I start the filter and watch Finn. His gaze is fixed on Riley and Katie. No. Not both of them. Just Riley. He watches her with a look that's so intense, I don't know how to interpret it. Longing? Worry? Protectiveness?

"Do you guys have a lot longer on trail?" I ask gently.

An innocuous question, but his face scrunches like I presented a calculus problem. He shakes his head slowly, his voice soft. "I honestly don't know."

He seems sad at the answer. Sad in general. Over by Katie, Riley laughs, and Finn exhales hard.

"We won't stay," I say, and he looks up, his eyes wide. Is that eagerness? Surprise? A flicker of unease moves through me. I can't read him. In another time, I would ask Katie. But Katie is caught up with Riley, and I am on my own to sort this out.

Does he want us to go now?

Should we go now?

"If we are interrupting, we can take off," I offer, glancing at my barely started filter. I have no idea how we could realistically move that without losing some water, but it feels right to offer. To acknowledge his strange expression.

Finn's face shifts, and his hands roll into fists. A shadow of fear rises in the back of my mind. I think of Katie freezing midstep. Inching behind me. Keeping her distance. Does she know something about Finn that I don't? What am I missing here?

No way to know. But I trust her gut on these things more than I trust mine.

Behind us, Riley and Katie chuckle, sounding completely at ease. I keep my eyes on Finn. And he keeps his eyes on me. And those fists of his stay clenched tight.

Finally, he licks his cracked, chapped lips, his eyes darting. "Look, I think you should—"

"Hey, what are you two talking about?" Riley asks, all sweetness. "You brewing up a little flirty predinner banter?"

"We're not talking at all," Finn says quickly. "She's filtering water. I'm trying to get some peace and quiet."

I flush, and Riley puts up her hands. She's smiling, but she's looking at me, and I'm sure there is suspicion in her eyes. An awkward silence descends over the camp.

"Wow, sorry! We'll quiet down." When she looks at Finn, worry passes over her features. She covers it with a loud clap, her small hands coming together.

"I hope he's not scaring you off," Riley says to me in a whisper-scream. Her eyes gleam bright in the darkness, and my stomach zips tight.

"No, of course not," I say, but is it true?

Finn stiffens on the rock. His expression is unyielding. He makes no effort to reassure me or shrug it off. He just leaves Riley's accusations to linger unchecked.

"Did you want me to move this?" I ask, nodding to my water filter.

He looks at me like I'm the one whose supposed to know how to answer. But the truth is I don't even know what's happening here. There is the thing we see. Riley and Katie making dinner. Me filtering water. Finn sitting on a rock. But there is something else. A darker story pulses just beneath this simple picture, too slippery for me to grasp.

He finally answers, his voice gruff. "No, it's fine."

Nothing here is fine. Katie's fear. Finn's silence. Riley's too-bright chatter. I don't know what these things add up to. But I'm certain something here is very, very wrong.

ZERO MILES

She squeezes her peanut-shaped rock and lifts her head. The bandana shroud slips. The raven has returned to watch with a single black eye. She's still here. Heart pumps. Lungs inflate. Life goes on. And the raven stands vigil.

Looks like she'll have to get out. Since she can't seem to die.

She drags her good arm back, back, back. Props herself up, air beneath her shoulders. All her shattered pieces scream but she strangles the sound.

Hush, hush, little body. Got to try now.

She drags herself back one inch. Two inches. Manages to rise through a tidal wave of agony. Unspeakable. She's sure it would be easier if she could cut the injuries off. Untether from the agony. She drags it behind her instead. Grits her teeth and uses her good leg now.

She's at the wall. Thin crack and black streaks. In the dark sky, there are no helicopters. No search parties with great red crosses. Night has come with stars and empty promises.

She takes her five-in-one. Six-in-one. Soon to be seven because she twists it around, parting the hovering sea of gnats. She presses it over the oozing wound in her thigh. Crisscross go the ends, and she pulls. Pulls tight.

Her body bucks in pain. She stretches her arm out, reaching for help, for relief. Or an end.

Her fingers curl around the peanut rock. The only soft thing in this desert.

KATIE

25 MILES IN

Riley yanks some napkins from the backpack and hands them to me. Her smile droops like an underwatered plant. "Sorry. Finn has been like this all day."

My senses prickle. Does she mean the fact that he's quiet or the fact that he's an ass? "Like…"

"Just all of that, you know?" She waves vaguely at Finn and Aster. "It puts me on edge."

She could mean his quiet. Or his asshattery. Or some other third option I can't think of. Who knows.

"Aster, are you any good with maps? I want to ask your thoughts on something," Riley says, an edge to her voice.

"Sure." Aster checks her water filter, which is over halfway done now. "I can take a look, and then we can get out of your hair."

Riley laughs again. She has the best laugh, and she uses it a lot. Part of me doesn't understand what she's doing with a guy like Finn. And that same part of me wants to take her with us. Maybe even shake her and tell her that whatever just-all-of-that is, if it's putting her on edge, she needs to listen. I want to tell her that she should get away before Finn turns into someone who would hurt her.

But how do I know he hasn't already? She said something about a mug shot, didn't she? I look her over for signs of trouble or damage. Funny since I know the worst scars are the ones you can't see.

Riley *tsks*, dragging my focus back. "You're not bugging us. You know what it's like out here. Meeting anyone new is super exciting! Plus, we still need to eat." As she hands me a sandwich, she nods. "You've met loads of new people on the trail, sounds like."

"Just the climbers and that runner. But I doubt you'll see them."

"Why's that?" Riley asks.

"Well, I guess I assumed you were heading south." I consider mentioning the *RF* entry we saw in the logbook, but then realize it's kind of a leap. It actually doesn't make a ton of sense to list your initials like that without an *and* between them. They could have started at another location or not logged in at all. Either way, mentioning it makes me look like a bit of a stalker, so I stay quiet. Especially since Riley is watching me with an unreadable expression.

"Yeah," She pauses, her eyes cutting to Finn. "We are headed south. How'd you know?"

"Lucky guess," I say with a shrug.

"Have you guys been hiking together for a long time?" Riley asks.

I laugh. "Well, yeah. For most of our lives. She's my cousin."

"Oh, wow! That's super cool." Riley hands out more food, but she seems distracted. Or maybe even a little nervous. And she keeps looking at Finn.

"I'm local," Aster says, taking a sandwich.

"Like local to Utah, or..."

"Local to Moab. Up by Arches?"

"Oh, right, right. Do you guys still live in town?" she asks around a bite of sandwich.

I shake my head. "Oh, not me. I live in Ohio. Columbus."

Finn walks away, muttering something about the bathroom. Riley watches him go, her face flickering with that same tension. When he's out of sight, her shoulders droop, and she lets out a heavy breath. Like the curtain has dropped on a stage. I want to ask about Finn. I want to make sure she's safe, but of all the times for Aster to decide to be social, she chooses now.

"So what about you?" she asks. "Are you from Utah?"

I shoot her a look. I'd bet a thousand dollars she already knows the answer to that question. She always seems to know when someone's local.

"Nope," Riley says. "Neither one of us, actually. We're both super Midwestern."

I take a bite of my sandwich and chew thoughtfully. "What brings you out here then? Do you do a lot of hiking?"

"I did a lot growing up but got out of the habit. But things have been so crazy for me back home, and I wanted a break. I heard someone talking about hiking in Utah at a coffee shop."

Riley shrugs, and I put down my sandwich, shocked. I can't imagine hearing about a multiday hike and deciding, what-the-hell-let's-do it. Our trips have always been carefully planned. If I'm surprised, then Aster is halfway to a stroke by the look of her face.

"You heard about this trail in a coffee shop?" She frowns. "It's one of the least traveled areas in southeastern Utah. Most of this trail is barely documented."

Riley quickly waves that off. "No, not this trail specifically. She was talking about Canyonlands. But I went right home and started googling and checking out hiker forums and, well, here we are." Riley rolls her eyes. As if this is all the silliest thing, and she just happened upon an incredibly challenging trail and figured why not? Aster's horror at this whole admission is obvious.

"And Finn?" I ask, looking for a way to shift this topic. To give her a chance to speak up if she is in any sort of trouble with this guy. "Is he a hiker?"

She looks momentarily confused, and then shakes her head with a laugh. "Finn? He says he's been backpacking since birth, you know? Funny since he's from Illinois, which doesn't really sound like hiking paradise. So what about you guys?"

"I live here, so I hike a lot," Aster says. "And because I live here, I prefer the quiet backcountry trails. But they can be dangerous. You're quite isolated."

"So true!" Riley says, brightening. "It's amazing!"

I stifle a laugh. Aster is trying to lay out a grave warning and Riley thinks she's offering selling points.

"What about you, Katie? What would bring you all the way out here?"

I think of the sound of a zipper and the whirl of too much alcohol and the thump of frames against a bedroom wall. My stomach rolls, and the truth lays itself bare in my mind. The truth? I am here to run away.

"I just needed something new," I say.

"Me too," Riley says, her eyes on mine, "but I think my adventure is just about over. I think it's time to move on." Riley's eyes flick meaningfully in the direction where Finn disappeared. She's trying to say something to me, and I wish to God I could figure out what that something is. Is she leaving him? Does she need help? Can I even help her if she does?

I finish my last bite of sandwich and straighten, hoping to find a way to ask her. To offer some sort of assistance. Which is exactly when the crunch of Finn's approaching footsteps interrupts us.

Riley straightens when he reappears. She gives him a look I can't decipher and then timidly pats the boulder beside her. An invitation to sit. He hesitates for a long while before finally lumbering closer.

There is weirdness between these two. I can feel it when he gets close to her, ignoring the sandwich and the way Riley tenses—the way we both tense. He takes a nondescript water bottle instead and then retreats a few feet away.

Riley gestures at the untouched sandwich with a sigh. "You guys can probably split the fourth sandwich if you want. I'm getting the impression Finn doesn't have much of an appetite, you know?"

Out of the corner of my eye, I see his attention sharpen. A muscle jumps in his jaw, but Riley keeps smiling. Like she's desperate for him to see that she means it kindly. Or maybe she just wants everyone to get along. Anger folds up my insides into a tiny, tight knot. I can't stand this. Watching her be afraid of this man. I flew across the country and hiked for two days to forget about men like this and fear like Riley's.

But it's still right here. Like it was waiting for me.

Except it isn't me this time, is it? It's happening to Riley. And deep down, in spite of how sick I feel, I know this is not my problem to solve. My therapist is big on that, on me remembering-what-I-am-actually-responsible-for. Finn and Riley's relationship is definitely not on that list. I know that. I know that my mother and my friends and yes, my therapist, all have one primary commandment for me to follow. Care for thyself. No matter how much I want to take care of someone else.

But what if taking care of someone else could protect them from what happened to me? Or something like it at least? How am I supposed to live with myself if I walk away and Riley ends up as messed up as me?

"So!" Riley claps her hands together again, pulling my attention back to the present. Then she sets to pulling her mass of curls out of the bun containing them, only to twist the whole mess back into place. "Top three moments on the trail?"

"What?" I can feel the way my smile hesitates.

"Your top three moments on this hike?" Riley beams.

"We're not done with the hike," Aster says, zipping up her jacket. Her eyes cut to the open desert—east, maybe. Probably she's just looking to be done with this scene. Aster has never been big on lengthy visits with strangers.

"Well, then your top moments *so far*." Riley wiggles a little on the rock, like she truly can't wait to hear what we say. "I'm a big believer in quantifying things like this. When we repeat our good experiences, they stay sharper in our memory than the bad times, you know?"

A year ago, I would have believed that. A year ago, I walked around just like Riley, sure that nothing too terrible would happen. Just as long as I played nice. But playing nice earned me finger-shaped bruises and a night in the emergency room, so now I know better.

"Maybe bad times shouldn't be forgotten," Finn says. His voice is so sudden and unexpected that we all whirl to look at him.

My throat feels tight watching him. Waiting for him to say something else to soften those words. He doesn't even bother to try.

Riley ducks her head. "Sure, that's a fair point. I guess…I just like to focus on the positive side of things, you know? It helps me to remember what matters."

Finn makes a noise then, so slight and quiet I could almost miss it. But I don't miss it. And I know a scoff when I hear one. I wait, hoping someone will say something. Hoping Aster will say it's getting late or we'll hear a coyote or hell, anything. But instead Riley just looks at me expectantly, waiting for my list, I guess.

But I can't. I feel myself freezing up, some terrible mix of numbness and anger that renders me incapable of playing along. I can't be cheery and hopeful like Riley anymore. No matter how badly I wish I could.

"There was a field with blue pod lupines."

Aster. I turn, surprised to see she has shifted closer to me. Not substantially. Just enough that I notice she is here. Is it coincidence? She hasn't read me worth a shit this week, not like she used to. But now… Maybe she still feels something, some thread of our connection that hasn't been lit on fire.

"They usually don't bloom now," she says, "not in numbers like this."

Regardless of why she's closer, I feel a swell of gratitude, and that gratitude unlocks my voice. "They were stunning. I'm sure you guys saw them. They were really vibrant against the red rock. That was great."

"I don't think I remember that," Riley says, still smiling. "I must have marched right past it, but it sounds amazing."

"It was," Finn says quietly. "I remember them."

My whole body coils tightly at the sound of his voice, but I force myself to offer a polite nod. I can't even put my finger on what it is, but everything about this guy makes me nervous. My whole body is screaming that he is tense or angry. Maybe even dangerous.

"I also loved the middle section of the second canyon," Aster says. It surprises me, because I don't remember her making a comment or even stopping. But she looks thoughtful now, not smiling but still pleased in her Aster way.

"The middle section near that tall, narrow arch?" Riley asks.

Aster coughs and then nods. "But not because of the arch. I live in Moab. Arches and natural bridges are everywhere. It was more the moment. We were just chatting, the breeze was nice, and some of the cactuses were in bloom. It hadn't rained yet."

We share a laugh and when Aster looks at me, I remember. Nothing special or concrete, just the quiet peace of a good day of hiking. I remember my legs were sore and my heart was full and it was good. It's still good. There have been low points, sure, but overall it's given me something I needed.

"There was a raven early on," I offer, feeling a rush of warmth in my chest for Aster and for this place. "I know they can be pests. Aster is not a fan."

"I am not," she agrees.

Riley and I both chuckle.

"But when I heard him…" I put my hand on my chest as if I can grasp the feeling I'm trying to describe. But it's vapor passing through my fingers. "I guess being near a raven reminds me that I'm really here. That I'm not in Ohio."

"That's right, you live in Ohio?" Riley asks. "Have you always lived there?"

"Born and raised."

"Wow, that's so great."

"I promise, it's not all that exciting, but Columbus is generally underrated."

"Well, I'm super glad you're here," Riley says, and she's beaming. Just full of electric joy that feels so foreign to me. I had so much of that joy once. But now it is like my childhood bedroom furniture, familiar but impractical.

Finn looks away, and I glance at the water filter, which must have finished while we were eating. Aster spots it too and stands.

"Well, thank you so much for this," she says, sniffing. "You have both been kind."

Riley practically leaps to her feet. "Wait, you don't need to rush off or anything."

I can't even pretend to smile. My insides are bunching and twisting. She wants us here. She wants us to stay because she's afraid and it hurts. It hurts because I can see the fear in her eyes, and in the same instant I feel my own inability to do a damn thing about it. No matter how much I wish I could, I have no idea how to save another person. Hell, I still haven't figured out how to save myself.

"Oh, wow, I almost forgot," Riley says. She wrestles in the blue backpack, bringing out an extra bottle of water. A refilled quart bottle, so nothing special, but around here, clean water is liquid gold. When she stretches it out to me, I hesitate, and Aster shakes her head.

"You should keep your water. We have a filter."

"Trust me, we can't carry all of this." Riley laughs. And then she hands us a bag with a box of granola bars and a couple of warm-and-eat backpacking meals.

We use our flashlights to lead us away. We follow the trail, which is hard to spot in the darkness. It's a barely-cleared ribbon of sand weaving through the patchwork of cactuses. Still, I'm surprised when Aster stops not much more than a hundred yards from Riley and Finn's camp.

"Did you forget something?" I ask.

"No, I think this is a good spot. We're back on the trail, and I know that narrow cliff section starts in the next mile. Maybe less," she says.

"Yeah, probably makes sense not to navigate that in the dark."

"Absolutely not," she says and then blows her nose. "And honestly, I feel terrible. I need sleep before I can hike more."

Aster pulls out the GPS. I can tell by the way her expression changes that there's a message. She reads it and then hands the GPS to me. The message stares up. Stash dropped. No rain forecasted. Julie's scared anyway.

I navigate to the keyboard. "I'll send something reassuring, if you're okay to set up the tent?"

"Sure."

At the message box, I go blank for a moment, thinking of my mom's worried eyes. The way her hands reach for me now. She used to pour her love out through her hands. Hugs and pats and squeezes to my arm. Now it isn't love; it's assessing damage—the way you'd gently prod an injured limb to see if there's a break.

Mom is probably coming apart at the seams right now, desperate to have me safe and sound and back where I belong. But I need to finish this. I want people to remember that I'm capable of standing on my own feet.

I start my message decisively. We're safe. No flooding. Trails dry and doing great!

I pocket the GPS while Aster slides the poles into the tent. The sight of the wad of fabric and the click of the poles underscores my exhaustion. Another night on a flimsy pad stretched over rocks sounds like a shit sandwich I'm not interested in eating. But it is what it is, or whatever.

We each use the restroom a little farther off-trail, keeping watch since this time there are people somewhat nearby. When we return to our bare-bones camp, we refill water bottles, and unlatch our sleeping bags and pads.

"I'll prep the tent tonight," Aster says, crawling inside to handle our sleeping bags and such. It's a one-person job, thanks to the cramped quarters. I wait until she's inside and hand my pad and sleeping bag in first.

Across the darkness, I hear faint noises from the other camp. An indistinct thump here or a snap there. These are the sounds of cleaning up and preparing for bed, and they can probably hear our sounds too. I don't relish the idea.

"Hand me the next one," Aster says.

I feed in the other sleeping roll and bag, and help Aster sweep out a pile of sand she's collected at the edge of the tent. Once the worst of it is dumped back into the desert where it belongs, she slips back inside to set up her sleeping area.

Something rustles behind me. I turn but see nothing. It could be a desert hare or maybe a fox or some other small, furry thing. What I'm sure of is that it's too loud to be a scorpion, so I'm happy to share our little patch of sand.

But then I hear it again, more softly, and my skin prickles. Somehow the change in volume feels…deliberate. I don't know why the word comes to mind, but the minute it does, it settles deep into my bones. Instinct. Whatever made this sound is trying to not be heard.

Aster rustles in the tent and a breeze ruffles my hair. My breath sighs out. There is darkness and tranquility. And then the rustle comes again. Something moving inside or near a plant. My eyes lock onto to two pinyon pines twisted together.

The hair on the back of my neck stands on end, so no. I am not imagining this. My body is warning me. And once upon a time, I would wave it off, but once upon a time, I did not feel like throwing up when I heard people pulling down their pants in the bathroom stall next to me. So once upon a time, I might have ignored this, but not now.

"You about there?" I ask, trying to inject humor into my trembling voice.

"Almost," Aster says from inside the tent. "My zipper was stuck."

My ears prickle at the sound of another rustle. Like a footstep. A human footstep. I take a step to the side to see better.

Across the desert, a single light dances inside a small dome tent. Finn and Riley's tent. Nothing near us moves. Aster softly rustles in the tent, but other than that? Nothing. My stomach sinks. I did not imagine what I heard. So what the hell is out here with me?

I am turning away when I hear the slightest shift of sand under a foot. This time it is much, much clearer. My eyes lock onto the cluster of rocks near the pinyon pines. Five yards from me. Maybe less. The rocks stand dark and solid and still. And then a shadow peels away from the cluster. My eyes catalog the parts and pieces. Two legs and a splayed hand. No. It can't be.

My stomach tumbles end over end and something unzips in the

distance. At Finn and Riley's camp. Which means this can't be what I think. The only people for miles are zipping up their tent. I can hear them! But, even still, I don't dare look away from the shadow now.

"Finn?" Riley's voice is small but clear in the night.

The black shadow springs into motion, stepping toward me.

Finn.

My chest squeezes a knot into the hollow of my throat. Finn is standing right in front of me, gasping like he's out of breath. He was hiding—keeping himself in the shadows, for what? Why is he here? What the hell is he doing?

He looks at the tent and then back at me. At the tent and then at me. Panic fires through every part of my body, a rush of pins and needles racing over every inch of exposed skin. My hands come up automatically, and then he is close enough to strike me.

He takes another step, and I realize should scream. I open my mouth to do it, open it wider because my voice is trapped somewhere deep in my throat, pushed down by an invisible fist. I can't make a sound. Why can't I scream? I have to scream!

Help! I need help!

Finn opens his mouth too, as if his voice is trapped like mine. He's going to say something or do something, and I can't do anything to stop him. I have been turned to stone.

"Finn?" There is a sharper, nervous edge to Riley's voice now. She's afraid.

Finn's head swivels toward the sound of her voice. He gives me one last look, one that tells me he knows now he can't have whatever the hell he came for. That expression lingers on his face for the span of a breath.

And then Finn turns his back on me and runs.

ASTER

---

25 MILES IN

Katie doesn't crawl into the tent; she hurls herself inside. Something has happened. She is pale. Panting. Terrified. I look her over, finding no obvious explanation for her state.

"What's wrong? Are you sick? Are you hurt?"

She shakes her head and reaches toward me. Her hands are shaking. I take them and squeeze as she scoots closer. Like she cannot be near enough to me. Or far enough from whatever has her so frightened.

"Finn." His name comes more air than voice. She is breathing so fast. Too fast.

"Slow down. Try to slow your breathing. Tell me about Finn. Is he hurt? Is he in trouble?"

She shakes her head hard, but she is still gasping. Her eyes are everywhere, searching every shadow in this tiny tent, jerking at the tiniest noise outside.

I touch her shoulders. Try to get her settled. "Hey, you are okay. Just breathe. Take a minute."

She jerks away from my touch. Shakes her head again and again. "No. No, he was out there. He—outside." Then suddenly, her face clears. She pulls in a deep breath and speaks slowly. "Finn was outside, and he was watching us. Watching me."

I watch her closely. "Finn was outside."

She nods.

"And he was watching us." Another nod, so I keep going. "Where is he now?"

"He went back to their camp. Riley called for him, and he went back."

"Without saying anything at all?"

"Not a word. He started to, but then Riley called for him."

I had heard that much, in the distance. It didn't seem like a thing worthy of my attention.

"Was he going to the bathroom? Or getting water? Or—"

She grabs my arm hard, and her eyes are dark and wild.

"Listen to me." A whisper-scream. My heart speeds up. Her fingers pinch. She looks deranged. "He was *watching* me. He was hiding in a bunch of rocks."

My throat feels raw now that it's late in the day. I'm exhausted, and even the adrenaline now pumping through me has not pulled the ache from my bones or the throbbing from my temples. "Did you say anything? Did you ask him what he was doing?"

"He was in the dark. He came at me." She shakes her head. "If Riley hadn't called for him…"

I wait for her to resume her sentence, to pick up where she trailed off, but she doesn't. She scrabbles across the tent instead of answering. Plucks her travel pillow off the ground and moves to start rolling her sleeping bag.

"Wait, what are you doing?"

"We're leaving," she whispers, working her bag into a tight roll. "I can't stay here. Not with him out there."

Real alarm flares through my chest now, throbbing through the pressure in my face and ears. I shake my head, because whatever this is, it isn't a good enough reason for us to leave in the middle of the night. I don't know what's going on with Finn, and I don't like it. But I'm not afraid of Finn. I have ways to deal with creepy hiker guys, even ones who think they can lurk around in the dark. Hiking here in the middle of the night is different. That frightens me.

"We can't leave right now," I say.

"Yes, we can. We don't have to go far. Just a mile or two down the trail."

"We can't do that."

"Yes, we can!"

I touch her arm again, very gently. "Katie, we are close to that cliff section, remember? It's almost three straight miles on a narrow path along the rim of a cliff."

Katie looks like she wants to argue. But she remembers. I can see that much in her face.

"There's no clear scramble, so we won't see it coming," I say. "The earth will just drop away. There are notes about how dangerous this section is. Attempting to navigate that at night would be beyond dangerous."

She wants to find a way out of my logic. I can see it in her face. I can feel it in the way she huffs out, her breath smelling of the peanut butter from earlier. But Katie knows where we are and how foolish it would be to go out there at night.

Suddenly her eyes go watery and bright. Her next breath goes in with a shudder, and her voice is so small when she speaks. "He could come back for us, Aster."

I remember Katie at the hospital then, trembling and small in that enormous wheeled bed. She looked like this that night. And in the wheelchair the next day when Aunt Julie signed her out. A deep ache settles in the center of my chest, followed by a wave of anger. I swore I'd never let Katie feel like that again. Not around me.

But now it's too late. I didn't have a problem with Finn before, but now? What the hell *was* he doing out there? Even if he conjures up a good reason, it doesn't matter. He scared Katie. And she has had enough scaring for a lifetime.

"What if he comes back?" she says again.

I squeeze her arms gently. "He'll regret it if he does."

I let her go and drag my pack closer. Unzip the bottom pouch and feel around until my fingers graze cold, smooth metal. Bingo. I pull the canister out carefully, feeling the slight heft of it in my palm, the plastic trigger ready to be deployed.

"Bear spray?" she whispers. "But there aren't bears."

"No, but the range is better than pepper spray, and it would work on mountain lions in the unlikely chance we run into one." I soften my face and my voice then. "I will not let anything happen to us out here, Katie."

What I really mean is, I will not let anything happen to *her*. Because I already let something happen to her. I won't make that mistake twice.

"You can't spray that in here," she says.

"Oh, I won't. If I hear him within ten feet of our tent, I'll stick my arm out of the flap and let this rip the second he's close enough to hit."

She doesn't like this solution. Doesn't trust it. But her shoulders slump the slightest bit. I'll take it. I'll take anything that can calm her down.

"I can't sleep," she says. "No chance can I sleep with him out there."

"Then I'll stay awake. So you can rest."

"You can't. You've been sick. You have to get rest."

"I'll take the first shift," I say. "I'll wake you in an hour."

She's calming. Her breathing slows and her hands go steady. I can tell she's thinking it over, and finally, she shakes her head.

"No, you should sleep first," she says. She nods then, looking certain. Katie is always better with a plan. "It makes sense for you to rest while I'm wired."

"I could stay up with you if you'd like. I'm still wide awake," I say, but fatigue is pulling hard at my eyes. My throat feels raw, my nose and ears suffocating me with pressure.

"You look tired," she says. "And you can fall asleep at the drop of a hat. Plus I'm so wound up, you could probably power a small city off my tension energy, so one of us should get some sleep, right?"

I relent, slipping into my sleeping bag, but I keep a close ear out for any hint of danger. There is nothing outside of what I would expect in the desert at night. Crickets. Wind. Quiet. I keep my eyes open too, watching her sit in the center of her sleeping bag. Her legs are pulled up tight to her body, her chin resting on her folded knees. Like maybe if she makes herself small enough, she will disappear.

Before, Katie was a fighter. When confronted with danger, she wouldn't run or hide, she would set her jaw and face down whatever was scaring her. And some piece of this new fearful girl is my fault. Maybe I didn't drag her into that bedroom or mark her with bruises, but I left her. There were a thousand other choices I could have made—a thousand ways I could have saved her. I close my eyes and my mind visits those better choices one by one.

I must drift off to sleep, because I wake up to pain. Katie. She is hovering over me, eyes gleaming. Her fingers claw hard into my bicep, her nails biting through the thin fabric of my shirt. I yank my arm free.

"What?" I nearly shout.

And then her hand is on my mouth. My throat. Panic erupts in my chest. I flail.

"Shh…" she whispers, her voice trembling.

She moves her hand slowly away from my mouth. My heart is pounding, and my ears feel horribly clogged. My head feels like it's in a vise. Like I'm a hundred miles underwater, and the pressure is building and building.

But even with my clogged hearing, I catch something outside our tent. Voices. Shouting. A fight. I sit up quickly in the darkness and my head spins. I brace myself on my arms and listen. It's Finn and Riley.

"What's happening?" I whisper, trying to clear my mind. Trying to catch up.

"They're fighting. It started a few minutes ago."

"What are they saying?"

"I can't really hear. I thought maybe…"

We both inch closer to the side of the tent. I push in until we are shoulder to shoulder, pressed as close as is reasonable to the canvas wall. The wind has picked up since I fell asleep. But when it quiets, I can hear fragments of their conversation. Bits of sentences that don't make sense.

"—*you don't know*—"

"—*show them*—"

"—*just stop*—"

"—*bad enough*—"

The sound of a tent being unzipped. And then distant footsteps.

"*You're not going over there!*"

Finn's voice is a low growl. Beside me, Katie tenses, her arm going tight against mine.

"—*can't stop me!*"

I hurl myself back to my bag, blearily grasping in the dark until I find the bear spray. My vision is sloshing from side to side, and my throat thickens with nausea. Katie shoves her way in front of the entrance to the tent. Between me and my target.

"You can't spray Riley!" she whispers.

Footsteps now. Coming closer, and I need to get Katie behind me. Something is coming. And I cannot let it get to Katie.

I have my hand on her arm to haul her back from the entrance when Riley's voice comes through loud and clear.

"Help," she sobs. "Please, please help me."

Katie is unzipping the tent door before she finishes her sentence. "Riley!"

Riley is sobbing and trembling in the doorway. Moonlight leaves her face in strange shadows. "I need help."

"Come inside," Katie says, but Riley shakes her head quickly.

"No! I can't! He'll come here."

"Finn?" I ask, my grip tightening on the bear spray. My ears prickle for the sound of heavier steps, but there's nothing.

A frustrated growl in the distance. Riley flinches.

"Please. Do you have a phone? Or something that will get signal? I can't get signal, and I need to call for help."

Help. We can call for help. I turn to my backpack, moving for the pocket where I keep it.

"Here," Katie says. "Do you want me to call?"

"I know how," Riley says around a sob.

"It's unlocked," Katie says, and that's when I see the Garmin in Riley's hand.

Riley is holding our GPS but she can't be. It's in my bag. Confusion fizzes through my mind. My vision whirls, and I plant my palms into the tent floor. The dizziness is debilitating.

Katie nods. "You can message *SOS* unless you're trying to reach—"

"Riley!"

Finn's voice is a roar, and it is not far enough away. And then I remember. Before we set up the tent. Before Finn showed up. Before any of this, it was Katie who sent the message home. Katie who has our GPS. Katie who just handed our only connection to the outside world to a complete stranger.

"You're not doing this, Riley!"

A single frozen moment. Riley's eyes and mouth wide with terror. Cheeks glistening with tears. Katie's own face drawn tight in fear. And then the moment splinters. Riley rushes from the tent in a flurry of arms and legs. Her footsteps head south, and different, heavier footsteps approach. Finn is coming for us.

Terror climbs into my throat as I lift the bear spray. Hold my breath because he is so close now. So very close.

ZERO MILES

She gasps when she remembers it. His hands on her face. Her neck. His mouth hot and hungry. New kisses always feel best. Like something you're not supposed to have, which is always the thing she always wants most.

She searches her bag again. Remembers the tiny first aid kit in the front pocket. Laughs at the blister bandages and ointments but clutches that slick rectangle. The size of travel tissues and the shape of salvation. It's all harder now that she wants to live.

She opens the emergency blanket fold by fold by fold. How many times has she done this? Unfolded a blanket. Played a risky game with a handsome boy. A look that lingered. A lip bitten. A silent invitation.

Maybe those things add up to her broken body at the bottom of this canyon. Maybe those things earned her the push.

KATIE

25 MILES IN

He is coming for us, and there is nowhere to run and nowhere to hide and nothing to stop him. Panic squeezes around my heart, a cold fist with long fingers. But then I am pushed to the left and Aster is there, shoving her way between me and the entrance to our tent.

Our tent flap, still unzipped, ripples in the wind, and Aster moves it open just enough to slip her hand through. She's holding something, and I remember seeing it earlier. The bear spray. Finn's footsteps have stopped, but I know he's out there. It is too quiet for him to move without us hearing. We will know if he is past us. We will hear him coming.

He was already close before, but how close? Can he see us inside the tent? Surely it's too dark for that, but I shiver in the cold, feeling his eyes on me through the shadows and the tent walls and the impossible darkness around us.

I shift so that I can see over Aster's shoulder, right through the narrow gap in the tent flap. There are rocks and dirt and a pinyon pine's twisted arms. And then he's there, a dark blur racing across my line of sight.

I cringe backward, and Aster surges closer to the door. Her grip on the bear spray tightens, her arm stretched straight and strong. She will shoot him if he comes one inch closer, but he doesn't. His footsteps move right past our tent, heading south.

Following Riley.

My stomach squirms like a bag of snakes. He is going after her, and we are sitting here, not doing a single thing. I instinctively reach for a phone and remember where I am and how worthless a phone would be. But we did have something—an emergency GPS. Riley is holding the single best way to get help. That fact gives me the space to breathe.

Long minutes after there are no more footsteps, Aster zips the tent closed. But she sits there in the darkness, and I can feel the tension in every breath she takes. Sleep isn't likely to come for either of us.

Then, all at once, Aster sighs, sinking back onto her heels. "I wish you hadn't done that."

I shake my head, having no idea of what she's talking about. "Done what?"

She turns to me then, and I'm glad for the darkness. Something tells me her expression would sting like a slap. She's clearly angry. I can feel that much, but why?

"What did I do?" I press.

"You gave her the Garmin, Katie. That was our only way to call home."

"What was I supposed to do? She was in trouble!"

"*You* could have sent an SOS for her."

"I didn't know she was going to run off. I thought she'd call and leave it."

"Well, she's gone," Aster snaps. "And so is our only way to connect with help."

I open my mouth, unsure of what to say or how to act. She's right, of course. I handed over our most important in-case-of-emergency device without a single thought as to when we'd get it back.

"Without that GPS, we are utterly isolated," Aster says.

The guilt is a gut punch. I made this choice for both of us, and now we're both at risk. We could get stuck in a flood or get lost or fail to find the stash Uncle Mike left. There are eleventy billion ways this thing could turn to absolute shit, and I tossed our Hail Mary into someone else's hands.

"I'm sorry." My voice is softer than I'd aimed for.

Aster turns away from me. Even in the darkness, I can see her drop her head into her hands. She coughs roughly and then blows her nose. She sounds absolutely awful, much worse than before.

"I want to tell you it will be okay," she says.

"But?"

She picks her head up then to look at me. I can't see her well, but her voice is close and impossible to escape. "But the truth is, something about this feels wrong."

I straighten. "Wrong how?"

"Wrong about Riley. About both of them."

"Obviously," I say. "Riley was terrified of him. I knew she was in trouble at dinner."

Aster makes a puzzled noise. "Trouble? What trouble?"

"Well, did you not notice Finn's utter assholery at every turn?

He barely spoke to us, and she was ultra-jumpy around him. She didn't even want us to leave."

"He was quiet," she argues. "*Quiet* does not mean *asshole*."

"Not always, but in this case—"

"In this case we have no idea!" Aster coughs again and then blows her nose before going on. "No one knows what's going on in someone else's relationship. Everyone thought my dad was the problem too. You don't remember that, but I do."

Aster doesn't talk about her mom. I only have one memory of her standing at the bathroom mirror in Uncle Mike's house, applying lipstick. I don't even know that she spoke to me. I don't remember her speaking much to Aster either. Which tracks, since she hasn't talked to her since the day she took off.

"Your dad is an amazing person," I say softly. "Finn is nothing like him."

"You think that, but what do you actually know about Finn?"

"I know he snuck up on us in the dark. I know he scared Riley so badly she ran to us sobbing. She's probably already called for help."

"Possibly. Hopefully."

"She wouldn't have asked for it if she wasn't planning to use it."

"I didn't say she wasn't planning on it, but she ran," Aster says.

And he ran after her. Would she have been able to send an SOS message while she was running? If not, has she kept herself away from him long enough to send the call? I have no way to know. She could have gotten lost or fallen, and all of this is bad. Especially since we have no way to send for help if Riley didn't already do it.

The implications stack themselves in my mind, one after another. Our family has no way to know that there's something wrong here. We checked in at our normal time with a standard all-safe-here message. They have no way of knowing that anything is amiss.

"When have we been sending messages to Mom and Uncle Mike?" I ask.

"Nighttime," she says. "Nine p.m. the first night. Eleven last night, maybe?"

"So, if we don't send them a message by eleven tonight, they'll worry?"

"Your mom might worry. Midnight is the absolute earliest my dad would give it a thought. And that's all he'd give it."

"He wouldn't worry?"

"Not if our GPS seemed to be in the right place. Even if we don't send a message, he can ping for our location on his end. He would assume our messages aren't working or something is glitching, as long as that GPS ping is tracking in the right direction."

My shoulders slump. "And Riley was headed in the right direction."

"Yes."

She might not be far off. Uncle Mike isn't a guy known to panic. But Mom…

My mom's face flashes into my mind. If she doesn't hear from me and thinks that something is wrong out here—it doesn't matter what Uncle Mike says or how he feels; at some point she'll panic. Then she'll call the police and rangers and anyone else who will listen.

She might even call Adam. My last misadventure cost him a semester—pushed his whole life back a few months. For mom it was even worse. This can't be anything like that for them. I can't put them in that place again, not even for a moment.

But what about Riley? Isn't she stumbling headlong into her own nightmare? What about her brother, her parents, or whoever else she has back home?

Riley is in trouble, and Finn is at the center of that trouble. I can feel it in my bones. And we might be the only ones who know. The only ones with any chance of saving her.

Aster lets out a long sigh and snuggles down a little farther in her sleeping bag. Maybe she thinks the conversation is over. Or maybe she's just cold. Either way, we're not done here.

"I'm going out there," I say. I shift onto my hands and knees to reach my pack. I quickly unzip it and retrieve my windbreaker. Aster sits back up as I'm pulling it on. "First, I have to get that GPS back. Second, and maybe more importantly, I have to help Riley."

"Are you freaking cra—" Aster stops before she finishes the word, her lips pressed together tightly. I know she's taking great care to gain control of her face and her tone. "You can't go out there, Katie."

"Yeah, I can. She has our GPS, and we need it back. Plus, she's literally running away from that asshole. She needs our help."

"Maybe you're right, but you still cannot do this," Aster says. "You can't follow this path in the dark. It's beyond dangerous. Look."

She wrestles herself out of her sleeping bag and turns the lantern on low. Crawls to her pack and digs out the trail guide with its bent corners. Then she finds the page she's looking for. With that same pen flashlight, she shows me the section—the one underlined red and filled with exclamation points and notes that begin with *BE ALERT* and *WARNING*.

"We are probably right about here," she says, tapping a spot less than an inch from the scary zone. I want to argue with her. My body is ready for a fight, but it is difficult to deny that page.

In Utah, trails like that are where people die. There won't be safety fences or rails to keep us in, and no carefully cut timbers laid across the path to ensure we don't slip. Out here it isn't uncommon to have a foot-wide trail with a sheer wall on one side and certain death on the other. In the light, the section ahead of us will be dangerous. At night, it would be reckless veering toward fatal.

She's right about me not going out there. But there's something I don't think she's considering. I sink back onto my knees and lick my chapped lips. "Do they even know how dangerous it is?"

"I have no idea."

"How long until the drop-off?" I ask.

Aster shrugs. "Maybe half a mile? I can't be sure. Maybe the fight petered out, and they are making up. Maybe they'll find their way back to camp."

I think of Riley's face when she showed up at our tent, her curls springing wild around her freckled face. She wasn't just upset—she was frantic.

"No," I say simply. "No way did they make up. She was terrified."

Aster is very quiet, and I get it. I know how she thinks. But I also saw a side to Finn she didn't see. "You were inside setting up our sleeping bags, so you didn't see him, but I did. I was out there for a long time, Aster. I was looking at the stars and thinking about the trip, and Finn had crept over here, quiet as a cat, to stand in the darkness and watch us. This isn't just some couple in a fight. He is a dangerous man. And I would know."

Aster is quiet. I know there are questions burning in her throat. Maybe apologies too. I know she wants to ask about that night, maybe even about the guy who hurt me. I don't know all the questions forming in her mind or what she really wants to know, but I learned eleven months ago that all the compassion in the world doesn't cancel out human curiosity. Even good people want to know the sordid details.

Some of them resist the urge and some of them launch right into the Spanish Inquisition, like my rape is a movie they're not sure they want to see, or a book with a plot they don't quite understand. Aster has that same curiosity, I guess, and it makes me tired.

She pushes her hair behind her ears. "I'm sorry about Riley. I'm sorry about…" Her pause is full of all the things she won't dare say. In the end, she changes the topic like she's flipping a switch. "They will have to come back. No matter how upset they are, they didn't tear down their camp. Logically, they'll be back to do that."

"So, we're supposed to just sit here twiddling our thumbs until morning."

"It would be recklessly dangerous to do anything else."

The frustration building in my chest feels like a scream wanting to claw its way out. But in the end, Aster's logic prevails. I unzip my jacket and lay it over my pack. After a few quiet moments, the chill in the tent sends me into the warmth of my sleeping bag. Aster curls into her bag too, but she has shifted her body directly in front of the door. In the soft light of the electric lantern, I can see one arm is still outside of her bag. The bear spray is out and her finger is on the trigger and the whole apparatus is aimed at the tent door.

Maybe Aster doesn't believe Finn is dangerous, but she isn't taking any chances. If anyone pays us a visit, it's clear she's ready to drop them to their knees.

I turn out the lantern feeling an eerie sense of helplessness.

Even with the lantern off and the moon long gone, my eyes adjust enough to make out shadows in the dark. The wind is a soft hush across the sand, and everywhere there are lizards and crickets. Now and then I hear the soft *hooo*s of a burrowing owl. It's hard to believe that less than an hour ago, there was a frantic, sobbing woman in our tent, and even harder to believe I was determined to go after her. It feels like a made-up thing.

"Katie?" Aster's voice is a shock in the quiet.

"Yes?"

"I never know how to talk about what happened to you," she says. Her voice is soft and small, but my whole body has turned brittle and sharp. "I never know what to ask or what questions to avoid. I'm not great with those sorts of things."

She pauses for such a long time that I think she's done speaking. I even rest my head onto my arms and force my jaw to unclench. And then she takes a deep breath.

"But I wish I was better," she says. "At talking about it, I mean. And at helping. I just…I don't know what to do. I haven't known what to do all this time."

"No one knows," I admit softly, and the words deflate me. "Not even me."

I feel boneless and weary when I close my eyes. The pull of sleep looms and an image of Riley's tear-streaked face blooms in my mind, her fingers gripping my arms as she pants. My heart climbs into my throat again and thumps too hard and too fast.

I see Aster with her hand on the bear spray. I stare at that can and strain my ears for the sound of danger. But the closest thing to danger I hear is that burrowing owl, its calls reaching into the quiet. Telling me that we are not the only ones waiting in the night.

ASTER

25 MILES IN

This morning it is a raven and not a coyote that wakes me. Its soft gurgling cry rises just outside of our tent flap, its silhouette starkly outlined against the fabric. Ravens are enormous birds. In close proximity, it's startling. And this raven is maybe three feet from me, kept apart by a single thin layer of tent fabric.

I watch its shadow as it pecks the ground and then tilts its head. They are usually noisy birds, their cries telling everyone around that they are here, they are here! But this raven is quiet. It walks awkwardly in front of the tent, occasionally pecking at the ground or tilting its head, its beak slightly open.

It makes a sound that feels like a question. But I have no answer, so I watch it. It sinks to the ground in slow motion. Maybe it's injured or sick. As if it can hear my thoughts, it lifts its head, that wicked beak open wide. The next cry is the one I know. Shocking. Loud. Iconic.

Katie opens her eyes. It is clear she has not slept much or well. "More coyotes or just the raven?"

"No coyotes."

Two words, but they sends me into a fit of coughing. I sound and feel worse than yesterday. My chest rattles and my right ear is clogged so deeply that my hearing is muffled.

"Are you feeling worse?" Katie asks.

"Maybe." I cough again, and my head thrums with pain. "Yes, actually. I think my ears are messed up."

"You sure this isn't something more than a cold?"

"Not sure. I don't think I have a fever. Hard to know if every part of my body hurting is about me being sick…"

"Or hiking across half of Utah," Katie finishes with a smirk. "I get you." Then her gaze turns to the tent door and her face tenses. "Did you hear them come back last night?"

"No. But I wasn't awake very long."

"Me either." Katie frowns. "I have no idea how I fell asleep."

"You are physically exhausted. This isn't hiking for lightweights."

"Yeah, but Riley was out there in real trouble. She needed help, and I just…went to sleep. Like an asshole."

My memory rushes back to me. Slipping inside Aunt Julie's house. Climbing the stairs. Curling into bed. I had no trouble falling asleep the night that Katie was assaulted either. I suppose the body has a way of winning those battles.

"I get it," I say. "But to be fair, you could blame it on me. I told you it was too dangerous to go in the dark."

I tug my coat on and push the tent flap open. A pale, cloudless sky clarifies all the murky details of last night. The low line of boulders near the trail. Pinyon pines twisting up near clusters of sage and claret cup cactuses. And a bright orange tent flipped up on one side twenty feet from our camp.

"Katie?"

A rustling inside the tent, and then Katie emerges. It's immediately apparent what brought the raven this morning. Riley and Finn did not come back. Their tent—unstaked, I'd imagine—is blown up on one side, pinned between a pinyon pine and a juniper. The flap hangs open and inside, I can see the edge of a gray sleeping bag.

The raven moves again. Plucks at the silvery wrapper of a granola bar.

It couldn't have been more than fifty-five degrees last night. Not appropriate weather for sleeping out in the open. I try to imagine a scenario that might convince them to leave the tent behind. Nothing good comes to mind.

I lace my boots quickly. Zip up my coat and turn to Katie. I don't have to say a word. She's already tying her own boots and pulling a soft knit beanie down over her messy hair.

"Let's go," she says simply.

We investigate the tent first, which is empty other than the sleeping bag and the rogue granola bar. Then we march past it to their camp. Or what's left of it, at any rate. There is a group of ravens. *An unkindness* is the proper term, and it feels right here. They are all scrabbling at something on the ground. They scream and flap wings at one another, peck and grapple. A dark-blue strap comes loose in the melee, and I recognize it.

"That's a backpack," Katie says.

Riley's backpack. I know because it was the one beside her when we got to camp. The one she fished food out of, much of which is now strewn across the desert floor. I see the shredded remnants of a bread bag. A torn box that probably contained granola bars.

Katie's eyes move from the ravens to the backpack. "They never came back."

There is no reason to pretend anything else at this point, so I don't. "No."

"They could have fallen," Katie says simply.

"Yes. It's possible."

My ears are clogged and ringing. The pressure in my face is intense. And in this moment, with this eerie evidence before me, I do not want to make choices. I want someone to give us answers. Or a plan to follow. Maybe I could shoo away the ravens. Zip up the pack and remove the hammock. Pull out the satellite-enabled emergency device that we do not have and call for someone to handle whatever the hell this is.

"So what do we do?" Katie asks.

"What choice do we have? We have to keep going."

Katie looks down. "We probably need to get help. Is going back an option?"

I shake my head. "We are past the halfway point now. After this next section, things should ease up difficulty-wise."

Katie sweeps her hand wide at the scene around us. "Something bad happened here. We can't just stand around pretending they wandered off to pick flowers."

"I'm not pretending that. I'm not pretending anything."

"Then you know she's in trouble."

"I know none of this is a good sign. That's what I know. Something happened last night. It probably happened after their fight, and it probably isn't good."

"She could be dead." Katie's voice is a whisper.

"They could both be dead," I clarify.

"And you just want to keep on hiking. Like we never saw this at all."

"We need to keep going so that we can find help."

I do not remind her that we could get help right now if we had the GPS. The truth of why we can't call is floating between us like smoke. Maybe she isn't pointing out the fire, but I know she can smell it.

Katie makes a strangled noise. She paces in a circle, breathing hard. I know why. That same helplessness is churning in my stomach. Cranking the pressure in my head even tighter. But I do not burn energy pacing. I wait for her to face the inevitable. Because there are no other choices. Just this.

Katie finally gets there, taking a few shaking breaths. She slows her pacing and steeples her hands under her chin. "Okay, talk to me about the next section. Specifically."

"Well, there is a one-and-a-half-mile section to start. That's the start of the narrows. There is an old, closed horse trail around the backside of the canyon wall that connects with an old off-roading route." I tap the page to show her the twisting road.

"Why's that trail closed?"

"It's never been popular. Nowhere near as pretty a view. It's also half a mile longer, involves a scramble on a narrow section, and it's been hit by a couple of recent rockslides."

I tilt the page so she can see the liberal Xs and shorthand notes about that section. "Plus, I don't think that's a popular off-roading spot. It's all but ten miles of switchbacks until you hit the next real road."

She sighs. "Peachy. So we stay to the original narrow section for a mile and a half or whatever. What happens then?"

I clear my throat, wishing to God my ears weren't so cloggy. I feel like this whole conversation is being projected through blown speakers.

"Well, the two trails join back together here in this small gap between the ridges," I say. "It's just a quick, sharp descent and then right back up to the next ridge. That's still narrow, and we are on it for a while too."

"But there's no access point there? No way out to a real road between the ridges?"

"Nothing."

Katie shakes her head. She still struggles with the roads in Utah. In Ohio, it's hard to find an inch of earth where you're more than half a mile from a paved road. In southeastern Utah, it's a whole different ball game.

"If Riley had called for help, we'd be hearing helicopters by now," Katie says.

I shrug. "Maybe. Maybe not. They wouldn't pull out all the stops because a couple is bickering on the trail."

"This was more than bickering."

"I know that, and as long as she's clear that she's in danger, they'll come. But if they're dealing with flooded roads, they might be stretched thin."

"Which means it could take longer," she says, slouching. She looks around, her eyes moving over the ruins of their campground.

I spot a worn carabiner on one of the backpack straps and remember Carter and Luke. They were headed south too. Maybe if we're lucky… "Katie, I have an idea to find help."

We use rocks to carve out *SOS—SEND HELP SOUTH* in the sand. Of course, rain will ruin it, or even a gusty night. But with a little luck, the climbers will arrive in the next twenty-four hours and see the message. With a little more luck, they'll find it soon and use whatever device they have to call in a rescue. By then I hope we are well clear of this trail, but right now? Hedging my bets seems like the only smart move.

Neither of us has much of an appetite back at camp. We dress quickly and I fill our water bladders and bottles while Katie breaks down the tent. We are packed up by nine and ready to head south.

I take the lead as we move out. A raven flies ahead of us, hopping from pinyon pine to juniper bush as if he's got a secret to share.

We hit the ledge just over half a mile in, and it is every bit as sudden and worrisome as promised. After the pinyon pines disappear, the trail runs between heaps of boulders on the right and left. A mini canyon for a quarter of a mile, weaving in and out. And then we shift to the west, and the trail on the left disappears.

It simply drops away into nothing, leaving a narrow walkway along the boulders to our right.

"Wow," Katie says. "That is sudden."

My head spins at the height. In truth, my head has been spinning all morning. Not dizziness exactly, but that slightly off-balance feeling I always get when my ears are infected. I haven't mentioned it to Katie, but I'm pretty sure that's what I'm dealing with. It hurts to move my jaw too much, and my hearing is fuzzy and distant.

I take a step, careful to stay very close to the wall. The trail is rutted and uneven here too. The kind that could easily trip a person. I think of the stories I've heard over the years. Smart locals. Experienced hikers. Death can happen to anyone out here, even people who understand what they're doing. Riley and Finn didn't even know how to keep a tent tethered. It would be so easy for something to happen to them.

I keep a steady, even pace. In the canyon off to our left, I hear a hawk's *cree*. I turn my head, and a wave of dizziness smacks into me. My body lists left. Panic shoots through my limbs. I jerk back to the right, instinctively grabbing the wall. My breath shudders and I try to slow my suddenly racing heart.

"Did you trip?" Katie frowns. It will frighten her to hear the truth, but I have to tell her.

"I think I might have an ear infection."

"Yikes, I'm sorry. Does it hurt?"

"A little. But the bigger issue is that I'm a touch off-balance."

A pause behind me. Then a shuffle of feet. "Okay. So that's not optimal."

I chuckle. "*Optimal* will never be the key word for this trip."

"Let's just think for a minute here," she says.

I turn slowly around, careful to stay close to the wall. But Katie's eyes move right past me, and her apprehension transforms into something else. She sees something.

My shoulders tense, but I stay still. "What is it?"

"Not a snake," she says, clearly reading my tension. "Not dangerous."

"Then why do you look like that?"

"Because I think I found our GPS."

I follow her gaze, twisting slowly back around. And there it is, just like she said, lying face down against the wall. The black plastic on the back looks clean and perfect. I'm careful when I move toward it, still mindful of my earlier dizzy spell. I crouch and pick it up.

Whatever hope I have withers the second I turn it over. The touchscreen is shattered. The far left corner is black, a section of glass completely missing.

"He broke it," Katie says.

"Not entirely. Our location is still being transmitted."

A single red light is illuminated on the top of the GPS. It sends a swell of relief through my chest. But then the wave crests into anxiety. Is that even a good thing right now?

"Wait. That means your dad will think we are okay."

"He wouldn't think to check until late tonight anyway," I say.

Katie pulls her bottom lip between her teeth. She's probably weighing the same question I am. "But when he does, if we leave the GPS here…"

"Then he would send help here. They would find the SOS message and then head south."

"How long would that take?"

"Two, maybe three days."

Her face falls. "We only have two days left of hiking to get to the parking lot."

"Less, if it goes to plan," I say.

"You cut your ankle, got a cold, and then we ended up losing our GPS to a couple who may or may not have fallen off the trail we're currently hiking. I think it's safe to say, this trip is not going to plan."

I nod and look down at the GPS. It feels like a paperweight. But what we do with it could save the day. Or maybe cost us our lives.

ZERO MILES

She dreams of rodents and kisses. Teeth chewing at the tips of her fingers. Clouds of stinging insects. Beaks wet with blood. But it is voices that wake her.

Her eyes fly open, seeing nothing but light. Bright but still cool, her skin chilled under the silvery emergency blanket. Still morning, then.

She hears nothing but the wind.

Ringing in her ears.

Her own breathing. Faster and more ragged than yesterday.

She could have imagined the voices. Dreamed them up like all the other horrors. She could have—

She hears them.

And again.

Two voices. A conversation then. A single word slips through her mind.

Help.

She could call to these voices. Scream for them maybe. But

fear holds its hand over her mouth. Squeezes her tongue until it hurts.

A whisper in her ear. A dark warning. If someone hears her, they won't save her. They might finish the job they started.

KATIE

26 MILES IN

We decide to take the jacked-up GPS. We are twenty-three miles from the end point of this trip. We were supposed to get there by tomorrow evening, and we can still do that. Regardless of all of this, even Aster's cold, we can probably make it. As long as we pick up the stash for more water.

Before we move out, I ask Aster to pull out the map again. "Just show me exactly where the stash is."

Aster frowns at the map, touching an unremarkable spot. "Here. It's about four miles. It might be five. It's hard to be completely sure."

"Is there any point to trying to hike out on that road?" I ask. "Will that save any time?"

Aster studies the map and pulls out a pencil to add up sections of mileage in the corner. Then she tucks it away and coughs. "The road is somewhere between thirteen and fifteen miles. Some of these aren't marked so I'm guessing."

"It's less than twenty-three miles though, right? What are the chances of us running into someone on it?"

"It's a gamble. It's passable for off-roaders, obviously, since he said he left the drop. But the elevation changes would be intense on foot. Lots of steep hills."

She points out several nondescript squiggles on the map for me, one halfway through the switchbacks Uncle Mike must have traversed. She pauses to blow her nose, her eyes red and watering. "So, if it's fourteen miles, we'll have to camp at the stash or maybe along the road. Not sure what that looks like since we have no notes on that route."

"Even if the route is boring, we'd still have to hike some distance on the real road until we find someone to flag down. And given the way this trip is going, that someone would probably be the reincarnation of Charles Manson."

"I think it's more likely we'd run into a truck driver. Or maybe no one at all. But Dad would see the signal changing as we hiked down the road."

"Which would get him here…"

"Still two days, I bet. He would expect us to go to the drop and probably wouldn't pay super close attention to our location. He might notice the next morning, but by then—"

"We'd be almost out on the regular trail. The one we have copious notes on." I sigh. It's a classic devil-you-know situation. And frankly this is a shit-tastic devil, but I don't like the odds of trading it in for something unknown.

"I see merits in either choice," she says. "The mileage is similar. We might have a better chance of alerting help a few hours sooner if we take the off-road trail."

But we won't have any shot of helping Riley. If she's still even out here, that is. A chill creeps up my neck, and my stomach squeezes at the memory of her tear-streaked face. I should have gone after her, night or not.

"I want to keep going," I say. "I want to stay to the main trail, because if there's any chance at all of helping Riley, I want to try."

Aster's brows pull together, and I know what she's going to say before she even opens her mouth. "Katie, you understand they may have been hiking on the cliffs at night. In the middle of an argument. There is a real danger—"

"I get it. I know what we might find." And then I tilt my head trying to really look at her. She's got a red, chapped nose and dark circles under her eyes. I've never seen Aster look sick like this. She needs to be in bed and instead we're going to take spend the day hiking along a cliff. "You need to be careful. If you have another dizzy spell, tell me. Don't hide that shit."

"I won't."

And so we go. It's unnerving walking along such a precipitous cliffside. Geology bares all its secrets in the desert. Gravity, erosion, simple physics—all of it right out in the open. There are no clusters of trees or blankets of velvety grass. There is nothing here but parched, sand-strewn rock dotted by the few plants that can survive these conditions.

Everywhere I look, the land seems to tell me a story. Once upon a time, this cliff did not exist. It was part of a much larger mesa, but water trickled into the rocks, forming cracks. And those cracks multiplied and widened until gravity took its pound of flesh. Right now we're seeing evidence of the tipping point, when an impossibly large wall of sandstone broke free of the mesa, crumbling into heaps of sand and rock at the base of this cliff.

The trail we're following now is narrow, with a wall stretching up on our right and a terrifying drop on our left. All I can think of is Riley out here in the dark. And Finn right behind her. I begin to check the ground to our left. God, are they down there somewhere? Could anyone survive a fall like that? Because I can't imagine it.

"How will we know if they are down there?" I ask.

"What do you mean?"

"In some places, it's too steep to see the bottom."

"Look for vultures."

I stop. My throat suddenly feels too small for the air I need to breathe.

"There will be vultures feeding," Aster repeats, voice flat. "Maybe flies if we're close enough, but—"

"Enough." I close my eyes to stem a wave of nausea. "Let's just...let's keep moving."

We reach the end of the first ridge midmorning. The trail widens briefly as it rejoins with the old trail on the other side of the ridge. Then it shrinks into a narrow channel that pitches steeply downhill, twisting between boulders and clusters of sharp yucca plants. We pick our way down slowly, but Aster still wobbles at the bottom, catching herself on a boulder.

"I'm fine," she says before I can spit out a word. I must be exuding worry out of my pores at this point. But I can't help it. She looks so, so bad.

"Maybe you should try some more medicine," I say. "Something with a decongestant?"

Aster pauses for a moment, pressing her fingers to her temples. Then she nods reluctantly. "Yes. That would be good."

I dig out the plastic blister packs of cold medicine. Four pills left, and the two I'm giving her probably won't last more than six hours or so. Let's hope it at least makes those six hours better.

We start back up the hill, and my legs are burning at the top. It's even hotter today than the last two. Aster peels off her long-sleeved shirt, and I pull my hair into a sloppy bun, eager to get the heavy mass of waves off my neck. I drink and realize my water is already running low. The math runs quickly through my head. We started the day with three quarts. It will buy time, but we need the stash. No question about that with this heat.

We eat granola bars as we go and keep a quick pace. My left knee is starting to ache, and Aster's coughing is acting up again. When I glance at the sky, the sun is high overhead, and I'm sure we've gone a mile on this new ridge. Maybe a mile and a half?

"Do you think we've hiked two miles since we stopped?"

"Since the beginning?" she asks. "We might be getting close to three. But maybe half a mile on this new cliff, if that."

Disappointment sinks through my middle. I swipe the back of my hand across my forehead and look down. The path is a solid four feet wide here, which feels extravagantly spacious. "I feel like we've gone farther on this new ridge. Maybe I'm being optimistic."

Aster laughs. "Uh, yeah. I'd say half a mile is on the optimistic side."

"Oh, shut up."

She stops and turns around. "I mean, we could check the ma—"

Aster stops abruptly, the smile on her face freezing into something like shock. And then worry. A chill rolls up my spine because I know she isn't looking at me. She's looking at something behind me.

"Do you see something?" I ask.

"Yes." Her answer is swift and certain and clearly uneasy. "Yes, I see something. I see Finn."

ASTER

28 MILES IN

Katie whirls around, searching the trail. "What about Riley? Do you see Riley?"

"No."

And it doesn't make sense. Riley should be there. It also doesn't make sense that he is behind us. Finn left hours before we headed south. How is he only here? How did we not pass him if he's behind us? And where is Riley? Logically, no matter what kind of fight they had, they should still be on the same path. Unless they split up.

I don't have answers, but there is one possible explanation for why we didn't pass him today.

"He must have taken the other trail," I say. "The one around the backside of this ridge."

"Then where the hell is Riley? They headed this way hours before us, Aster."

"If they were still fighting, they could have separated at the narrows. Maybe Finn ran into trouble on the back side."

"But we found the GPS on this side."

"It was before the split," I say.

"Either way, it was destroyed. No way Riley did that."

"They could have just dropped it. It's not indestructible."

"Or he could have done something to her and then broken it."

"Katie, stop. We can't do this. We don't know what happened, and we're wasting time guessing."

"Yeah? Well, you're only saying that because deep down you know something bad happened. You are too smart not to realize there is no good reason he's here and she's not."

She's right. If Finn somehow ended up behind us on the trail, then he must have been delayed for some reason. Something must have happened. And it probably happened to Riley.

Finn looks up in that moment, and my breath catches. Freezes into a lump in my throat. I didn't think he could see us. He's easily a quarter of a mile away, so it's surprising we can see him. I thought the angle—the fact that we're in shadow—might keep us hidden. But I am clearly wrong because he is no longer moving. He is watching. Because he has seen us.

"What is he doing?" Fear sharpens the edges of Katie's words. "Does he see us?"

"Yes, I think so."

He is so still. Is he looking at something else? Is there a snake or some danger? But then, he leans forward and breaks into a run.

"Why is he running?" Katie's voice is small and quiet.

Finn continues forward, and when the sun hits his face, I can read enough to know. He can see us. And it's more than that. He is coming for us.

A burst of adrenaline thumps through my chest. My head spins and my fingers buzz. I do not know what he wants or why he's doing this. There are so many missing pieces, but there is one certainty in my mind. I do not want him to catch us.

"Aster?" Her voice is small and trembling. A child calling out in the dark.

"Let's go," I say. "You in front of me. Run."

I whirl around as she shuffles past. She's breathing fast, and we've only taken a few steps. She makes a good pace though, and I scramble to keep up, feeling seasick. We all but sprint our way down the ledge. The sun beats down the way the sun can only beat down in Utah. Searing. Bright. Relentless.

My backpack slaps against my hips—I need to tighten the straps. I need to drink something. I need this damn medicine to kick in, because waves of dizziness are hitting me in an endless loop. Maybe it's the exhaustion of running. Maybe it's just this damn cold.

Katie slows in front of me, breathing hard. We've probably covered a quarter of a mile. Maybe more. It leaves us nearly a mile to go, I think.

"Is he still back there?" she asks, sucking wind.

I slow my pace and twist my head to look over my shoulder, but I don't see him. Maybe I was wrong. Did we lose him? His head appears around a slight curve in the trail. My stomach drops into my knees.

He is closer now. Can't be more than two hundred yards. It's impossible. I don't know how he's made time like this. It's crazy. He must have been running flat out.

"He's closer," I say.

A strangled noise in front of me. Katie's footsteps slow. "I can't go faster."

"It's okay. Just keep moving," I say. I keep my voice calm, but I am not calm. This whole situation is getting the best of me, and I am struggling to keep my cool.

I should have seen this coming. When I talked to Finn, I didn't pick up on a thing. My instincts were off. I missed the danger here like I missed the danger at that party. And now my bad instincts might have let someone else get hurt. Why am I so blind to this? Katie told me she knows dangerous men. Dad does too. But not me.

I turn to look over my shoulder again, and my head spins, my vision tilting so that I cannot see if Finn is still back there. I plant my hands onto my knees. Let my head drop and my eyes close until the dizziness passes. Katie's footsteps continue on. She doesn't know I've stopped, and I want it to stay that way. She was smart enough to see this coming. If he catches up with us, she should not be the one he hurts next.

I open my eyes. My balance is still off-kilter when I straighten, but it is better. Finn is behind us as expected, but he is no closer than before. Impossible. I was sure he'd have closed the distance, but he has slowed. He's much too far away to see clearly, but his speed is definitely not what it was.

A ribbon of hope unfurls in me. Running is different in the desert, and Finn is from Illinois. Maybe his body is not up for a mile-long jog in canyon country.

"He's slowing down," I say softly. "I think he's running out of steam."

I grab the wall with one hand and push forward, speeding up to try to catch Katie. She isn't jogging—not even close. But she's going to win this race tortoise style. Slow and steady. And from the sounds of her gasps and whimpers, on the edge of completely losing it. But she doesn't lose it. She just keeps marching.

We pass a pair of windows high up in the ridge. Holes in the rock like spectacles. The trail guide mentioned this, and the sight of it grounds me. This is better than a street sign. It is a definitive landmark. Proof that this ledge will end.

"We're half a mile from the end of the ridge," I say.

"I can't go that much longer," Katie says. Her voice is raspy. I can tell she's stumbling. And we have another problem ahead. The wide ledge we've been on narrows in the next fifty yards.

I slow and turn to check Finn's progress. I'm grateful for the wall to hold me strong, because while he is still two hundred yards away, he is running again.

"We need to go, Katie."

"I don't think I can." She sounds like she's on the verge of tears, but there isn't time for that now.

I don't want to scare her, but I don't see a choice.

"Finn is all but a football field away from us. He is running. And if we do not move, he will catch us. Do you understand?"

She does not answer. But I see her spine straighten. I can nearly feel the resolve take root in her bones. She begins forward again with renewed speed. I follow as fast as I can. The trail narrows, and my vertigo intensifies. My stomach churns with every step.

A quarter of a mile later, my legs have turned to rubber. To liquid. I have no idea how we'll make it, and I don't dare look back over my shoulder. But then the trail curves to the left and downhill, and I see the end in sight. The sharp ridge we're on widens. Desert stretches out far to the right and to the left. A narrower footpath leads off to the right, but I know that's not what we want. It was mentioned in the log, with specific notes to stay to the wider trail.

We continue on the main path away from the ledge, the desert unfurling before us. Boulders and swirling sandstone formations. Juniper bushes and clumps of desert sage. There is plenty to see. And plenty of places to hide.

We could hide. My heart leaps in my chest. Hope renewed. I speed up to catch Katie, my eyes on the sandstone fins that will keep us out of his sight line in moments. Before we are separated, I turn back to see. Dizziness ripples through me, but I keep looking and looking. He has to be back there. He has to be.

And then I see him. A hundred and fifty yards back and stopped, hands on his knees and head down. He might be catching his breath. He might be vomiting. No way to know.

"Come on," I say.

We wind around the sandstone fin. The trail proceeds due south here, but there is a large adjacent area to the right full of boulders, crevices, and junipers stretching in every direction. A hundred hiding places.

My ears ache and my chest squeezes, but I know how we do this now. For the first time since we saw him, I think we have a chance.

"He's going to catch us," she says.

"No. He will not."

"How? I can't do this. I can't!"

I unbuckle my chest strap and yank my backpack around to my chest. I am rooting around in the large zippered area, but I nod at three larger boulders sitting together nearly dead center of the clearing to our right.

"Do you see the boulders there?" I point. "I want you to go over there, but I want you to pick your way from stone to stone. No footprints."

Katie turns, panting and red-faced. "You want to hide?"

"Yes," I say. I'm still hunting for my compass bag in my pack. All the ultralight hiking philosophy I subscribe to has never swayed me from keeping this too-heavy and completely unnecessary compass on my person. In the ten years I've owned it, I've never needed it. Today it might change that streak.

I find the pouch. A terrible Pepto-Bismol pink, which couldn't be more noticeable in the brown-orange expanse around us. Better yet, my name is embroidered across the front in neon green letters. The fact that it's bright is good, because I need him to spot it. The fact that it has my name on it is even better because he will know it belongs to us. With a little luck, he'll think we dropped it while we're running. With a lot of luck, he'll believe it enough that he'll stay on the path in hopes of catching us. Instead of hunting here to find us.

I toss it in the air and catch it, testing the heft and weight of it as I look at the trail. He could be here any minute. We need to move.

"Katie, get to those boulders."

"I'll throw it," she says, still breathing hard. "You're trying to throw something, right? Something on the trail for him to find. Something he will think we dropped."

I look at her in surprise, and when she holds out her hand, I automatically hand her the bag. "I'll do it better. Your hand-eye coordination is horse shit."

She's right. But when I watch her jog away, I feel sick. I should move. I know that. But I stand, frozen as she runs ten more yards up the trail. Then she winds up her arm and throws. The pouch and with the hefty compass inside sails and sails. At least forty feet up trail before it lands. Not quite in the center but so damn close.

All my breath comes out in a whoosh of surprise. I all but sprint for the large boulders, picking my way from stone to stone. Footsteps behind me. Katie. She's moving too, hopscotching her way off the trail. She has to cover twice the distance, but I move quickly, finding a flat stone and a lucky plate of slickrock that lets me cover a quarter of the distance easily. I slip once, my foot plunging into the sand a few yards from our hiding spot.

I pull it out and scrape the divot out with my boot. I'm not even sure he could see it from the trail, but I'm not taking chances. I hear Katie hopping from rock to rock. I am almost to the boulders now, but she sounds far. I don't look up. Don't pause. I move from one rock, then step behind a cactus, and then I am there. Behind a tall boulder, my body hidden from the trail and protected by the shade.

But Katie isn't with me.

I hear her hopping, and she's getting closer. But then I hear something else. A very faint *scuffle chink. Scuffle chink. Scuffle chink.* Footsteps and something rattling on a pack, if I had to guess.

My body goes cold.

I dare a peek and see a shadow at the very edge of the trail. Goose bumps rise on my arms. He's *so* close. Any second and he will emerge. Katie will be seen. My heart leaps into a higher gear as I crawl to the edge of the shorter, jagged boulder. She is fifteen feet away, but she needs to be here *now*. Thirty seconds ago would be better.

Shuffle chink. Shuffle chink.

It's louder now. We have seconds. Maybe less than that. It may already be too late. Katie looks up and catches my eye, and she must see the absolute terror on my face, because she gives up any effort at finding a rock. She sprints through the sand, diving behind the boulders. I grab at her legs, pulling them up, making sure her hands and legs—her shoes are hidden behind the rock.

Shuffle chink. Shuffle chink.

We turn into ice. Into stone. Into the immovable boulders that are hiding us. Finn is on the trail walking south. Fifty feet away from us at best. He is one hard sprint from being on us, and I didn't even pull out my bear spray. My bag is still strapped to my chest, the front flap gaping open like a wound. But I don't dare reach for that hole. I don't move a muscle. If he hears us. If he sees us…

Shuffle chink. Shuffle chink. Shuffle—

The pattern stops. Something in his walk was making that sound—maybe his backpack slapping his shoulders. Maybe something else. But the rhythmic sound has cut itself off. Because he has stopped walking.

Fingers curl hard around my wrist. I look down at Katie, who is lying sideways in the sand. Her face is a mask of terror. She is Katie in the hospital. Katie in the big bed with her hollow eyes and pale, pale skin. And just like then, I can't do a damn thing to help her now.

A scuffling on the trail. A shifting crunch of boots moving. He is turning around. My heart leaps into my chest. And then my throat. And then it is trapped in my mouth, threatening to tear its way out of me, dragging a scream with it. Even without seeing him, I know that Finn is turning in a circle. He is searching for us.

Katie twists a little, and I immediately touch her arm, dig my fingers in hard enough to warn her. But she looks me dead in the eye and shakes her head slowly. And then she slithers, belly in the sand, until she is at the edge of the short boulder. She is going to look.

Panic fires through my body, but Katie pushes her face to the edge of the boulder. Just enough so that she can see. This isn't just Katie from the hospital anymore. This is the Katie who survived. And this time, she wants to see what's coming.

ZERO MILES

She needs a thing to write with. Laughs even as she searches. As if she'll happen on a can of spray paint. A fresh-tipped Sharpie.

Still, she tries. Checks her pouch. The peanut rock with all its secrets. The smooth flat emptiness of both pockets. Nothing reveals itself.

She looks at the sun. Funny how much she remembers. Her multiplication tables. Her brother's laugh. The formation of the eight basic climbing knots.

But the days and hours leading to this moment are a smear, only bits and pieces emerging from the dark.

The bleeding in her leg has slowed. Flies still buzz. Vultures still watch. She closes her eyes and opens her mind. She has to find a way.

KATIE

—

29 MILES IN

Finn is big enough to kill me. This is what comes to mind when I'm on my knees behind a slab of rock, my palms stinging from the heat of the sandstone and my eyes watering in the wind. He is maybe halfway past this alcove. If he moves another twenty yards, he'll find Aster's pouch. Another fifty, and he'll pass through the opening in the low ridge that surrounds this area, and we will be safe.

Of course, to do any of that, Finn will have to start walking again. But he doesn't.

A sweat bee lands on my wrist. I feel the sting of the bite, but I don't move. Can't move. Finn is waiting on me to make that mistake. Or any mistake.

He turns away, I guess to scan the other side of the desert.

I don't know how he detects that we are out here, but he clearly does. Some part of him senses we have abandoned the trail. That we've run to the nearest big rock to cower like frightened kittens. It's only a matter of time before he spots a footprint or some evidence. Before he tracks us out here like the predator he is.

I inhale deeply and push the spiraling thoughts away. I have to hold onto some morsel of logic. Maybe he only suspects we are out here. Or maybe he thought he heard something. Or maybe he's given up and decided this is a swell place to rest. Given our luck these past two days, it would track.

It's entirely possible that him stopping has nothing to do with us being here. But if Finn takes one foot off that trail, I'll find the can of bear spray in Aster's pack and spray it until he's blind and puking.

He turns back to the trail. His shoulders heave up and down like he's winded. But he's moving like he's going to keep going. I think this is it. We're going to be—

Aster coughs. Fear lances through my middle. My eyes lock onto Finn, but he doesn't look. I'm sure he's heard—how could he have possibly not heard? But he's focused on something on the trail. He starts forward and stoops, and my shoulders sag in relief when I see something pink in his hand. Aster's pouch. He's already picked it up and is turning it over. He unzips it, and I can imagine the battered old-school compass inside. The one Aster got for her ninth birthday and is only dubiously functional but still finds its way into every backpack. Her lucky charm, I guess.

I guess it's working because Finn starts walking. But then he steps off the trail and into the sand. His body pivots, and I duck behind the rock, my heart stopped cold. He is coming right for us. I hear the hiss of his footsteps coming closer. Something on his pack lightly clangs with each step and my mind conjures images of what it could be. A carabiner or a pocket knife or a real weapon.

Aster's eyes are wide with terror. I frantically lift my index finger to my lips. A silent plea to be quiet. So quiet. I don't know where he is—I have no idea how close he is. My heart is pounding so hard, I'm sure he will hear it. And then I hear the unmistakable sound of a zipper being unfastened, and everything in my body turns to ice.

I am back in that room. Under that man. Hearing frames thumping the wall. My stomach heaves—I am going to vomit. I vomited that night and I vomited in the hospital and I can feel it again, the wave of nausea thickening my throat and sending a rush of heat and sweat to my face. I lean forward, sure it will come, and then Aster's hand is on my arm.

I cling to the familiarity of her face. Her lips are chapped and a streak of sunburn reddens the bridge of her nose. I feel better looking at her. And then something wet dribbles against the sand nearby. There is one blissful second where I'm not sure what that sound is. And then I understand. Finn is urinating.

My stomach seizes. Finn isn't even ten feet away from us, and I can't be here. I swallow the sour saliva pooling in the back of my throat. The sound is so loud. I'm sure he will hear us. If not the sound of me swallowing, then surely the clamoring of my heart, which is pounding like drums at my ribs.

If he hears, he does not react. He finishes his piss. Then he zips his pants, and I wince at the noise. God, I want to run. I want to put so much space between me and this man. But in the end, Aster's gentle squeeze on my arm keeps me in place. Holds me still.

Long seconds pass, but Finn does not move. I don't know why he won't go, or what he is doing. I hear no shuffling of clothing or bodily sounds or anything else for that matter. There is silence, the desert kind of silence that makes my ears strain for some noise beyond my own body.

Can he see us from his angle? We are literally separated by a single large boulder. If he decides to explore behind it, we're done. Or if he spots my footsteps in the sand. I think of that last frantic sprint and my throat squeezes. He's going to realize we are here. Maybe he already knows.

He could lunge around this boulder any second.

Aster tilts her head until she meets my eyes. She flicks her gaze meaningfully to the right, and I search until I see her backpack, the front flap gaping wide. The bear spray is in there, black and silver and full of dark promise. Something hot and hungry runs through me at the sight of that canister. I see myself hauling it out. I imagine the feel of the trigger under my finger as I spray and the satisfaction of seeing him put down, writhing and powerless in the sand.

But Finn does not look around the boulder. He steps away and clears his throat. And then he begins his trek back to the trail, one step after the next. I lift my head, sure I must be hearing wrong, but I'm not. Finn is walking away. I close my eyes, following the sound of each step with my ears alone until he is barely audible. His footsteps turn from a *hiss* to a *scritch* when he hits the hard-packed sand on the trail. I can tell he is farther away, closer to the trail. And then he is too far to hear at all.

Long minutes after the steps fade to silence, I inch my way back to the edge of the boulder, daring a peek. Finn disappears through the gap in the ridge as he continues along the trail. I sag in relief, my head lolling back against the boulder.

"He's gone," I say softly.

"You saw him?"

I nod and let out a shuddering breath. Then I wait for my body to stop shaking and my breathing to return to normal.

"I want to wait a bit longer," she says. "I want to give him time to get farther away."

"How far are we from the stash?"

"I honestly don't know. But we won't miss the turnoff. There will be a sign," she says.

Another few minutes pass before Aster pushes herself to her feet, and a few minutes beyond that before we strap on our packs and start heading south. We are careful moving around the ridge, pausing to scan the trail, or as much of the trail as we can see. It curves sharply to the left and heads due west behind a cluster of tall sandstone spires. Finn is probably back there somewhere. He is out of our view, blocked by the jutting bones of the earth.

The land between these formations is still dotted with pinyon pines, but mostly there is sage. Like a metric ton of it. The squat green bushes are clustered across the sand in every direction. I can smell it too, sharp and green and familiar.

The trail climbs steadily after the first quarter of a mile, and somewhere close to a mile, just before we walk behind the spires, Aster stops to rest. We've probably gained close to a thousand feet in altitude and my quads are on fire. But the view is the stuff of travel videos everywhere. We stare out at the miles of desert we've put behind us. This is the view I have hiked for, and even now, even with every terrible thing we've encountered, it steals my breath.

"Holy shit," I say.

"Yeah."

"I mean *holy shit*."

Aster doesn't respond, but she doesn't really have to. There aren't many words that could do justice to a view like this. We can see *miles* of trail from here, nearly everything we've passed. I feel like I'm viewing a model train display, most of my last two days captured in miniature before us. Both of the narrow sections of trail along the cliff are visible, gently curved in the slightest impression of a crescent. Behind that, I can see the backside of the ridges we traversed yesterday. They seem to be hundreds of miles away, and it's hard to believe that we were there, that we walked up some of those inclines and down into the canyons.

"I feel like I'm in a museum. Like this is a diorama or whatever," I say.

"Mr. Rogers's make-believe land," she says.

I side-eye her. "How old are you, again?"

She works through a nasty series of coughs. Then she shrugs. "My dad's obsessed. He plays it every Sunday."

"That tracks."

I take another breath and hold it in. I think of Riley's top three game from last night. She would love this memory. This unforgettable view would probably feature on her list.

But she isn't here, is she? She might never see this view. She might already be—

I shake my head, a physical effort to dislodge all these dark possibilities. Just for a moment, I want to stand here. I want to feel the warm sun on my skin and breathe in the smell of sage and gape at the endless spread of orange and gold rock under blue sky.

Some bit of movement flickers at the far edge of the canyon. No, above it. In the sky. Maybe a raven in the distance? Could I see a raven that far away? Or is it something bigger?

A frisson runs through me. The bird is a tiny speck, swooping hard to the right along the ridge. It's possible it's a golden eagle.

Or a vulture. I tense, watching. It flies north, out of my sight, until it's too far away. I can't be sure.

And now I want to be sure. No. I *need* to be sure. I root around in my pack until I find the tiny, cheap pair of travel binoculars that I absolutely did not tell Aster about. She's serious about packing light and might have argued that binoculars were just unneeded weight.

But to my surprise, she doesn't cluck her tongue or frown when I pull them toward my eyes. Instead, she squints at the canyon while I adjust the focus.

"Are there birds over there?" she asks. There is something funny about her voice. Something more than her cold.

Is she thinking the same thing I'm thinking? Is the same fear coursing through her?

"I thought there might be a golden eagle," I say, hopeful.

I adjust the focus and scan the trail. A distinct rock formation and then the ridge we've already hiked. I shift until I'm viewing the area near the cliffside. At first there is nothing but blue sky and shadowy canyon walls through my lenses. But then a bird— enormous and dark—soars through the frame. I open my mouth to tell her, but another bird follows just seconds after the first, wings wide and unflapping.

It rides the current in a swooping, lazy circle. And there is another behind him. And another just beneath. I remove the binoculars from my eyes, feeling a rush of nausea. The birds are vultures. And where there are vultures, there is usually something dead.

ASTER

31 MILES IN

V ultures." Katie's voice is flat and plain. When I reach for the binoculars, she doesn't argue.

I lift them to my eyes. Adjust the focus. At first I find the cloudless sky. Another pass, and I catch a glimpse of black wings with flight feathers like fingers. Certainly a vulture. There are more nearby. They are circling and circling.

Which could mean nothing. Vultures circle as they ride air currents. It's a transportation tactic, nothing more. Unless they are feeding.

The question is—*are* they feeding?

We are too far away to see clearly. We've nearly doubled back on our starting point, six miles by foot. But from here we are all but a mile from that cliff as the crow flies. Probably less. Still, it is far enough to make it difficult to decipher the scene. I focus again on the swirl of vultures. Scan the section of trail beneath them. And then down the beautiful orange face of the cliff until I come to an outcropping.

It is unremarkable. A small ledge a third of a way down the

cliffside. The binoculars are not strong enough to bring details into focus, especially with the ledge mostly in shadow. I can see black streaks of rock varnish. A flat-topped outcropping jutting out from the cliff wall. And a tiny misshapen lump in the shadows.

My heart thumps once. Again. Catches itself and resumes a steady but faster rhythm.

"Is there something down there?" Katie asks.

I can't answer her. Maybe it's nothing. I lose it in the lenses and have to carefully scan again starting at the lip of the ledge. And then down. Down ten feet. Down twenty. Maybe thirty, and then I see the ledge. The lump is still there. Motionless.

My mouth goes dry. Even with the binoculars I can't be sure what this is, but there are two smaller birds near it. Ravens. Moving in and out of the shadow. Pecking around the edges of the thing I can't identify. My skin prickles with goosebumps.

Vultures are generally quiet, nonaggressive birds who keep their distance from humans. Ravens, on the other hand, are smart enough to steal packs of cookies out of grocery bags. They know humans mean easy food. Their presence plants a horrifying possibility about that lump. A thousand grotesque images spark to life in my mind.

It could be a hundred different things down there attracting these birds. A bighorn sheep. A coyote. Even a lost backpack. I tighten the focus on the binoculars. And then my eye spots something long and blue at the edge of the lump. It is draped over a rock at the base of the cliff wall. Just outside of the shadows. My stomach drops. Light blue is not a color that naturally occurs in the Utah desert. And that shape looks like an arm. A human arm.

"Do you see something?" Katie asks, startling me.

"Yes." I could be wrong. I want to be wrong.

I turn away from the view, dizzy again for reasons that have little to do with my clogged ears. This time it's about the thing on the ledge. The thing that is almost certainly dead.

But it's not a *thing*, is it?

Thing implies an object. An animal, maybe. But my eyes are drawing a human form onto every visible bend and curve of that lump. It fits. This lump could be human.

"Talk to me," Katie says. "Those are vultures, so what are they after? What is down there?"

It's half question, half plea. There is a thin edge to her voice that tells me she doesn't want this answer. She wants me to assure her that she's wrong. Wants me to fill in the blanks with answers that will let her sag in relief. Don't worry, Katie. It's a deer. A sheep. A random water source that's attracting local wildlife. But I can't say those things.

"Why are you frozen like that?" Katie asks. Her voice cracks. "Just tell me what's happening."

"I'm sorry." I take a few steps back, my pack bumping into a rock behind us. Katie deserves to know what this is. But how can I tell her what I'm seeing?

"There is something down there," I say.

"Some*thing* or some*one*?"

"Someone. I think." My voice comes out a whisper, but the truth is so loud it lands like a punch.

Her heart-shaped face pales. "Is it…is it Riley?"

"I don't know. I can't see well enough. The body is on a small ledge maybe thirty feet down."

"But you can see well enough to know that there's a body.

There's a person down there." Katie's fear seems to harden into something closer to anger. Determination, maybe. "Are they alive?"

"I don't think so. The body has not moved. And there are a lot of birds nearby. The vultures, but ravens too."

Katie steps toward me and takes the binoculars for herself. I want to argue. To stop her. But I just stand in numb silence while she looks. Long seconds pass. Then she wrenches the binoculars from her face with a terrible sound. She turns away, her eyes screwed closed and her free hand curled into a fist.

For a moment, her posture is so strange and tense that I think she might be physically sick. But instead she takes a shaky breath.

"Are you okay?" I ask.

She shakes her head. "I think I see an arm."

"I saw that too."

"I think there's something over the person's face. Like foil. One of those emergency blankets."

"I couldn't see that." I wish she hadn't seen it either. The arm was enough. I want to peel back the last few minutes. Keep her from seeing any of this.

"The vultures should have been enough," she says. Shakes her head. "I shouldn't have looked."

I don't ask if the vultures were actively feeding, because it's not something I'd want her to endure. I've seen vultures in action. A coyote died at the edge of our road once, and vultures got to it before the city picked it up. I remember seeing those bald scabby-looking heads darting into the coyote's belly. The cruel curved beaks pulling out things I never wanted to think about again.

But I am thinking of them now. And this time, I know the dead thing they want is not a coyote.

I push the thought out of my head. The mental images are starting to make me queasy. We do not need to see anything more to confirm what I already know. Someone fell off the trail. It happens all time. How often has my dad gone on a rescue mission that turned into a body recovery?

Enough times that I know better than to look for details that will haunt us forever.

I turn back to the trail and scan the rocks and shadows. The quiet reminds me that we are not entirely alone out here. Finn was behind us on that trail, and Riley was not with him. And it is nearly certain that someone is at the bottom of that canyon. Someone that could be Riley.

The facts are a house of cards with razor-sharp edges. The last time we saw Riley, she was fighting with Finn. Running from him. She was going to call for help. Now Finn is alone. We found our GPS shattered. And there is a body on a ledge thirty feet below the trail. The trail we think Riley took.

My head swims. Five yards in front of me, a boulder juts up like a bad tooth. I inch my way closer. The pressure in my face and ears feels worse. My balance is a mess. I reach the boulder and lean into it, grateful for the sturdy grit of the sandstone under my palms.

"What the hell are we going to do?" Katie asks. There is no color at all in her face. Dizzy as I am, part of me wants to tell her to sit down before she falls down.

"Aster, we have to do something," she goes on.

"There is nothing we can do." I say honestly, wishing I could have some more cold medicine. Or an incredibly hot shower. Or a new head altogether.

"We need to think of something," she says. "You and I both know it's probably Riley down there."

"We don't know that. It could be an animal. Or the light playing tricks on us. It's too hard to see clearly from that distance." My alternatives don't add up and I know it. Maybe these aren't lies, but I am certainly offering possibilities I don't believe.

"You know damn well that is not an animal or a trick of the light. That's Riley."

I meet Katie's eyes and know I can't protect her from whatever this is.

"We are out here with a murderer," she says.

"What?" I shake my head. "Katie, we have no idea what happened to that person. They could have just fallen. That's by far the most likely scenario."

She scoffs and I stand upright.

"I'm serious." I say. "Things happen out here."

"I know that." Her voice is measured, and I do not see the frightened girl that hid behind me with the climbers. Or when the trail runner ran past. This Katie is determined. "But let's do some math. The last time we saw Riley, she was running for her life. Running from Finn. Now, we've had Finn run after us. Riley is nowhere in sight. But this person at the bottom of the canyon is somehow from some other totally unrelated situation?"

Long seconds tick by. A fly buzzes close to my ear, a whine that darts in and out of my muddled hearing. I swat it away.

"You're right," I say, unable to forget the fear etched into Riley's face in our tent. The darkness in Finn's expression at the campsite. Riley was afraid of him. She was scared that night, and I missed it. I left another girl alone. And now she's dead.

I lean back against the boulder feeling sick. I can see it all in my mind. Riley's easy smile turning to shock as she slips. Her slender arms going wide as she topples over the edge. I close my eyes to shut it out. "It is still possible that it was an accident."

"Accident?" Katie scoffs. "I think we both know what happened wasn't an accident."

"We don't know what happen—"

"Yes, we do! Her psycho boyfriend chased her onto that cliff last night. And he either ran her off the side or pushed her!"

I stand up off the rock, my face hot with anger. "Stop! Just stop! Finn had to be on the other side that ridge. If he wasn't, we would have passed him. It is the only way he could have ended up behind us."

"He could have doubled back to cover his tracks."

"Katie, we cannot keep going down this road. There is no point. We need to focus on getting help."

She scoffs, but I shake my head. "I am not saying it isn't likely that's Riley. I'm just saying we could stand here all day, make guesses, and maybe never get to the truth of what happened."

"So what the hell do you think we should do?"

I go quiet then. Truth is, I don't know what we should do. There's a dead person out here with us. Or an almost dead person at least. Either way, this is the worst kind of emergency to experience on a trail. There's only one right thing to do in a situation like this: Call for rescue and recovery. Recovery probably.

Except there is a slim chance. She could be alive down there. I do not dare utter a word of that to Katie. Because it will torture her the way it's torturing me and it will make no difference. Either way, we have to keep going. Even if she is alive, there is not a damn thing we can do about it without rescue climbing gear.

"We have to keep going," I say. "We have to keep going and get the stash, so we don't get into trouble ourselves. We need to move fast and get help as soon as possible."

"Are you seriously suggesting that we just hike along like nothing has happened here?"

"I'm suggesting that we don't have any other options on the table." I pause, letting my words sink in. Waiting to see if she'll fire back a quick argument. She doesn't, so I continue. "We are in the backcountry. This is why we took a GPS and why it's a risk coming out here. We need help. We need to contact the outside world because all of this is way, way beyond our abilities."

"What if she is somehow still alive?" she asks, worry filling her eyes. "Maybe we can get to her? Help her?"

"It would take hours for us to hike back there, and we have no ropes. No way to safely get to her. And even if we could, how could we help? We barely have the supplies to deal with a scraped ankle and a head cold."

"But shouldn't we try?" Katie wants to try. That much is clear. And it breaks something open in me. She's right. We should try to help. And as excruciating as it is to admit, the very best way we can do that is getting to the outside world.

I turn my body toward her. Look her in the eyes because I need her to hear me. "You're right that something awful has gone on here. You might be right about Finn. As much as I can argue that it could have been an accident, I know this could be worse. Someone could have done this. And if he did, he could try to hurt us too."

"I know. But there are two of us, and we aren't hurt. She's down there alone!"

And almost certainly dead. I don't add this last part, but I can tell by the way her face crunches that she knows it too.

I touch Katie's arms. "If there's the slightest chance that something dangerous is going on out here, then I need to get you out of here."

"You need to get *me* out of here." Her eyes are flat. Angry maybe.

"Yes *you*, Katie. You've already had a terrible thing happen to you. One is enough. More than enough."

She looks away. Her face is red, and her mouth has flattened into a thin, angry line. I do not understand or have time to deal with her being mad. So I start walking without waiting for her to say anything else.

The sun is creeping slowly toward the west. We have a few hours of daylight left, which means there is no time to talk about this anymore. We have to move as fast as we can, because there is already one dead person on this trail. And if we run out of water or if Finn finds us, then we could end up joining her.

KATIE

33 MILES IN

Aster doesn't say a word. She lets her little proclamation sit in the air, and the weight of it feels physical. It presses at the center of my chest like a fist. I know there is some love behind these words—in the same way there is love behind every time my mother looks me over, touching my face and my neck, her eyes always searching for signs of weakness.

Now in her own way, Aster is looking for that too, I guess. She's adding up my deficiencies, deciding what I can and cannot endure. She has decided to tackle the Katie Project.

I search as far ahead as I can on the trail, looking and listening for some clue as to where Finn might be. But there's nothing. The trail weaves back and forth, moving away from the cliff and into a flat stretch between canyons as we march steadily southward. The day is hot, and my calves and knees are killing me.

"I'd like to check the map and our water," Aster says.

I stop while she looks and take a long drink. There's almost no shade on the trail, and sweat is tricking between my shoulder blades. I wasn't expecting heat like this in October, but Utah never plays by the rules.

Aster sighs and looks skyward. "I screwed up."

"When? How?"

"I read the map wrong. I miscalculated this big open stretch." She taps the map. "I thought it was a couple of miles, but I think it's longer. Soon, we'll start climbing again, and the trail will veer west. We'll get one more view of the narrows, and the off-road path is right after that. We aren't far now. An hour at tops."

"So the stash isn't right around the corner?"

"No. Maybe a mile from here. Or two. I don't know. I'm mixed up," she says, and then she shifts back and forth looking uncomfortable.

"What's wrong?" I ask.

"Too much water," she says.

I nod, feeling my own bladder twinge. After leaving the canyon wall, we veered into a wide, flat expanse. There is practically nothing on either side of the path. A few scrubby sage bushes and clumps of wildflowers. Otherwise, it is a world of forgettable beige sand and low rocks for at least a mile on either side of the trail. There's a ridge dead ahead, and the trail hooks hard left to go around it. That may be the best option we have for a bathroom for miles, so I speed up.

We make impressive time getting to the ridge. Needing to pee inspires new levels of speed and endurance. By the time we're close, I've spotted some suitable privacy boulders. Which is a damn good thing because I am practically wincing with every step.

Aster handles the whole thing with her typical stoic determination, but even she unbuckles her chest strap a little frantically when we are close. We move off-trail and around the wall to the trio of boulders that surely have been sent by God for exactly this purpose. Privacy, shade, and no nearby cactus thorns to make this more complicated.

I shove down my pants, wincing at the sound, and wedge my bare back against the hot, gritty stone. Even as my bladder empties, my eyes lock onto something pale and green. It's a zippered waterproof pouch wedged between the rock I'm using and the boulder to my left.

I've had a bag like that before, but mine was orange. It's perfect for keeping a few things safe and dry and cushioned in a backpack. When Aster and I carry a phone, this is the exact kind of pouch we carry it in. They're not cheap, so people tend to use them for things like money or electronics. And they don't tend to lose track of them either.

Aster pulls up her pants. I shake off the sound and focus on the pouch.

"Hey, I found something," I tell her, to distract myself as much as to inform her.

I scoop it out of the gap between the boulders. The bag is light—too light to hold a working phone—and up close it's clear it's seen some miles. The seams are dirty and the zipper is missing a couple of teeth. I pull it open and stretch the two sides of the pouch wide to see inside.

"What is it?" Aster asks.

I tip the pouch, and three plastic cards slide into my hand. I fan them out one at a time, a credit card and a library card and a state ID wrapped in two twenty-dollar bills. I double-check the back of the ID. It's from Illinois.

My stomach squirms. Didn't Riley say they were from Illinois? Or Finn was at least. But when I push the folded cash away from the photo, the picture is not Riley. The woman smiling back is young and brunette with a sharp chin and golden eyes that seem to leap out of the photo.

"Who is that?"

"Isabel Castillo," I say, not that the name means anything.

Unlike someone falling off the trail, I could see this pouch and ID ending up here accidentally. Whoever Isabel is, she could have easily put her wallet down while she peed. Or she could have draped a jacket over the boulder and lost the pouch when it fell out of a pocket. I have lost all kinds of weird things while hiking. It isn't that uncommon.

Except, of course, that she just so happens to be from the same state as Finn. But what does that mean? A lot of people are from Illinois.

"Is she older? Younger?" Aster asks.

I check the birth date on the ID. "She's twenty. It's weird that she's from Illinois."

Aster shrugs. "Maybe. People come from all over. And stuff like this turns up on a trail. I found a wedding ring once. Dad found a phone in a pair of water shoes."

"Yeah," I say.

But the pouch still feels sinister, which means my paranoia is kicking into overdrive. Even I know this isn't a logical fear. Finn was heading this way, sure, but he couldn't be more than a mile ahead of us. So unless he dropped this ID in the last hour, he has nothing to do with this pouch. And why would he? He was with Riley, not Isabel.

But my therapist's words come back to me again. *Both things can be true.* Maybe I'm wrong about this pouch and about Riley. But I could still be right about Finn.

I shuffle the cards in my hand as if one of them is going to fess up and tell me how they got left in the sand behind a bathroom boulder. Of course, the cards have no answers for me, so I turn to Aster.

"If you left your credit card, ID, and cash on a trail, would you go back for it?"

"Maybe," Aster says. "It depends on how far away I am when I realize I dropped it."

I shake my head. "Look, I know you think I'm being paranoid—"

"I don't." Aster puts her hands up, seeing my disbelief. "Honestly, I do not think you're being paranoid."

"Fine. Then hold on to that thought when I ask you if it isn't a wee bit of a coincidence that this girl and Finn just so happen to be from the same state. A state, mind you, which is almost as far away as Ohio."

"So this region is popular with tourists," Aster argues. "And Illinois is a heavily populated state. Chicago, remember?"

I don't recognize the city name on the ID, but to Aster's point, the library card is from the Chicago Public Library.

I open my mouth to interrupt, but Aster keeps going. "And Finn was heading south with Riley before all of this happened. He hadn't gotten to this point on the trail. We know who he was with, and neither of them mentioned anyone else."

"It's just…" I shake my head, not knowing where to go from here. "It feels too coincidental to not be connected. You said this is a low-use trail. Barely traveled."

"Yes but that doesn't mean it's never traveled. What it does mean is that this could have been sitting here for weeks undisturbed."

I sigh and tip up my water for another drink, and to my surprise, it runs empty. A breeze kicks up, ruffling my hair, and I feel the cool sensation of my own sweat evaporating. Lost water.

"How much water do you have?" I ask.

"Maybe half a bottle," Aster says. "Half of that quart bottle too."

My stomach sinks. "We really need the water your dad left. I'm out."

Aster frowns and looks around, pulling her backpack over her shoulders. I move to follow her but stop when I spot movement in the distance. My stomach tightens and my thoughts turn to Finn, running full tilt down the trail. Running right for us.

But this figure is much farther south than he could be right now. A person for sure, but not Finn. Hope bubbles up in my chest. Is that someone who could help us?

"Aster, look." I point ahead at the tiny figure that seems to be moving toward the west. "Is that another trail? What is that?"

"No, that's our trail," she says.

I open my pack for my binoculars again. "I thought you said we would curve west after this ridge and that the off-road trail is right there."

"It does. That's where the drop should be. See?" She reaches for the map again to show me, but I don't need that. I need to know who we are looking at.

"Wait on the map. Who is that person walking there?" I point at the small figure heading toward the curve. "Is that Finn?"

"I…I don't know."

I finally retrieve my binoculars and pull them to my eyes, quickly adjusting the focus. I scan the seemingly endless stretch of desert for what feels like hours. And then I find them in my scope, the figure blurred in the round area of focus. I adjust the binoculars until the details emerge

Light blue trail runners and bare legs and a pile of wild blond curls in a high ponytail. I should have known. Some part of me should have guessed.

"It's Riley," I say.

Aster's face turns grave. "If Riley is alive and well, then who is at the bottom of that canyon?"

The ID in my pocket burns like a hot coal, the sinister feeling I had taking on a whole new flavor. "It could be Isabel."

"It could be anyone," Aster argues.

"But it's not Riley. Riley is alive." It feels surreal to know this. To realize that my convictions about what happened were so utterly wrong.

"Looks like it was a simple accident after all," Aster says softly.

No. The word springs into my brain, instantaneous and irrefutable. Which is truly unhinged. I know an accident makes sense. But every cell in my body is screaming that there is something else here. Something darker.

I throw up my hands. "I just can't get my head around this. Why was Finn running for us? Why would either of them destroy our GPS? Something about all of this feels wrong. And what about that other guy we saw? The one from before?"

Aster's face scrunches in confusion and then clears when she remembers. "The trail runner? That was almost two days ago."

"But he could have done something. Or he could be in on all of this with Finn."

"In on what?" Aster asks, concern creeping into her expression. "Why are you so determined to find something nefarious here?"

"I'm not!" I protest, but I know what it sounds like. This sounds exactly like paranoia. Like I'm wildly swinging from one bizarre theory to the next. And logically I know that's exactly what I'm doing. But logic doesn't shake the feeling that this doesn't add up.

I push my hair out of my face with a sigh. "Look, I'm struggling right now to see some rational line of thought that could explain this. Help me, Aster. Tell me why the evidence points at all of this being an accident and *not* a complicated murder in the Utah backcountry."

Sometimes when Aster's thinking, you can see it. Uncle Mike says you can hear the whir of the turbines winding up. I don't know about that, but you can see the spark of something intense in her eyes. She is putting pieces together and taking them apart and working through every possible combination until she understands what she's looking at and what to do with it.

"I am changing my mind," she says, instead of answering me. "I want to take the off-road route. As long as the road is not flooded—and it shouldn't be—we'll walk through the night."

"Okay, you're giving me whiplash with that answer. First, you haven't answered me. Second, you always say it's dangerous to walk at night."

"It is dangerous. No question."

"But you think we should do it?"

Aster bites her lip. She's holding back something else.

I step in before she can get away with it. "Are you telling me it's worth the risk because you don't believe this is just an accident either?"

She is too even-keel to entertain that sort of worry, but something has her nervous. And I want to know what that something is.

"I believe the most likely explanations are usually true," Aster says.

I roll my eyes, but she keeps going.

"It's probably an accident, because that's the most logical explanation. Most likely, the trail runner is just a trail runner. Most likely Isabel, or whoever fell, was hiking alone and had a terrible accident. And most likely, Riley and Finn are a couple who got in an argument and are storming down the trail separately now."

"And Finn running at us?"

"If Finn went around the backside of the ridge earlier, he might have thought he was lost. It's common, especially for solo hikers. If he saw us, he might have freaked out and tried running for us so he wouldn't be alone."

"Or he could have gotten delayed shoving another hiker off the trail and destroying our GPS when Riley tried to keep him from pushing her too."

"You have to know how irrational that sounds," Aster says.

My cheeks burn. Because I do know it. I absolutely know it, but it still feels right. God, what the hell is wrong with me? Is this some sort of heat-induced hysteria?

"Katie, given the last two days, I get why you'd imagine sinister possibilities. But I've been thinking all of this over. Trying to make of sense of motives."

"Motives?" I ask.

"Yes. Tell me, why would Finn destroy the GPS instead of tossing it over the side? Why run after us and draw attention if he already pushed someone off a ledge? For that matter, how would he be walking south with Riley now if he pushed someone else heading north?"

"I don't know," I say. What I don't say is that not understanding isn't enough reason for me to give Finn the benefit of the doubt. He scared me and I trust that. If Finn is the kind of guy that maybe wants to hurt women, then he will do it whenever he finds the chance.

An opportunistic predator. I overheard an officer use that phrase in the hospital after interviewing me. Because no, I did not know him, and no, we were not fighting, and no, there was no history before that night. But I got drunk and stupid, and he didn't miss his chance.

He's spent most of the time since that night out on bond, waiting for a trial that may never happen. I'll spend the rest of my life wondering about every single guy I meet. Wondering if they're waiting for their chance too.

Aster exhales slowly. "It just doesn't make sense that Finn has anything to do with whoever is at the bottom of that canyon."

It sounds like a final argument, and a good one. But her expression tells me that's not the end of it.

"I feel like there's something else you want to say."

She nods. "Funny thing. Logic isn't convincing me. There is no reasonable explanation I can offer. But you are frightened. And beyond that, I feel like something out here is…"

"Wrong." My voice is soft but certain when I finish for her.

Our eyes meet, and no other words are necessary. We start

walking again, down the narrow trail, and then around a cluster of otherworldly stone spires.

"Why, hello and good afternoon!"

We stop dead in our tracks at the unfamiliar voice, one that belongs to the unfamiliar man standing on the path in front of us.

ZERO MILES

The word comes back to her in a triumphant rush. Three syllables on her mother's lips. On a birthday card. On the board in her third-grade classroom.

Isabel.

Her name is Isabel.

ASTER

---

33 MILES IN

A trail squatter is the last thing we need in this moment, but from the second I spot him, I'm pretty sure that's what he is. I also suspect he is using some sort of illicit substance. Maybe several substances. My father's warning comes back to me. *Petty theft. Drug paraphernalia.* This is actually rather uncommon in the backcountry. But since we are all but breaking records for bad luck, of course we would run into him.

We do not return his greeting. Not unless a wary look is a response. But this man doesn't seem to mind. He watches us with red-rimmed eyes and I survey his appearance. Scabs cluster at the corners of his mouth and up both of his arms. He's wearing faded jeans, no backpack, and flip-flops. A hiker? Unlikely. A criminal? Maybe. Too old to be chatting up teenage girls? Definitely.

"How are you two doing?" he asks. For the briefest moment, I am tempted to ask him if he has a phone. Or tell him about what we saw. But even my imperfect instincts tell me to be careful with this person. He is easily forty. Maybe older. I can't think of a single man my father's age who looks at me the way this guy is watching us now. He does not feel like someone we should trust.

"I said how are you doing?" he repeats.

"Fine," Katie answers shortly. Like me, she does not engage in further small talk. Is she picking up the same vibe I am? Hard to tell. Katie is edgy around men in general these days.

"You in too much of a hurry to exchange a few basic pleasantries?" The man tilts his skeletal head. His smile looks cruel. "I'll go first. I'm Bobby."

"Good to meet you. We're moving fast today," I say.

I start walking toward him because he is on the trail. Unless we turn around, we have no choice but to pass him. No matter how much I wish we had better options.

The warnings firing in my body are not fully formed. I don't know the shape or size of it yet, but there is an air of danger around this man. I think we need to be as far away from him as possible.

"What's your rush, girlies?"

His tone stops me. We are not twenty feet away now, and I need to think before I close that gap. Katie takes a sharp breath and holds it. A cold wave runs up my spine, but I look him dead in the eye. Make sure he knows I will remember his face if needed.

"Our rush is that we feel like rushing." The politeness is gone from my tone now. I am all business. The picture of a girl whose patience is running thin.

I turn to look over my shoulder, just enough to see Katie. I want to reassure her. And maybe tell her to open my bag in case I need the bear spray, but her eyes are locked on Bobby. And underneath the fear in her face, there is another emotion. But what?

Bobby laughs and laughs, and something metal jangles. Motion catches my eye. A dog. It shakes its head as it ambles into view a few feet off the trail. The dog sits near a rock, hipbones jutting. It looks too thin to be any kind of threat. But when it yawns and shows rows of white teeth, I remember dogs are predators. And this one is clearly underfed.

"Why don't we just chat for a little bit?" Bobby's smile is a horror of stained teeth above his scabbed chin.

I am calculating my next move when I feel my bag rustle and unzip. Bobby frowns, and the dog shakes its head again as Katie snakes her hand inside my pack. And then before I can ask or register what she's doing, the canister of bear spray is out, and Katie's fingers are wrapped around the trigger.

The fear I saw before is gone, leaving fury behind. When she holds up the bear spray, for one second I think she might really use it.

Bobby scoffs. "Is that supposed to be some kind of threat?"

"Yeah, it is. But you can try me if you're not convinced," Katie says.

I hear the plastic safety hit the ground. Bobby hears it too. He leaps back and edges away from the trail, his sunken eyes going wide.

"Jesus, what the hell is wrong with you?"

"We've seen enough shit on this trail to be a little bit jumpy, Bobby," Katie says. "And if it somehow escaped your notice, we aren't interested in anything you might have in mind. So give us some damn space."

Shock reverberates through me like a wave. Katie a year ago would have been friendly. Katie a day ago would have frozen in panic. Katie today holds that bear spray out like she means it. Like she's out for blood.

"Ohh," Bobby draws out the word and gives a little laugh. Katie nudges me ahead, and I march along, my skin prickling at our nearness to this man. He flexes his toes inside his flip-flops, and I try not to look at his yellowed toenails. He clucks his tongue knowingly. "There ain't nothing but trouble out here this week."

I keep walking, wanting to be past him and away from this. But Katie turns, her arm still stretched out. Bobby puts up his hands, smirking like this girl with her bear spray is the cutest thing he's ever seen.

"What do you mean *trouble*?" she asks.

He shrugs, clearly pleased to get a reaction. "Couple drama. Bitchy women. You know how it is in these parts."

"Heading north or south?" she asks.

"Does it matter?" he asks with another horror-show smile.

I want to know what he's seen, but I want to get away from him more. We keep going. My head is spinning again and my ears are ringing.

Bobby follows. He keeps his distance, and Katie keeps that bear spray at the ready. But he's still behind us.

"Sure you don't want to stay a spell?" he asks. "We can compare notes. Or I might have some stuff you want. Something to make the miles go easy."

I notice a small squarish tent set back in an alcove of rock a few yards from the trail. It has been here a while. A battered blue tarp is thrown over the top, and a stack of empty backpacks sits next to a lawn chair with a sagging seat. Crumpled beer cans litter the area just outside his tent door. This absolutely looks like the camp of a guy who'd sell us something to *make the miles go easy*.

"We could just talk," Bobby says, drawing out each word.

"We're not comparing notes," Katie says, her voice strong and even. It's like she's tried on a pair of boots she wasn't sure she could wear. And now nothing suits her so well. "We're going to keep moving, and you're going to stop following us."

"You sure have a shit way with small talk. I was just offering information."

I think his offer was about drugs, but since he's obviously been here this whole time, he might have seen something.

"Who have you seen?" I ask, unable to stop myself.

Bobby watches me. Sizes me up before he plays his next card. "Like I said. A couple two or three days back. A little blond girl today. Even bitchier than the two of you if that's possible."

Katie stops then, lowering the bear spray a fraction of an inch. Bobby eyes the canister but doesn't move faster. His dog trots ahead, finding a metal bowl near the tent. A reminder that we still need to get to our stash for water. The dog drinks and drinks, oblivious to our standoff.

"Tell us about the couple," Katie says.

Bobby bumps his chin toward the trail—toward the way we came. "Like I said, two, maybe three days ago. They were headed north. Guy was quiet. Didn't bother nobody, but his lady was a real piece of work. Took a sample of mine, and didn't want to pay the agreed price. Typical woman on a trail."

Katie taps her thumbnail against the canister of spray. "You sure you want to keep going with that women-are-so-bitchy angle?"

Bobby smirks at her, but I don't want to challenge him. I want to know what he's seen. What he might know.

"Did they leave together?" I ask. "How long ago was that?"

"Was the fight getting physical?" Katie adds. "Was he threatening her?"

Bobby's eyes narrow with interest. "What the hell did you see out there, girlies?"

"What happened to the couple?" Katie asks.

He shrugs one shoulder. "They kept hiking north. Fighting like cats and dogs. Don't blame him either because she was more trouble than she was worth, I can tell you that."

"What did they look like?" I ask.

Bobby shakes his head. "No, it's your turn to answer a question. Did something happen out there? Or maybe you won't tell me because you're up to bad business."

"We're not the ones offering to sell a little something for the trail," Katie snaps. "What did they look like?"

He demurs. I can't help but wonder if he's trying to figure out how he can use this information. What he thinks he might be able to get out of us. But then he looks at the bear spray again and thinks better of it.

"Young pretty somethings." He shrugs. "Nothing special about 'em."

"What else? Was he tall? Did she have curly hair?"

He shakes his head, clearly confused by our interest. "You're all mixed up. Shirley Temple came through earlier today—tiny thing and moving fast. The couple? They both had dark hair. She was pretty and knew it. You know the type." Bobby lets out a low whistle.

I don't know what Katie's looking at, but I can almost hear the wheels turning in her mind. She thinks she's figured something out. But I have no idea what that something is.

"And they just left?" she asks. "Where to?"

He shrugs. "Beats the shit out of me. I told you, they took off looking like they were ready to kill each other. Is that what happened out there? Did you run into something?"

He licks his lips like he's hungry for news of a tragedy. It's sickening. I want to be away from this man. Now is not soon enough.

I cough and the dog startles. There's a notch in its ear and a bare patch of skin at the edge of its collar. It doesn't look like it's in the best shape. Neither of them do really. When I cough again, the dog barks and I jump.

Bobby laughs at me, then picks absently at one of the scabs on his chin. "You are spooked, ain't you?"

I look at Katie, but this time it's different. This time I'm the one who's afraid.

And Katie's not.

She lifts her chin and grips that canister tighter. Then she bares her teeth in an expression that isn't even close to a smile. "You have a good day, Bobby."

And then she lowers her arm and starts walking. Part of me is sure Bobby will continue to follow. It's hard to resist looking over my shoulder, but I manage. I trust my ears to catch the evidence of him moving. And after a few minutes of hearing nothing, I relax.

When we are several minutes past his camp, Katie stops dead in front of me. I search the ground for some danger, look behind us in case I've missed footsteps or voices. But there's nothing.

"Are you okay? Is something up there?"

"I think we got it all wrong," she says. And then she turns, eyes glittering. "I think we've got every damn bit of this wrong."

KATIE

34 MILES IN

My heart is beating about a thousand miles an hour. Aster blows her nose while she waits. But I need another minute to be sure the terrible pieces sliding into place in my mind make sense.

The facts are tumbling around, changing shape and place. The ID we found and the couple headed north and the trail runner bolting past. Riley and Finn and Isabel, and who knows who else.

"Aster, if Isabel and her boyfriend were heading north from Bobby's camp two or three days ago, was there any way we could have missed them?"

Her breath catches as she thinks it over. Works through all the possibilities. One simple question, but it's the kind that lays out dozens of implications.

"No," she says, holding my gaze. "Not logically. Other than the rained-out road, there are no trail exits between where we started and where we're standing."

"We would have passed them, right?" I ask.

"Well, unless they left on the road that flooded, but most likely, yes. We would have."

"And Riley and Finn said they hadn't seen anyone either," I say, just to be sure I'm right.

Aster takes a slow, heavy breath. She's thinking. "But we did see one person. The trail runner."

"Okay, that's not exactly where I was going. Tell me what you're thinking."

Aster sniffles. "Well, since we know Riley and Finn are both alive, I think it's possible that the girl at the bottom of the ridge is Isabel Castillo. She matches Bobby's description."

"We agree on that," I say.

"According to Bobby, they were fighting when they headed north, and we saw the trail runner, who I suppose could have been Isabel's boyfriend." She gestures ahead on the trail, urging me to keep moving. We walk while we talk.

"So you think the trail runner was Isabel's boyfriend, and he pushed her? It would explain why he was running," I say.

"I didn't say that."

"You didn't *not* say that. If she fell accidentally, wouldn't he have said something to us? Wouldn't he have been looking for a phone or someone to help."

Aster marches a few more steps before answering. "I don't know. That would make sense. But it's also possible they split up and he didn't realize Isabel fell."

I nod, taking this in. Aster is animated now, waving her hands as she walks. "It's impossible to know. We saw him for thirty seconds. He was a just a man running. Nothing more."

"Nothing except you think his girlfriend fell thirty feet."

"Well, that," Aster says. "But to be fair, I struggle to imagine a serious trail runner stopping midrun to hang out with a stranger like Bobby. So maybe it wasn't him."

"We can't really know if he was a serious runner," I say, taking a page from her earlier we-actually-don't-know-shit-about-shit mentality.

Aster coughs. "His pacing, breathing, and shoes didn't look like novice material."

"But did he have the look of a guy running to get away from a crime?" I say, trying to remember. "I thought he looked serious, but calm."

"I don't know. My theory is not bulletproof."

I stumble on a root, and catch myself. My ideas were enough to make me nervous, but Aster has added a whole new world of terrible possibilities.

"So what about you? What are you thinking?" she asks.

"I'm thinking it's possible Finn was with Isabel before he was with Riley."

"Wait. What?"

"My mind's been running through this. Because I don't trust Finn. Everything in my gut tells me he's bad news, and I trust my gut."

Aster looks at me. She wants to argue. I can see all of the logical statements lining up behind her eyes. But she holds her tongue. "Go on."

I let out my breath. "I initially thought Finn and Riley were a couple."

"Because they were," she says. And then she frowns. "Weren't they?"

I tilt my head back and forth. "I'm starting to look back and wonder if they weren't. If I didn't assume incorrectly."

She opens her mouth to argue and then closes it just as fast. Because she sees it too. She's cataloging everything we saw, everything Riley said, and every clue that could make it clear that they are a couple. And unless she thinks of something I'm missing, she's going to reach the same conclusion I did. They might not be as close as we thought.

"They never did expressly say they were romantically involved," Aster says.

"Nope. If you think about it, Riley didn't say anything about Finn that she couldn't have learned on a single day of hiking. They're both from the Midwest. Tidbits about his childhood. Even his strong, silent thing. She would have seen that firsthand."

"Maybe."

I tick the points off on my fingers as we walk. "They didn't touch. There were no nicknames or affectionate gestures. He showed zero warmth. Hell, he barely spoke to her."

"He barely spoke period," Aster argues. "And none of this explains how he would start with Isabel heading north and somehow double back with Riley. Finn and Riley were headed south, remember?"

"Hear me out. Let's say Finn was the boyfriend fighting with Isabel. And let's say the fight got so bad he pushed her off the cliff."

"I am not following. If that happened, how did he end up camping with Riley?"

"He would have run into Riley because he would have been headed north and Riley was heading south. She is trusting and kind and obviously liked having company, so she would have looked like a very good alibi."

"But wouldn't she have questioned him suddenly changing direction?"

I wave that off. "It would have been easy for Finn to make up some story, that he was headed south, but backtracked because he lost something, or maybe he was following an animal or whatever."

"Following an animal?"

"I don't know," I admit. "I'm just saying, it's easy to lie. And I could see him thinking being with Riley would make him look less suspicious."

"But if he headed south with Riley he'd have to pass Bobby again, who would obviously recognize him."

"I know. It doesn't all add up perfectly, but I feel dead sure that Finn is dangerous. He has a record. Riley said that. And he was watching us in the dark and ran at us earlier today. Normal guys don't do that."

Aster launches into another coughing fit, and we pause in a patch of shade for her to ride it out. She still looks like death warmed over and this whole trip has been a disaster. But I'm grateful to have her beside me. To know someone out here is looking out for me.

Riley doesn't have that.

She's alone. If she's smart and lucky, she'll continue to stay away from Finn and get her ass off-trail and back to the world as quickly as possible.

But what if she isn't lucky? What if Finn finds her?

I think of his face when he stepped out of the shadows. Of the fear that jangled through me when he was running for us on the trail. And then I think of Riley, frantic and terrified in our tent. We have no reason to think Finn is not still after her.

"Aster, Riley is alone out here, and Finn is fast. We have to go after her."

"No." Aster stops. She pushes her bone-straight hair behind her ears. Her expression tells me she isn't going to give an inch. "Someone died out here. Our priorities are clear. We need to find the stash of water, and then we need to get to civilization. Period."

"You want to just leave her." My face feels hot.

"No. We will alert the police and rangers, obviously, and tell them Riley is out here and may be in danger. But *we* need to get home safely. That's the priority."

Need to get home safely. The words drag back a hazy memory of Aster's thin-lipped nod before she left the party all those months ago. When she left me to get home safely on my own.

"That's not my priority," I snap. "It's yours. But we all know you're very good at taking care of your own comfort and safety, right, Aster?"

Her face goes very pale. "What does that mean?"

"It means, you got home from that party just fine. And you left me there without a second thought."

I march ahead, and Aster waits a full minute before following. I am too angry and embarrassed to look back. It isn't fair. I know that. I know exactly where the blame for this lands, and it sure as hell isn't my socially awkward cousin who wanted to leave a party full of strangers. And somehow knowing it isn't enough to shut me up.

But that's one of the ugliest truths about that night. I was relieved when Aster left. And despite that, despite how happy I felt when the door closed behind her, I'm still furious that she didn't stay.

ISABEL

The memory of her name is the crack of a track pistol.

She needs to tell someone. She is here. She is here. She is here.

But how? One finger drags a trail in the sand, but her mind is too topsy-turvy for letters. She bunches the emergency blanket in frustration.

It crinkles with possibility. Shiny and bright. It has already saved her once. The wind catches it, and panic curls hot fingers around her throat.

Slow. Slowly now.

She moves it back from the edge. Bunches it under her good leg while her fingers find a crack in the wall. Can she stuff it in? Make a flag? As high up as she can reach. Nowhere near high enough.

Ages pass while she pushes that shiny blanket into place. She drops it over and over. Starts from the beginning.

Her thoughts are random. Distance runners. Thanksgiving

dinners. The curtains in her mother's dining room. She then finds slivers of rock around her. Stuffs them in, hammers them with her peanut rock. Her arm shakes with the final blow, but finally, *finally*. It stays put.

When she sags back, the blanket droops like a bow.

She wants it to work. Wants it to grab the hope fluttering inside. And hold on tight.

ASTER

---

35 MILES IN

My eyes are blurred with tears, but I follow Katie. The trail veers back and forth, eventually tucking into the shade under a wide rock overhang. The temperature drops instantly. We're walking into a cool breeze now. Perfect place to stop.

But stopping means speaking. We have managed to avoid it since our argument, and the silence hurts less. Of course, the silence doesn't drown out the memory of her words. Or the fact that she's right. I did take care of myself. I did leave her. And I'll wish for the rest of my life I could undo that.

But it would not change my mind here. Riley isn't Katie. Not to me. There is no circumstance when I would put her before my cousin. Katie thinks I'm wrong for that. But for me, nothing else feels right.

Katie stops with a sigh, pulling a single granola bar out of her bag. My stomach is growling, and the turnoff for the off-road area is uphill from here. We should recharge before tackling the climb.

Katie turns to offer me half of the granola bar, and something falls from above us.

It hurtles and hits so fast that I register that it's a rock at the same instant that it explodes with a dull crash at our feet. My heart stops cold, but I exhale in a rush, stunned that we are alive. Safe and unharmed. And in that exact instant, pain explodes through my foot like a cannon.

A scream is ripped out of me. It punches upwards from my gut. Stretches my throat. Roars into the sky as raw and endless as the agony shooting through my foot and leg. My vision tunnels and my knees fold. As I crumple, I see the pieces of rock around my shoe. It hit me. My foot was crushed by the falling rock.

I fall sideways in the rusty dirt. My scream goes raspy and then silent. Katie's pack hits the ground and then she drops in front of me. My head reels and the expression she's wearing terrifies me. Did it rip my foot off? Is there blood? She is breathing so hard, and her hands are reaching. But she doesn't touch me. Or I don't think she touches me. There is no feeling in me outside of the brutal, excruciating stabbing in my right foot.

I curl myself in. Move my head so I can see better. My foot is still attached. Intact. I am surprised there is no blood. This sort of pain deserves it, but it is better to not be bleeding, I think.

"Is it just your foot?" she asks. She sounds breathless. Panicked.

"Broken." I grit the word out and hiss as another wave of pain pulses through me. It is more than broken. I have broken bones before. Both arms. My left hand and a couple of toes in the same rappelling accident. I don't have to untie my boot or get an X-ray to tell me that this is much, much worse than that.

"Is there anything else?" Katie asks. She is hovering, waiting for marching orders.

"The foot is bad enough." I close my eyes, feeling a swell of nausea. The pain is beyond my foot. It's infecting every inch of my body, and I feel sick.

I roll to one side, feeling the grit of sand under my face and the wet heat of tears clumping my eyelashes together. It's impossible the way this pain is traveling. Up my leg, into my groin. I feel the electric buzz of every damaged nerve, angry and relentless. I clutch the sun-warmed earth beneath me.

"Maybe we should take off your boot and get a look at it?"

I shake my head roughly. The idea of touching my boot sends stars bursting behind my eyes. "No. I can't. I should take ibuprofen."

"Really? Ibuprofen? Is that going to help?"

"Not the pain, but I need to do what I can for the inflammation. I need ice and elevation."

What we actually need is an emergency room. And that's a problem that pushes its way to the front of my mind. We can't get to an emergency room. The off-road route is a sloping, winding nightmare that could have treacherous drop-offs and jutting rocks. My gut tells me I won't be able to navigate that with a heavy limp. Especially without crutches or even a walking stick.

The more I think, the more my anxiety grows. I don't think I can walk at all. I am not sure I will be able to stand. I can barely look at my foot without reeling.

My vision blurs and I blink rapidly, trying to clear it. I push myself up on my arms and cry out, the change in pressure sending fresh blades of pain slicing through me.

"How can I help?" Katie is wringing her hands. "I don't know what to do."

"I suppose you could help me sit up."

"Of course."

I take a hard breath. I need to blow my nose. If that isn't insult to injury, I don't know what is. I force myself up onto my elbows and look around. Another chunk of the rock that fell is only a few feet from me. I look up to see the curve of the enormous overhang, splinters near where the first piece fell. There is still a crack above us. My heart double thumps.

"We have to get away from that," I say. "It's not stable."

"Shit," Katie whispers, her face pale and pinched.

I try to crawl backwards on my butt, but it's awkward and every movement stabs me with a reminder of the agony I can't escape. I cry out. Scoot another foot. Fall back, gasping and moaning. It's all I can do to not sob.

"Stop," Katie says. "Don't move. I have an idea. We need to go slow."

She drags her pack over and turns it so the straps face up. Then she looks at me, her face serious, but calm. "Aster, I'm going to push your good foot through the strap. And then I'm going to prop your other foot up on the bag too."

"Why?"

"Because I think it will be easier if your legs aren't bumping along the ground when I drag you."

"When you drag me?"

She is done asking permission now. Usually when we're hiking, I'm in charge. More experience. More stamina. More of all the tools you need to make it. But now, Katie's lips have pressed together, and she's carefully maneuvering my good foot under one of her backpack straps. She adjusts it to cinch it down and then looks me in the eyes. "Are you ready for me to move your other foot?"

"Absolutely not."

"Is there a better option?"

I cringe. "No."

She nods and slowly, slowly moves her hands toward my calf. My whole body tenses. The endless searing pain is already more than I can bear. How much worse will it be when her hands connect with my leg? But when her palms finally cup my calf, she is so careful.

"This okay?"

Tears spill over down my cheeks. I nod.

"I will go slow."

"It hurts."

Tears fill her eyes. "I know. I know it does. I'm sorry."

She moves my whole leg carefully over the pack, easing it down one millimeter at a time. I groan and hiccup back a sob. But she makes gentle noises and finishes the job. I feel boneless and spent when she releases me. It is over. Except she has not actually moved me.

I swipe tears off my face with the back of my dirty hand. My leg is resting on the pack. Elevated, actually, which is logically a good thing.

"Okay?" she asks softly.

I nod, still gritting my teeth. A cracking above. My body turns to stone. The crack in the sandstone above us. Is it growing wider?

"Katie…"

She nods and rushes behind me. I feel her hands at my shoulders, her fingers digging under the straps of my backpack. "Here we go."

She doesn't give me time to ask questions or to change my mind. I feel my backpack straps tighten, the chest strap digging into the soft flesh above my breasts. And then I am moving backwards on my bottom in a surprisingly smooth slide. Ten feet. Then twenty. Then thirty until she stops.

She eases me into a pocket in the rock. Off the trail. Safe from the overhang. Sandwiched between two low sandstone wedges, maybe eight feet apart. In a bizarre twist of luck, the view from my position is astonishing, a straight shot through a low spot in the desert. A window, and through it the long and winding trail we've taken.

"Let's get you that ibuprofen," she says.

She rushes around in full-on nurse mode. Everything is a process. I shift and squirm, trying to make my top half comfortable against the stone. Katie hesitates, noticing both my discomfort and the fact that she won't be able to dig around in her backpack with my foot on it.

"The sleeping pad," I say.

She is already on it. Reading my mind. We work in perfect unison, me leaning forward while I shrug off my backpack. She leans it against the wall next to me, detaches the sleeping pad, and starts to unroll it.

A hazy part of my mind thinks this is like Katie from before. But this is not that Katie. This is Katie now. She is different. And she is the same. Maybe all these versions of her are a little bit true.

I touch her arm. "Thank you."

"Don't thank me yet. God knows if I can find that ibuprofen."

"No." I shake my head, more tears spilling. "Thank you. You're helping me. I didn't help you. I left."

I don't know where my brain is going. I don't know why I'm suddenly thinking of that metal staircase as I left the party. Of the thumping music. Of me leaving her behind. I don't even know that I'm making sense, but her face changes. She knows exactly what I'm saying and she has figured out something important in the same moment.

"We are okay," she says. She almost sounds surprised at her own words.

"Are we?" I hate how small I sound. How weak.

But then my cousin's hands are on my shoulders, and her eyes are wet, but her gaze is steady. "You didn't know about that asshole any more than I knew about this rock."

Long seconds tick by while we look at one another. There are miles and miles on us now. We smell of sweat and pain. And fear.

"I don't know how to fix this," I admit, the words swallowing up all the broken things between us.

"Hell, me either," she says. "But we'll figure it out."

And then, we move on as if we'd never spoken of it at all. She's folded my sleeping pad until it is a soft-sided block, one that will be just wide enough to further elevate and support my injured foot.

I wave my hand vaguely at my leg. "A scarf or bandage or something?"

She nods, and I am grateful that she knows I'm offering options for securing my leg to the pad. Even the idea of my leg falling off the side makes me want to come out of my own skin. My stomach sloshes, and I close my eyes. I feel dizzy with things that are more than my ears or this injury. Like my whole system is spinning off-kilter.

"What's going on?" Katie asks.

I hear her kneel but can't answer or open my eyes. All of my energy is focused on calming my intensely queasy stomach.

"Did you hit your head too? Is something else hurting?"

"Feel a little sick," I say, even those four words draining my energy. And then, as if my body takes my words as permission to fall to pieces, I begin to tremble violently.

"Okay," Katie says. She sounds nervous but determined. I open my eyes to see her hair swinging near my face as she moves for my backpack. She unzips the main compartment, finds the first aid kit, and then roots around until she finds something that seems to suit her. I can't quite see it until she moves in front of me, and then I nod. It's one of the headband scarves that she always packs and rarely uses.

I watch her work. Snipping the fabric. Moving the folded sleeping pad next to me. Transferring my leg from her backpack to the folded square.

She pulls up the two sides of the cut scarf on either side of my leg. The pieces are carefully tied, one above my knee, another even more carefully a few inches above my ankle. When she pulls that one tight, a fresh wave of agony and nausea blooms through me. Funny how such a distant extremity can cause system-wide chaos.

"Okay, now let's get you more comfortable," she says.

She detaches her own sleeping pad next, folding it quickly into thirds and wedging it behind my back. The rock is still uncomfortable, but it is more bearable. I blink away the fog of pain. The world slides back into focus, all the facts on the ground coalescing.

There are problems to solve. Problem one: It will be dark in three hours, and we have not reached the stash. Problem two: We are down to a third of a bottle of water. Problem three: Only one of us can walk.

There aren't going to be any good options from here, just smart choices. I am good at making smart choices. But I am my father's daughter. And I know that all the smart choices in the world still might not get me out of this alive.

KATIE

36 MILES IN

've seen some truly shitty injuries, but this takes the cake. I was there when Adam took a weird fall at hockey. His glove shot off his hand, and his fingers ran into the business end of a pair of ice skates, which are every bit as sharp as you might think. He got sixteen stitches in three different fingers that day, and the ice rink closed for the whole afternoon to clean things up. It was bad.

This is worse.

Aster howled like an animal when that rock exploded, like someone had ripped her leg clean off her body. For a few minutes, I thought she was actually slipping into shock, but now she's nibbling thoughtfully at a granola bar. She washes down four ibuprofen with a water bottle that has an inch left at best.

"Well, we definitely need help now," she says.

I frown, looking at her. She is so pale. Sweat has beaded up on her freckled forehead, and she is shaking. "Yeah, I don't think you're going to be able to walk."

"I know that," she says simply. "You need to go alone."

My heart sinks. I want to argue with her, but she's right.

"Splitting up out here feels dangerous," I say.

"It is. All of this is dangerous."

I rub my temples, trying to understand. "I know. Just walk me through the logic."

Aster adjusts herself against the rock with a wince. "Unless you want to see if Bobby can help—"

"I wouldn't be surprised if Bobby eats kittens for lunch, so he's roughly ten miles past the last resort in my opinion."

"Agreed," she says. "All the more reason I don't think that's a good choice."

"What other options are there?"

"We can't go together." Her tone tells me she's already thought it through and dismissed it. "You'd have to carry me. You're obviously very strong, but—"

She stops abruptly when I wince.

"What is it?" she asks.

"I hate that," I say. "People calling me strong. I didn't choose to be strong. A horrible thing happened. And I kept waking up every day, whether or not I wanted to. That's not strength. Just survival."

Aster looks confused. But then she blinks. "Survival *is* strength, Katie. That's what it boils down to for every creature. Every time."

A long pause passes between us, but then she shrugs her shoulders. "That said, I was actually referring to your physical strength. You are a strong climber and better at handling a heavy pack."

"Oh." I chuckle. "Well, thank you? I guess?"

"Strong or not, I still don't think you can carry me any sort of distance. Not quickly."

I waggle my mostly empty water bottle. "And I'd say moving quickly is a pressing matter."

"One might even say *crushing*," Aster says, arching her brow at her foot.

"Glad to see your dad jokes are still intact," I say. And then I rise to my feet. "So how far away is the stash?"

"Less than half a mile. Do you see that fin?" She points at a wedge of sandstone uphill from here. It's angled to cut directly across the trail. And it's all uphill, because what else could possibly make this day better? As if reading my mind, Aster goes on. "The trail does a switchback around that fin, and yes, it is a miserable altitude gain. The mouth of the road is just beyond that. When we saw Riley, she was near where we are now. Quite a view."

I take a moment to follow her gaze north. It is beautiful. We can't see quite as much as before, but the long stretch of cliff we traversed is clear as day. My heart clenches. Isabel is down there. I can't see her without the binoculars, but I know she's there, and I hate that I did nothing to help her. Nothing to help Riley either.

But I can still help Aster. And if I'm fast enough—if I can get help out here, maybe there's a chance of keeping Riley safe.

"Okay," I say, turning back. "I can do this. It's nothing compared to the hell we've been through, right?"

"Right."

"I'm worried about leaving you here," I admit. "I'd rather you have the GPS."

"I'm worried about you going alone. You should take it."

"No." My response is firm. So is my resolve. "If the GPS stays put, your dad might notice we aren't moving. He might see that we haven't gotten to the stash. It might be enough to send him back to look for us."

"Not sure I can argue with that," she agrees, her eyes drifting closed.

"Good. Because there's another thing you aren't going to win." I unzip my pack long enough to retrieve the bear spray. Aster shakes her head, but I put it beside her.

She tries to push it back. "You should take it. You are more likely to run into someone than me."

I tuck it next to her. "I can run. You can't. It's logical for you to have it."

"I don't care about logic," she snaps.

"Okay, now I know you need medical attention," I tease. But when she doesn't smile, I drop the cheery act. "I'm not leaving you defenseless."

"You should," she says. Her voice is very quiet. But then she looks up at me. "Fair payback."

Emotions roll through me in a succession of waves. I want to tell her she's right, and I want to tell her she's wrong, and I want to tell her that there are a thousand tangled, twisted feelings tied up in that awful night. I resent her for escaping unharmed. For leaving me. But for every one time I hate her, I hate myself twice for not knowing better. Because I guess that's what this is. One asshole has his ten minutes, and I'll spend years trying to fix my brain because of it.

But I don't want to talk about that night or the stain it left. I want to save Aster and Riley both. And I want to make sure Finn doesn't get away with this.

I take everything heavy out of my pack and leave it in a heap next to her. Then I take a bracing breath and fasten my chest strap. "I'm going to get us water. If I get lucky, I'll see someone. If I don't get lucky, I'm bringing water back to you, and then I'm going to take that same road back to the highway and see if my body remembers even a sliver of what I learned in cross-country."

Aster rests her head back against the rock and looks south. All that desert stretching out. All those miles that didn't beat us. So help me God, this last bit won't beat us either.

ISABEL

She waits and stares at the crossword puzzle of her mind. Clues filling themselves in one at a time.

The endless bickering.

That sickly old man and his emaciated dog.

Her lost wallet.

That's when the real fight erupted. When he left, her rage was a shadow behind him.

That was also when she met them. Riley and Finn. Oh, lucky day.

It's almost funny how lucky it seemed.

ASTER

36 MILES IN

I watch Katie until she is a small dark form against the orange rock and scrubby sage bushes. I keep watching until she slips behind the large sandstone fin ahead. And then out of my sight.

I release a slow breath when she's gone. The quiet is absolute. The rock behind me is still warm from the sun. I am tucked in a dark pocket of shade, but all around me the world burns.

The desert has always suited me. I like heat and solitude. I love the unyielding presence of these rocks. The maddening way the desert is both never changing and always changing. If I'm going to be alone, this is always where I'd choose.

And a small part of me acknowledges that if I don't make it—if the shock I feel hovering at the edge of my senses takes me, or help doesn't come fast enough, or a million other *ifs*—then I am happy I will die here. There will be stone behind me and orange sand beneath my palms. It is enough.

My chances are reasonable. The stash is close, and Katie is a good hiker. She'll make it there and back. It is the after that scares me. She will have to leave again in the morning, and it could take hours for her to reach civilization. More hours for civilization to reach me.

It might be too many hours in the end. I know what an injury like this can do to a body in the desert. I could dehydrate. Slip into real shock. I could be gone before Katie ever makes it back. From a damn broken foot.

I could be another body my dad drags back from the maw of a canyon.

And that's the only part of this that gets to me. Imagining either of them hurting more than they already have. For my dad? I am a daily reminder of the wife who had little interest in the desert rat she gave birth to and even less in the one she married.

And Katie? I already left her once, didn't I?

I look east, feeling drowsy and fogged over by pain. But I won't tire of this view. The sun is dipping to the west, casting golden light that sets the ridge on fire. I wonder if anyone else is seeing this right now. And then, a wink of light flickers low on the canyon wall. My heart catches.

What is that?

I watch for long seconds, but there's nothing. Then another flash of light. Something glinting. Is that where we saw Isabel's body? I rack my memories, trying to recall anything shiny at that scene. Was there anything? Anything at all?

I twist for the pile of detritus Katie left behind. Tent poles, a couple of gear clips, and a toiletries bag. My fingers catch a thin black strap and tug. The binoculars tumble out of the pile.

I twist to grab them and my leg shifts. Pain skewers me through the marrow of my bones, Ankle to knee to pelvis. It's like a razor slicing in a hundred directions. I let out a low groan, my stomach rolling. My foot feels different. Pressure now adds a new layer to the pain.

A glance reveals the laces of my shoe, pulled taut on my injured foot. My ankle bulges like a water balloon over the sides of my hiking boot. So, that's…not great.

My laces are double knotted and looking at the plummy red flesh of my ankle makes me regret refusing Katie's offer to remove my shoe. Because my foot is rapidly swelling. And this shoe is starting to cut off circulation.

I find the toiletries bag, moving slow. Careful. There are scissors inside—*thank you, Katie*—and I grip them tightly. My hands shake when I move to cut the laces, so I stop to gain my strength. Take deep breaths to steady my hand.

And then I cut, the small metal blade sawing slowly through the first lace. It pops open when it breaks, an electric jolt of pain following the success. I keep going, gasping my way through each new jab of agony. Two laces. And then three. And then the last two, and I hook the scissors inside the loop on top of the tongue of my shoe. I pull it loose.

The motion is excruciating, but relief follows. I close my eyes and drop back, exhausted. Like I've run a 5K instead of cutting open the laces on a single shoe. I slowly open my eyes and look out at the canyon across from us. That same glint of light winks at me.

I remember now. Katie saw an emergency blanket on that body. That's probably all it is. Logically, that's what I'm seeing.

But I'm not taking chances.

I take the binoculars again. Raise them to my eyes and ignore the sledgehammer battering at every nerve in my leg. The image in the tiny circle of focus jumps and jumps. My hands are shaking again. My whole body is shaking. Palms slick with sweat. Agony will do that I suppose.

Finally, the image steadies on something reflective. A silvery swatch against the orange rock. The emergency blanket must have blown off Isabel's body. But something about that doesn't track. I look again. The blanket is up on the wall, billowing out on two sides like a giant floppy foil bow against the varnished wall. Could it seriously have blown up against the wall like that?

It doesn't feel likely. The wind is blowing the opposite direction. If anything, it should have blown into the canyon below. And there hasn't been anything windy enough to pinch it in the middle like that, has there?

I twist my head to look at a crack in the wall behind me. How would I get an emergency blanket wedged in there? What would do that? Wind? A raven?

Neither seem probable.

But I could do it. I think it through. If I had a blanket now, I could push the middle in with my hand and it would billow out. Just like the one I'm looking at. I could wedge it in there with a stick or some part of my gear.

And I would do it. If I had fallen with no way to call for help, it might be just the thing I'd try to let someone know I was down there. To let them know I was alive.

Footsteps behind me startle me from my thoughts.

"Katie?"

A scuffle. Shoes on sand, maybe. I look up but there is no one on the path. The hair on the nape of my neck stands on end. The next scuffle is closer. A shuddering breath with the shuffle of feet.

The binoculars slip from my fingers. And three things hit me in an instant.

One. It is too soon for Katie to be back.

Two. The noise is coming from behind me.

Three. Whoever is back there is crying.

KATIE

37 MILES IN

I spot the sign and sag with relief. It's stupid. I know that. I haven't even found the stash, just a crude wooden sign with an arrow and a single word: *Road.* So I'm not there, but the hot prick of grateful tears is waiting just behind my eyes.

I take a sharp breath and tamp them down and force myself to keep moving. The sign awakens every ache in my body. My knees twinge with each step. My shoulders burn under the weight of my pack. Even the trickle of sweat between my shoulder blades is a stinging reminder of misery. I am hot and exhausted and frightened, but more than all of that, I am absolutely desperate to get water. And then help.

I am going to save Aster.

And I am going to save Riley.

I only wish I could save Isabel too.

My hair slides free of the bun I slopped it into earlier, and the hot weight of it on my neck is unbearable in an instant. I reach to fix it while I walk toward the wide opening to the road.

It pitches sharply downhill, rocks planted on either side of the rutted roadway.

I loop the elastic band around my hair once. Twice.

"Katie."

I drop my hands. A dark figure steps out from behind one of the rocks. Finn. He moves toward me, and I am rooted into the stone beneath my feet. I am Isabel at the bottom of the canyon. I am Aster with her broken foot. I am myself in that apartment bedroom, the frames still thumping the wall. My world burning to ash.

"I need you to listen to me," he says.

A hot, prickly rush of adrenaline pulses through my veins in a single jolt. I remember my therapist again. *Both things can be true, Katie.*

And they are.

I am still the broken, terrified girl in that bedroom. And I am the furious woman who would rather die than let another man get his chance.

I crouch with gritted teeth and an animal growl in my throat. I am hefting a rock before I can think. I hurl it before he can do anything but duck.

"Shit! Stop! Stop it and listen to me!"

But I do not stop. I throw rock after rock after rock and when I am out of rocks and out of luck, I do the only thing left I can.

I run.

ASTER

36 MILES IN

R iley."

Her name shudders on my lips. Or maybe it is Riley's voice that shudders.

She hiccups on a sob, her eyes brimming with tears. "You—you have to help me."

"I…" I do not finish, because I do not know where to begin. She hasn't seen my foot. Her eyes are wild.

"You have to help me," she repeats.

Her hair is loose and dirty, and her shins are stained orange with sand. She looks like a woman possessed, her hands clenching and releasing. Clenching and releasing.

"What happened?" I ask.

"Finn." She whispers the word. Eyes darting like even that tiny noise will summon him. Her hands are still moving, curling tight. Over and over. "Finn. He did something. He's going to do it again."

Chills race up my arms and legs. "What did he do?"

"You have to believe me," she sobs. Chokes on the last word and brings her hands to her throat. "You don't know what he did."

"I know he ran after you," I say. Because this is true. But a bone-deep instinct tells me to stop speaking. To only listen.

"He—there was a girl. There was a girl before you came. Before we met you. She came from this way. She was—"

Riley stops herself again, her shoulders hunching. A raven calls nearby, and she jumps. Catches herself, and looks back at me. She is bone white. Eyes ringed in dark circles. She is Katie in the hospital. Katie on the ride home, her face turned to the window and eyes seeing nothing.

"What happened?" I ask, wishing I could move. Get up. Do something.

Riley tries to speak, but she dissolves into ragged sobs, her slender arms crossing over her stomach. She looks left and right. As if Finn is a phantom who could leap out of any shadow. As if he might run down from the ridge above.

"Did he hurt you, Riley?" I ask.

She shakes her head but does not answer. I wait and wait for her to speak. When she does, she does not answer me.

"He killed someone." She says it plainly. Her fingers fidget while she speaks. "He pushed a girl. That's why I wanted you to stay with me. That's why I wanted your GPS. Because he killed her. He looked her right in the eyes and pushed her off the edge, and she was so pretty. She was beautiful, and now she's dead."

"Where is he now?"

She does not answer. She takes a halting breath and then drops to her knees beside me, her hands clutching my shirt. "He is still out here. I'm trying to get away from him, but he is chasing me. He's going to kill me too. If we can't get away from him, we'll all die."

ISABEL

She knew they would kiss. More than that if they could find a way. The heat between them was instant. Undeniable. She remembered the sick pleasure of knowing Riley didn't stand a chance.

And she was right.

Longing looks. Kisses like stolen bottles of liquor, fast and delicious.

More delicious for their wrongness.

She remembers her topsy-turvy vision when Riley caught them, her eyes big and full. She burned with shame, but Finn only laughed.

A cruel, hard sound.

She was sure he'd be the one to watch. The one to fear.

KATIE

---

37 MILES IN

I run until my legs and arms and chest burn like fire. Until my whole body is impossibly heavy and cramps squeeze my calves and quads. And I keep running, legs pistoning and my pack slapping hard against my back.

"Katie, stop! You need to listen to me!"

I don't answer. I enter the road, feel my joints adjust to the change beneath my feet. The ground here is packed and hard with little sand to cushion my footfalls. Deep ruts and jagged rocks pepper the trail and torture my knees.

I move left around a giant pothole and sideswipe a cluster of yuccas, the long, stiff leaves scraping my arm and neck. I veer right, moving away from them, and my foot catches on one of the deep grooves in the road.

I catch myself, but only barely. And Finn is right on my heels. I will not outrun him. I duck behind a juniper, pressing myself to the backside of a squat boulder. His feet thunder past and then stop. Soft footsteps sound nearby. My heart is an ache beneath my collarbone and in my throat.

"Katie?" His voice is different. Beseeching. "Will you please just talk to me? Please?"

He sounds nice. But I know how nicely boys can ask for things you don't want to give. And I know how quickly that asking can turn into a hand on the back of your neck and a knee pushing your legs apart.

He steps closer, the crunch of his hiking boot just inches from my own feet. I clench my fists and hold my breath. There are yuccas all around, their long rough arms stretched in every direction. I can't get out, not without moving right past him.

"I can see your shadow," he says, panting. "I don't want to scare you. If you just stay there, I'll just talk."

I reach down slowly, scooping fistfuls of orange sand into my hands.

He sighs hard, "I need to tell you about—"

I launch myself at him, throwing both handfuls of sand right at his eyes. I miss, but he stumbles back, crashing into the yuccas with a cry.

I force my rubbery legs to move. I have to go. Right now. I run with everything I have, but there is so little left. My lungs ache and dark spots are speckling the edges of my vision and I know this can't last. He is stronger. Faster.

He's going to catch me.

"I'm not trying to hurt you," he says.

I weave around an enormous sage and hop down a low shelf into thick, sticky mud. I squelch my way across, knowing I can't hide again. My footprints are outlined so clearly—the stuff of old detective movies.

"I know what Riley told you!" he yells. "I know why you're running, but you're wrong!"

I leap over a cactus. I don't see the dip in the road. My foot hits and wobbles sideways. I throw my hands out to brace my fall as I crash face-first into the ground.

ASTER

36 MILES IN

Riley's sobs come in a strange rhythm. Breathing in once and out twice. Soft cries emerge with each exhale. She crosses her arms over her stomach, her head bobbing as she cries and cries. She looks pitiful.

Like she's terrified.

Like she's faking it.

The last thought needles in, a speculation with just enough evidence to feel right. Something about Riley does not add up. But I should know by now this kind of math isn't my strong suit.

I was wrong about Katie being safe at that party.

I was wrong about the rain.

I was wrong about the accidental fall, so it makes sense that I would be wrong about Finn and Riley.

I shake my head and work to be sympathetic. I don't trust myself anymore. I have no reason to trust myself. What I should trust is what is right in front of me. Riley is a tiny, innocent girl. She needs help. But when I open my mouth to speak all those compassionate thoughts, a question tumbles out instead.

"When did this happen?"

"The night before we met you," she says, hiccupping on a sob.

I try to remember. Before the flowers. Before the rain. That night I scraped my ankle. And we heard a woman scream.

Isabel.

It can't be. A human scream can't even carry a full mile in most conditions. My father taught me that. And he also taught me that the canyons are not like most conditions.

"Why didn't you say anything?" I ask, trying to keep my voice gentle. To press every ounce of suspicion into simple curiosity. "Why didn't you ask us for help?"

"Because I was terrified!" Her voice rises sharply, her eyes dancing despite her tears. "He would have killed me if I said anything. He could have killed you! I think he even started to sneak over to you later that night, but I called him back. I was trying to keep you safe!"

It tracks. Katie saw Finn in the darkness. Watching us from the shadows. He terrified her, and she told me Riley called for him. There is truth in the things she's saying. So why does it feel like a lie?

And then I remember our dinner. Peanut butter sandwiches on paper napkins. The three of us ate, but not Finn. Finn walked away. Made his excuses and disappeared. At least ten full minutes, he was nowhere in sight. Riley could have told us anything.

But she didn't say a word.

Riley swipes her hands beneath her eyes. "We have to get out of here. He's going to come back for us. Do you remember when I asked you what the two of you were talking about?"

I nod, but I remember that exchange differently. She wasn't just asking. She was accusing Finn of flirting.

"I was afraid he was trying to learn something about you. Something he could hurt you with. I've been trying to find both of you to make sure you were safe."

She's rambling. No, not just rambling. She is lying.

I know that I have been wrong before. And I know what Katie thinks—how sure she is that Finn is responsible. But right now every cell in my body is screaming at me that we were wrong. We didn't need to be afraid of Finn. We needed to be afraid of Riley.

"We need to hurry," she says. "We have to tell someone what he did!"

I do not move—cannot move if I'm honest—but I watch her carefully. Looking for some cracks in this veneer. And I should leave this be. I should not press. But when she lets out another low sob, I can't help myself.

"Why didn't you tell us when Finn went to the bathroom?" I ask. Riley drops her hands from her tear-slicked face then. She does not respond, so I go on. "Do you remember? When we were eating dinner, he walked off for several minutes. But you didn't say a word about this girl then."

Riley turns toward me slowly, but her face flips like a switch. The breathless sobs vanish. Her mouth hardens and her eyes go flat. And I know I am in very serious trouble.

ISABEL

She remembers. Now that it's too late. Now that it doesn't matter. But maybe this is her gift. No one has seen the blanket. It will be cold again in a few hours, and she will freeze. Or infection will set in. The cloud of flies around her thigh have been promising it.

But she will die knowing how it happened. Knowing she got exactly what she asked for.

That old pervert gave her a little baggie for a little peek.

Trey left with all his sanctimonious bullshit.

Riley and Finn let her join them, and within hours, the kiss.

Maybe she asked for all of it. But she didn't ask for Riley to catch them.

Her stomach tumbles as the images flash. A slideshow in double time. Riley's pretty face turned ugly with fury. Finn's cruel laugh. Isabel was sure that Riley would hit him. Instead Riley turned to her and screamed.

Slut. Four letters. One hard consonant. A proclamation of her guilt over Finn's.

Finn stepped away, absolved of his crime. And Isabel turned her back on it all. On Riley. On Finn. On this problem that was never hers to begin with. And that's when Riley struck.

She remembers small hands between her shoulder blades. That word again on Riley's tongue. And then she remembers the sickening shock—the weightlessness that comes before a fall.

Isabel closes her eyes, and despair sinks like weights in her lungs. She considers the cost of four pills in a dirty bag. A few stolen kisses. Wonders how it adds up to dying alone in the desert.

KATIE

38 MILES

I taste blood and see stars, but I push myself up with both hands and shake off the dizziness. I hear Finn behind me, his breath heavy. Track pants swishing.

I am on my stomach, and he is so close. He could push me down. He could hurt me. I scramble for my feet, but pain lances through my knee, and I go right back down. Finn stumbles to a halt behind me. I hear him panting.

My throat tightens. I think of frames thumping the wall. The sound of a zipper.

I cannot do this. I push myself up again, keeping a rock in one hand. I force my knee to take my weight and find my way to my feet.

"Aster, Riley is the one who hurt her. I know what she told you, but it's a lie. She pushed Isabel."

Riley didn't tell us anything, and I don't know what he's talking about. I don't know and I don't believe him and I don't want to be one more person he hurts in the desert. I haul back my hand with the rock and hear something in the distance. The rumble of an engine.

We both turn in time to see the glint of something silver moving behind the sage bush and pinyon pines. Round headlights and a dented grill come into view.

A Jeep.

Hope blooms in the center of my chest. It's Mike's Jeep. I break into a jog, limping. I spot the raven's feather dangling from the rearview mirror. Another step, and I can see tufts of unkempt gray hair and a single tanned arm propped on the driver's door.

"Mike!" I scream, my voice hoarse and shrill. He turns immediately, but I scream again. "Help me! Help me!"

"Katie?"

Uncle Mike is already out of the Jeep. I am barreling at him now, my ankle screaming and my heart pounding so, so fast. I am sobbing when I reach him, when I see the mix of fear and shock on his face. He leads me to the Jeep, the metal hot and solid against my arm.

"What's going on here?" he asks. "Where's Aster?"

I am breathing too hard and fast. My vision is going gray at the edges. I push my palms into the scorching hood of the Jeep and try to breathe.

"Katie, where is Aster? Is Aster...?"

I've never seen naked fear like this on my gruff uncle's face. It ages him decades.

"She's okay," I say automatically and then correct myself. "She's hurt. Her foot."

"Thank God," Finn croaks. His voice is strange and hollow and much too close.

Uncle Mike moves toward him, his fear calmed enough by my words to return him to his normal state. He knows this desert and all the terrible things that can go wrong. More than that, he's the one people call. This hysterical boy is probably nothing my uncle hasn't seen before.

"Who are you?" Uncle Mike asks.

"Thank God," Finn says again, his voice catching. Goose bumps rise on my arms.

Finn is…crying. I shudder and watch. And everything I understand about him slips through my fingers.

"Thank God, thank God." Finn's litany of gratitude breaks off in another sob. He is weeping.

I feel the world tilt precariously. Finn has dropped to the ground. He is on his knees, his shoulders hitching. When he pulls his hands away from his face, it's clear the tears are no act.

This is not the Finn I saw at the camp with his tense jaw and wary eyes. This is a man with the face of a wounded boy, his eyes streaming and mouth quivering.

"What's going on here?" Mike says gently, still keeping himself between Finn and me. Still keeping his hand on the side of his hip where I know he keeps his pocketknife. "Did this boy hurt you, Katie?"

I open my mouth, thinking of Finn in the camp. Thinking of his expression too when I saw him outside our tent. Finn did harm. He frightened me. But did he hurt me? Is that the right word?

"I need help," Finn cries, his voice breaking on the word.

"What help?"

"There's a girl." Finn lets out an animal sound. Something more guttural than a cry. When he looks up, I am sure he'll confess. I brace myself for the words.

"What girl? Just tell me what's going on." Mike's hand stays close to his hip. I see the shape of his knife through the denim. "Nice and calm."

"There is a girl who died out here. She fell." Finn takes a shuddering breath, and his eyes go hollow.

"She didn't just fall!" I scream. "Tell the rest of it, Finn! Tell him what you did!"

Finn shakes his head, a strange look of terror dropping over his features. "I didn't do what you think I did. I've been trying to tell you that. I've been trying to tell you. It was Riley."

I laugh. The idea is so ridiculous, no other response seems valid. Through a fog I can hear Uncle Mike asking who Riley is. Prodding for more information. But my whole body has honed in on Finn's face. On the helpless look in his eyes. My mother has worn an expression just like this since she stepped into my hospital room.

That's how I know. Finn isn't lying.

"Riley pushed her," Finn says.

"Pushed who?" Uncle Mike asks. "Who was pushed?"

"Isabel." His voice breaks on her name. "Her name was Isabel."

"Was Isabel a friend of yours? Was she in your group?"

Finn shakes his head, his whole face slick with tears and snot. "No, we didn't know her. We just met her on the trail. She was headed north after a break-up, I guess, but she joined us—she said she'd go back south with us. She just wanted to be with cool people..."

"You're sure she's not alive?"

"I don't—" Finn breaks off, unable to finish the sentence. He swipes his hand over his face. Stares at the ground like all the air has gone out of him.

"I don't think so," I say quietly. "There were vultures. Not feeding yet, but…"

Uncle Mike turns to me. "You saw her?"

"I think so, yes. She was on a ledge about twenty, maybe thirty feet down."

"Could go either way at that height," he says.

My stomach squirms miserably. I don't want to think about this. Not the arm I saw splayed over the rock or the vultures circling, or the fact that at one point Aster and I were only twenty or thirty feet above her and maybe we could have helped. Maybe there was still time then. But we did nothing.

"I'm getting my kit, and I'm going to radio for help. Wait right here."

Uncle Mike climbs into the back of the Jeep, and I look at Finn. Minutes ago, he was a monster. A villain. A thing that goes bump in the night. Now he is a mystery. He pushes himself to his feet, and I take a step back instinctively. He is still too big. I still feel danger when I look at him, my mind going back to his lurking in the shadows.

Is this always the way I'll be? Afraid of every man I pass?

"Why were you watching us?" I ask him. "That night—"

"I know the night." He looks at me and then casts his eyes down. His cheeks have gone pink. "Riley swore she'd frame me for this. She said it was my fault."

"Why would she say that?" I ask.

"Because of my record. Because I'm the kind of guy who looks guilty," he says. "You obviously thought I was."

He isn't wrong. I turn away and remember the moments with him. I thought he was an asshole. A dangerous asshole. But he was afraid.

"I snuck away while Riley was using the bathroom," he says. "Wanted to tell you both what went down. But she called for me."

"And you ran. Because you're afraid of her."

He flushes. "I'm afraid of prison. Look at me. You think a judge is going to believe my word over hers?"

I go very, very still. I do not want to answer. The police believed me when they came to get me. The officers and nurses and counselors and attorneys—they all believed me, but what the hell does it matter? In the end, all that belief and a whole lot of proof are still circling around an endless court system loop.

Behind us, I hear Uncle Mike on the radio calling for help.

Finn sighs. "When I got back to camp, she read me the riot act. Started in on your friend, that I'd been flirting with her."

"Flirting," I repeat the word because it makes no sense. Aster doesn't flirt. Not ever. Saying they'd been square dancing was no more unlikely. He hadn't spoken to us. He'd pouted and glowered. "She thought you were flirting with Aster?"

"Why do you think she pushed Isabel?" he asks.

"She was jealous?"

"Yeah, jealous. Jealous and crazy."

Uncle Mike is answering someone on the radio. A crackle and a disembodied voice. He says something about climbers. A helicopter. Two hours isn't soon enough. Round them up. And then his voice is fading, and the desert is tilting into a slow spin around me.

Finn's words repeat in my mind, the implications plain. *Why do you think she pushed Isabel?* My blood runs cold.

"Finn, where the hell is Riley right now?"

He shakes his head. "No idea. She got away from me. I caught up with her, but she disappeared. And I just want to get the hell out of here."

"You never caught up with her?"

"I didn't try. I just wanted to get the hell away."

I turn back to the trail, terrible possibilities sliding into focus. Aster cannot move, and she cannot fight. If Riley is still out there and finds her, she—

A faint sound tears through the silence, sending a wave of chills crashing through me. Someone is screaming. My uncle calls my name, but I do not answer. Without another word, I break into a dead run.

ASTER

36 MILES IN

I fully realize what I've done only when Riley screams. She drops to the ground, hands at her face. Her eyes. The canister falls from my hands, toxic drips turning the sand red.

Riley coughs. Gags. Sobs and rolls to her side, her skin and hair stained orange with the desert.

"Slut!" she cries through her tears. "I'll kill you, you stupid whore! You caused this. You're the reason he ran!"

Her words are nonsense, nonsense trailing off into coughing again. I shift my hips away from her, crying out as pain splinters through my ankle and shin. It burns and burns all the way into my groin.

Riley is rolling onto all fours. Coughing. Gagging. Enraged. Saliva and snot drip from her face. I pat the ground, catching the silky leaves of a sunray. A sharp rock. I'm reaching and reaching for the silver canister that is just out of my grasp. She crawls forward, fingers inches from my injured leg.

Helpless, I fling a handful of sand at her. She jerks left to dodge me, and then surges closer. I cannot get away from her. I twist, but the pain stops me, chewing me from the inside out. I try to ignore it. Try to jerk my injured leg, to pick it up and out of her reach, but the pain overrules me.

Riley tries to speak, but I scream to drown her out.

"Help! Help! Katie!" My voice is a harsh cry. One that seems to land flat a few feet away. I squirm. Cry. Throw whatever small rocks I can reach.

Riley is coated in sand. Still gagging, dripping, and likely blind. But she continues forward, driven by her own fury. Animal grunts rise from deep in her throat. Even disoriented, her fingers brush my leg, and a howl comes out of me from my deepest places.

It is in that moment that I am out of rocks. That the ground beneath me has been wiped clean of sand, pebbles, and any loose thing I can use. Riley lunges forward, and her knee presses hard into the back of my hand. I cry out, and she realizes her success. Moves her other knee to join the first. Grinds her slight weight into my wrist until bones twist and ligaments scream. Then she is patting, feeling her way over my stomach. My breast.

I do not understand. I don't know what she wants. I am clawing with one good hand, but then her hands are on my throat. And she is squeezing. She coughs wetly. Droplets on my face. Spots in my vision. My heart beating like a bass drum.

I open my mouth, wishing I could scream. Instead I twist and claw uselessly. And then I do hear a scream, a furious wailing that cuts through my fear and pain. Riley's hands loosen. I drag in a greedy breath and hear my name.

"Aster!"

Katie. She screams my name again as she plows into Riley's

side. Katie is crying when she raises her fist. She is clumsy and inexperienced when she punches, but she is raging. She hits again and again. I hear the impact of her fists every time. See crimson under Riley's nose. On her mouth. Riley curls onto her side, crying. Limbs curling in like a newborn. But Katie won't quit.

"Stop," I cry, my voice rough and weak with disuse. "No more, Katie."

She pauses, and then removes herself from Riley, pushing closer to me. Riley twitches in the dirt. Katie keeps her back against my side. Her legs are pulled up, feet ready to kick if Riley moves an inch.

"Are you okay?" Katie asks me.

But I cannot answer. I can only cry, pressing closer to my cousin. Riley whimpers. She is a wreck. A girl. A killer.

"Your dad is here. He'll come any minute," Katie says.

I find her hand on the ground beside me and twist our fingers together. A closed part of me breaks open. A thousand questions swirl up through my mind, but then Katie squeezes my hand, and I go silent.

She is shaking and strong. She is soft and hard. She is Katie from the party. Katie from the trail. She is whoever she will be in the weeks and months that come. I look at the angry solitary girl just beyond her feet. And my sobs come in great gulping gasps.

I clutch Katie harder, suddenly terrified she'll slip away.

"I've got you," she says softly to me.

"I should have gotten you," I say. "I should have never left."

"Maybe," she says. "But you're here now, right? We're still here."

"Yes," I say, and this time I believe her.

I cannot go back. We cannot go back. But now I see we are

moving forward from that terrible moment. And we will move forward from this terrible moment too. Somehow we will carve a new path. And this strained, beautiful thing between us will be more than enough.

ISABEL

She opens her eyes to heaven. White clouds and blue sky. Sunbeams gleaming like God's own arms. There is a soft *whump-whump-whump.*

Angel drums.

The wind kicks up, and a single black cord dangles down, several yards from her face.

Heaven closes its gates as a helicopter hovers into view.

Her angel lands hard, black boots crunching all that orange gold sand. Gloved hands reaching to deliver her home.

KATIE

49 MILES COMPLETE

We stand at the edge of the parking lot with sore shoulders and sunburned noses and matching blisters on our left heels.

"Well, that was a bitch," Aster says.

I laugh. "Yeah. It was. But now no one can call us quitters."

"Thank God for that."

I grin, turning to my cousin. Her hair is shorter now, cropped right to her chin with a tendency to slide into her eyes at all the most annoying moments. She leans heavily into her right trekking pole—a new addition recommended after four foot surgeries and six months of physical therapy—but she looks good. Stronger than I would have thought after fourteen miles.

It was not the fourteen Aster wanted, but I insisted on the location. And when I explained my item-recovery mission, she agreed. But Aster was determined to hit that forty-nine miles on the nose. Cue a certain rescue helicopter pilot who agreed to a special delivery—two hiker girls in a large clearing near a long walk along a cliff. Near the spot where Isabel almost died.

"How's the foot?" I ask.

"Annoying. Typical. Fine."

Aster's doctor said a long hike was unwise. Both of our therapists expressed concerns. My mom nearly resorted to physically restraining me. Even Uncle Mike wasn't enthusiastic, especially doing this in July. But we didn't need anyone else to be sure. This didn't have anything to do with them.

Twenty minutes later, Uncle Mike's silver Jeep rumbles up the road, coming to a stop just a few feet from where it waited nine months ago. The driver gets out slowly, her dark hair in a sloppy bun, her gait still awkward on her new prosthetic leg.

"Hell yeah!" she says, pumping a fist for us. "You did it!"

Aster smiles. "We did."

"Be warned, we smell like an armpit."

"Damn if you don't," she says, coming closer. Her dimples soften her angular face. "Good thing your dad's Jeep is a convertible. Oh, oh, shit, look what I got you!"

She reaches into the back seat of the Jeep. When she opens the lid, steam pours out.

"Um…" The alarm is clear in my voice, and Isabel just laughs.

"It's dry ice. That's the only way they can ship it, yeah? It cost me a damn fortune, by the way, making sure it would get here at exactly the right time."

"You didn't have to do that."

"Aye, it's worth it," she says, and then she pushes her dark hair out of her eyes. I notice the long scar on her left forearm. It's still a miracle Isabel is here at all.

She retrieves three small tubs of ice cream.

"Jeni's," she says. "It's an Ohio thing as you should know. To die for."

She produces mismatched spoons, and I take a bite of Gooey Butter Cake. It tastes every bit as expensive and delicious as it looks. While we eat, I watch Aster and Isabel. Scarred and changed, but very much alive.

While I joined Adam for his three-month work-study in Germany, Aster kept up with Isabel. First, it was phone calls and text messages, but the moment they allowed her to drive, Aster made weekly trips to Salt Lake City. Isabel had moved there a few months before the hike after finishing college in Illinois. We bonded over our Ohio roots, and she and Aster bonded over the hell of last year's trip.

Over the months we shared video calls if we could match the times up. And Aster often sent me detailed outlines of Isabel's complicated treatment plans and progress. She also sent updates on Riley's trial, which seems to be on as many endless delays as mine.

It is the most effort I've ever seen Aster put into a friendship outside of ours. And it is the best gift she's ever given me. Knowing Isabel was alive. That even if I'd gotten everything about Riley wrong, I still managed to help save a woman who'd been left behind.

"Trey was actually the one who introduced me to Jeni's," Isabel says.

Trey the trail runner. It's almost impossible to think of him with a name. To realize the guy who streaked past us with barely a nod wasn't a killer or a stranger. He was Isabel's boyfriend until they broke up on the trail. And according to Isabel, his worst crime was following her command to get the hell as far away from her as possible.

"Have you heard from him much?" I ask.

"Trey?" Isabel nods. "We're cool. I mean, he sent me flowers and ice cream every week for the first three months, so that helped."

"Did Finn ever stop writing?" Aster asks. I'm surprised by this. I knew he'd written a few times, but I figured it wasn't much more than going through the motions.

Isabel laughs. "He is on some twenty-first century spirit walk if ever I have seen one."

"What's that mean?" I ask.

Isabel tips her head back and forth. "I don't know. He sends a lot of postcards from miscellaneous National Parks. Quotes on solitude and wisdom, and shit. White guy stuff."

"But no apologies?"

Isabel's dimples are an invitation to laugh with her. "Like I said…white guy stuff. He isn't big on apologizing. Trey, on the other hand, is going to drown me in *sorry*s."

Seeing my stiff smile, Isabel rolls her eyes. "Trey's not a bad guy, Katie. I didn't want him to stay, and he had no idea any of that would happen. No one can blame him."

Aster slowly puts her spoon back into her ice cream, her gaze drifting to the ground. I think of that night at the party. And then I think of us walking past Isabel without even knowing. How many days and nights and moments can blow sideways with none of us the wiser.

"You're right," I say. "Trey couldn't have known."

"Exactly," she says. "Besides, now I know if I ever need anything, like for the rest of my freaking life, he kind of sort of has to say yes, right?"

"Definitely," Aster says. But she's looking at me. And she looks happy. Really happy. "My guess is he'd always be glad to lend a hand."

"That's nice," Isabel says. "Though really, if he's going to offer, I could use a leg."

We groan and laugh at the same time, and mutually decide it's time to pack up. We're sticky with ice cream and heat when two four-wheelers clamber around a corner and up beside the Jeep. Two climbers jump out, hauling thick coils of rope that they sling over their broad shoulders. One of the guys is holding a cooler of beer. Another is in flip-flops.

Aster arches her brow at me, and I smirk.

"Afternoon," a tall guy says, his grin wide and wolfish.

That same shiver of fear rolls through me, but out of the corner of my eye, I see Aster's freckled arm. Isabel's dark hair. And I don't care about this boy or his interests or intents. Maybe part of me will always be looking over my shoulder, but another part will always be looking ahead.

"You ready to go?" Aster asks, opening the door for me.

"Ready as I'll ever be."

Aster takes the wheel, and in the back, I hand Isabel a small, hourglass-shaped rock. I was sure it wouldn't be there. Even as Aster belayed me down, it felt like a fool's errand, but if there was the smallest chance of bringing this back to her, it was worth the try.

I found it right at the base of that crack, right where Isabel had left it after she used it to push another rock into the center of the emergency blanket. She thinks the rock kept her alive. She thinks we did too.

Every week, Isabel sends us a text. Thank you both for saving my life. But as I put this smooth rock into her hands, I hope it reminds her that Aster and I only helped her along. She did what every strong woman does. We save ourselves.

Isabel squeezes the rock with quiet reverence, and Aster starts the engine and turns the Jeep around. The road stretches out, orange and rutted and steep. I breathe deep, ready for whatever it brings.

THE END

ACKNOWLEDGMENTS

This book exists thanks to the land in southeastern Utah and the City of Moab. When I lost my father, it was the brutal and beautiful desert around Moab that helped me to find my way again. The land was not originally called Utah, of course, and it was home to many people over the centuries before Moab came to be. It's overwhelming to be in a place where history is etched onto canyon walls and rock refuses to behave the way you'd expect. It's beautiful beyond compare and my gratitude is enormous. At the same time, it feels completely inadequate.

On the book side of things, my team is *bonkers* good. Every last person at New Leaf is an absolute rock star, but most especially thank you to Suzie (high sorceress of all things publishing) and Sophia (whose suggestions are always on point) and Olivia—you always have the answers and I'm so grateful! To my truly excellent Sourcebooks team, a world of thanks to the many people who work hard to make my books shine, especially Wendy for her solid eye and story wisdom that helped me find the story I desperately wanted to tell. And to Karen for coordinating all the things I'm not thinking about. And last but absolutely not least, thank you to the newest member of my team, my brilliant, creative, ultra-organized publicist! Leann, you've had such an impact in my writing world. I can't thank you enough!

I owe a very special thanks to Ben and Catherine who answered many lengthy technical texts about hiking and climbing with exceptional detail, humor, and warmth. I also owe a huge debt to many wonderful Moab residents, especially the staff at Back of Beyond Books who were endlessly helpful. Thanks to David who agreed to my zany idea for that first trip to Utah with kids in tow! And also to Margaret, Lisa, and Edie for your compassion and wisdom and endless patience with my ridiculous schedule. To Jody for all the reasons in the world (I meant that dedication). And to Ben for a whole lot of reasons, not the least of which is the several hours on the phone listening to chapter after chapter as I tried to get this book just right.

There are so many others to thank, but all books boil down to the great loves of my life. To Ian, who is always up for a hike or an adventure, and Adrienne who loves those ravens as much as I do, and to Lydia who reminds me every day to live life with my whole heart and soul.

And Dad? I still miss you every day. Thanks for teaching me the ways a trail can heal my soul. I love you.

ABOUT THE AUTHOR

New York Times bestselling author Natalie D. Richards is the author of several "page-turning thrillers" (*School Library Journal*). A champion of literacy and aspiring authors, Richards is a frequent speaker at schools, libraries, and writing groups. She lives in Ohio with her three children and (very) large dog, Wookiee.

sourcebooks
fire

Home of the hottest trends in YA!

Visit us online and
sign up for our newsletter at
FIREreads.com

· ·

Follow
@sourcebooksfire
online